NEPTUNE'S WALL

AJ BAILEY ADVENTURE SERIES - BOOK 8

NICHOLAS HARVEY

Printed in the United States of America

First Printing, 2020

ISBN-13: 979-8574828823 (Amazon only)
ISBN-13: 978-1-959627-08-1 (IngramSparks)

Cover design by Wicked Good Book Covers

Front and rear cover photographs by Drew McArthur

Mermaid illustration by Tracie Cotta

Author photograph by Lift Your Eyes Photography

This is a work of fiction. Names, characters, businesses, places, events and incidents are either the products of the author's imagination or used in a fictitious manner unless noted otherwise. Any resemblance to actual persons, living or dead, or actual events is purely coincidental. Heritage Kitchen and Miss Grece are used by permission in a fictitious manner.

DEDICATION

For Cheryl, my mermaid.
Happy 20-year anniversary, my love.

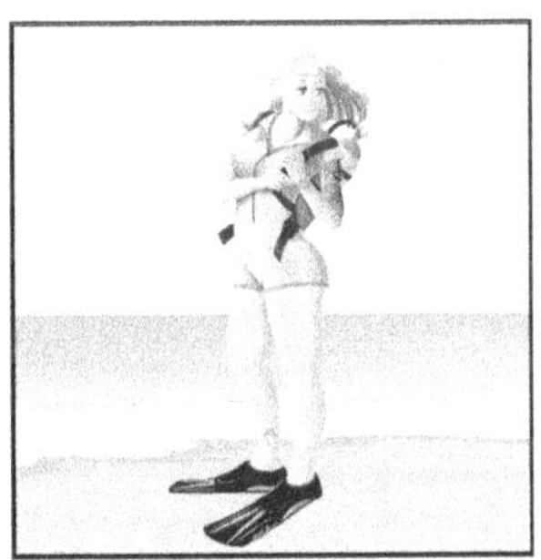

$$1$$

THE CAYMANES – 22 APRIL, 1586

Digby was a stout man, cursed with six feet of height, towering over every other sailor on the ship. He stood behind the other able-bodied seamen, half listening, while the boatswain shouted at, berated, and gave orders to the group. His size kept him out of the rigging, to his relief with his fear of heights, but he was usually first choice when it came to manual labour. He didn't mind that so much, as long as he wasn't expected to figure anything out. Or be in charge. Decisions came slowly to Digby, but that's why he stuck by Harlow, and stood directly behind his friend as the boatswain assigned the morning's tasks. Harlow was a thinker. Harlow could make decisions, and Digby was happy lifting, hauling and carrying, as long as Harlow told him which things to move. They all dripped sweat in the tropical heat, and each of them stank so badly, none of them noticed anymore. Their pale English skin had burnt, peeled, re-burnt and eventually browned over the months at sea in the harsh sun.

"Digby," the boatswain yelled, and beckoned the tall man towards him. "Come 'ere."

Digby shoved Harlow forward in front of him.

"Oi," Harlow protested under his breath, as he was herded forcefully in front of his brawny friend. "He called you, not me."

"You, Digby, yer useless side of beef, not that excuse for a sailor," the boatswain chided. "I need rowers."

The boatswain scanned the group for a second burly man and tried to remember who he had already assigned tasks to, easily looking over the diminutive Harlow who was now right before him, courtesy of his friend's corralling.

"I'll row, he'll make sure I row the right way, sir," Digby announced in his deep, baritone voice.

The boatswain looked from the deck of the ship to the shore of the island less than half a mile away, then back at Digby.

"You're telling me you can't navigate your sorry carcass from this ship, to that island, without help?" he yelled, and didn't wait for a response. "Fine, take Harlow, gets him out of my sight for a while." He waved at four more men. "Lower the rowboat with these two, Captain wants his chest ashore."

"We're taking the Captain ashore?" Digby asked in a panic.

The boatswain stepped forward and stood up on his tiptoes until his face was almost in Digby's. "Did I say you were taking the Captain ashore?" he screamed, flinging spittle on Digby's chin.

"I thought you said Captain, sir," Digby replied.

The boatswain's cheeks were turning red. "I did say Captain! I said, take the Captain's chest ashore," he yelled, finding a louder volume from somewhere. "I did not say take the Captain." He poked a finger at Digby's barrel-sized torso. "Do you think I'd trust you two bilge rats to take the Captain anywhere, Digby?"

"No, sir, thank you," Digby replied.

"Thank you? Why are you thanking me, you dimwit?" the boatswain continued. "I'm insulting you and you're thanking me. Why, pray tell, are you thanking me?"

"For not trusting me with the Captain, sir," Digby replied.

The boatswain lowered himself to his heels and shook his head. "Lower one of the bloody rowboats, and leave this ship, before I clean the barnacles off the belly of this beautiful vessel with your ugly, worthless…"

It was Harlow's turn to shove Digby. He steered him away from the boatswain, who continued an impressive stream of insults as the six men set about the job of manhandling the heavy wooden rowboat over the side, and lowering it using a block and tackle. Once the boat was bobbing in the turquoise water alongside the ship, Harlow and Digby looked over at the rope ladder.

"You go first," Digby said quietly, although his booming voice still rumbled like thunder. "You know I don't like high-up things."

"Fine," Harlow said, stepping over the gunwale. "Just don't fall on me – you'll sink me and the rowboat."

Digby looked around the seas while his friend climbed down the rope ladder, loosely attached to the side of the ship. Digby couldn't count, so he wasn't sure how many ships were in the fleet, but he guessed it was more than he had fingers and toes. The hotchpotch, from galleons to pinnaces, were scattered along the coastline of the small, low-lying island, the name of which he didn't know. Most of the fleet were anchored closer to the sandy beach, but the Elizabeth Bonaventure, the flagship, and easily the largest vessel of the group, stayed well clear of the shallow reefs.

"Your turn," Harlow called up, and Digby sighed as he looked down at his friend.

He nodded and surveyed the water. He couldn't see the bottom and wished they weren't so far from shore. He didn't mind the rowing, it was the deeper water he found unnerving. According to his shipmates, the deeper water was home to the Kraken and the sea goddess Umberlee, along with a myriad of other creatures waiting to take any poor soul who dared enter their domain. He gingerly swung a leg over the gunwale and searched for the rope webbing with his foot. The ropes swayed under his weight and he clung desperately to the gunwale while he tried to convince his other leg to follow.

"Come on Digby," Harlow hissed up at him. "You'll have us swinging from the yardarm with all this messing about."

Digby gritted his teeth and persuaded his other limb to cooperate, finding a footing on the webbing. Both hands still clung to the gunwale as he attempted to find the next rope step, keeping his eyes straight ahead into the hull of the ship.

"Lower it over the side," he heard the boatswain shout from the deck, before a shadow cast across him and he readied himself for the next round of scalding.

"Get down there, man! Call yourself a sailor? My mother could have climbed down the ropes and back up to the crow's nest by now," the boatswain screamed, causing Digby to flap, flounder and grapple with the ropes. His right foot found a step as his left hand found a purchase and he let his weight lower down, desperately trying to distance himself from the wrath, and the whip, of the boatswain. Digby's left foot slipped off the next rope just as he released his right hand and he gasped as he felt his weight plummeting. Harlow yelped as he tried to get clear of Digby's tumbling body, which crashed into the rowboat from six feet above.

"You alright?" Digby heard Harlow ask, as the rowboat rocked violently in the water and he dared to open his eyes. He was staring up at blue skies and wispy clouds that swung back and forth across the view above him, with the ship occasionally appearing. He wiggled his fingers, and then his toes, and was surprised as much as relieved that they all seemed to function. His right heel stung and his back felt like it had been clobbered with a heavy bludgeon. He raised himself with his hands and felt something wet around his feet.

"If you've damaged my boat it'll come out of your hide, Digby!"

He heard the boatswain bellow from above, and squinted up at the man leaning over the gunwale.

"Boat's fine, sir," he called back. "I am as well, thanks for asking," he added, mumbling under his breath.

"Stay still, Digby," Harlow growled. "Keep your foot against the boards."

"Huh?" Digby replied, trying to sit up.

He felt a thump on his leg. "Keep your bloody foot in the hole, you fool," Harlow whispered urgently.

"Where's all that water come from?" the boatswain yelled.

"Splashed in with all the rocking about, sir." Harlow replied loudly. "Everything's fine, sir. Lower the chest down."

Digby watched the wooden chest approach from above as he kept his heel dug into the floor of the boat as Harlow had told him. He decided he was either losing all the blood in his body, or sea water was pouring in through a hole under his foot. Either way, he didn't like his chances. The chest wasn't very big, but was beautifully crafted from walnut with brass and iron strapping, hinges and hasps. Harlow manoeuvred it to his end of the rowboat and hurriedly untied the rope, releasing the line to be hauled back aboard.

"Where to, sir?" Harlow called up.

"The beach," the boatswain shouted back.

Harlow and Digby both surveyed the coastline where all they could see was pale yellow sand between the ocean and the thick mangroves and trees lining the land.

"Yes, sir. Beach," Harlow called back. "Get rowing, mate, let's go," he whispered to Digby.

Digby picked himself up and felt a rush of water as he moved his right heel.

"I can't row from down here, and you said not to move my foot," he grunted. "Where's the seat gone?" he asked, noticing he was laid across where the thwart should be.

"You broke it to pieces when you decided to leap aboard," Harlow hissed. "You're sitting on what's left of it."

Digby looked up and saw with relief the boatswain had left. Found his next target to berate, no doubt.

"Let me come up front, then you can sit up and row," Harlow said. "I'll plug the hole."

The boat rocked around as Harlow stumbled his way past the big man and sat heavily down on Digby's foot.

"Ouch."

"Well move it, man," Harlow retorted.

Digby sat up and shuffled himself rearward until his back was against the chest. He clutched an oar in each hand and used the starboard oar to shove them away from the Elizabeth Bonaventure. With his back to the bow and Harlow sitting in the stern peaking around his friend to give him directions, the two set off for the shoreline. Digby looked at the bottom of the boat steadily filling with water.

"We're going to sink."

"No we're not, I'm plugging the hole," Harlow replied defiantly. "If you'd hurry up and get us to shore, we'll be fine. We'll fix it up and no one will be the wiser."

"Harlow?" Digby murmured.

"What? You're heading straight, just keep rowing," he replied, glancing up at the shore before turning his attention back to the leak in the boat.

"Harlow. The Captain's watching us," Digby said quietly.

Harlow froze. Digby could tell he wanted to turn and look, but knew he shouldn't. Finally, he could stand it no more and stole a short glance.

"Damn it," he cursed.

"I told you he was watching. He knows something's up." Digby said.

"He can't know. He wasn't there when you fell in," Harlow reasoned. "And the boatswain wouldn't have said anything 'cos it's his responsibility."

"Maybe he's just worried about his fancy chest," Digby wondered aloud. "What do you think is in there?"

Harlow shook his head. "I don't know, probably his best china for a spot of tea on the beach."

"Might be his letters from the Queen," Digby said.

Harlow laughed. "Doubt he'd leave his private papers in the hands of the likes of you and me, mate."

"Well, he's still watching us, so it's something his sir-ness is worried about," Digby said firmly.

Harlow looked around again. "Blimey, he is watching us. Look at him up there," he said angrily. "Pompous arse. Ever since he got knighted, he's been worse than ever."

"If this rowboat sinks, I hope the Kraken gets me," Digby said. "I'd rather be dragged to the depths by a beast than have what he'll hand us."

"Shut up and row faster, you fool," Harlow growled. "I don't fancy being eaten by sea monsters or seeing the cat o' nine tails. We get to shore and we'll have time to repair this hole before the Captain's brought over."

"He'll keelhaul us," Digby said sullenly.

"I'll flog you myself if you don't shut up and row faster," Harlow replied, wriggling around over the hole as water continued to leak by his heel.

Digby pulled the oars with all his might, but the Captain and the Elizabeth Bonaventure didn't seem to be getting any smaller. He dearly wanted to turn around and make sure the island was getting closer, but knew they needed every stroke. He sneaked a glance over the side but still couldn't see the bottom, which drove him to pull even harder on the oars. The rowboat creaked loudly above the sound of the oars through the water and Harlow looked down just as the wood splintered and a gush of sea water burst through the floor.

"Row man, row!" Harlow screamed, and Digby reached and pulled at the oars with every ounce of strength in his body. But it was useless. The water flooding the rowboat was unstoppable and the more water they took on the harder it was to move the small craft forward in the sea. Digby swung around and looked at the shore, still a quarter of a mile away. Just behind him the chest bobbed in the rapidly rising water. He turned back and looked at his friend.

"This is it, then," he said, and felt himself floating as the stricken rowboat sank beneath him.

Harlow looked back at the ship where several sailors had gathered against the gunwale, a safe distance from the Captain, as word spread of the disaster befalling the two men. The Captain hadn't moved a muscle; he remained staring at the scene unfolding before him.

Digby grabbed hold of the chest that buoyantly danced in the water, clutching gamely to it.

"Can you swim?" he shouted to Harlow, who was flapping his arms and splashing about.

"I don't think so," Harlow spluttered back. "I've never tried."

Digby pushed the chest through the water towards his friend. "Here, hold on to this, it's floating."

Harlow reached out and clawed at the wooden chest, pulling it towards him, along with Digby. For a moment they both hung gamely to the finely carpentered, curved walnut lid, and then the chest tilted, belched a slug of air from inside and quickly dropped beneath the surface, chasing the rowboat to the bottom. Both men splashed, kicked and wallowed to keep their faces from the water but they soon tired and the pull of the ocean was too great. Digby took a last look at the ship he and his friend had sailed halfway around the world on, and noticed the Captain had still not moved from the spot where he had first seen him.

Sir Francis Drake watched two of his able-bodied seamen drown before him. He cared little for the men, but the loss of his personal chest, containing his favourite compass and astrolabe and several charts, along with a sizeable stash of gold coins, was cause for great annoyance.

2

GRAND CAYMAN – FRIDAY

Annabelle Jayne Bailey was not the best sleeper. Her whole life she had struggled to go to sleep at night, her mind whirring on whatever subject, issue or problem that captured her thoughts. Once asleep, she tended to crash out in a deep state of rest until she awoke, earlier than she would like each morning. Running a dive operation meant getting up early, and getting up early was one of her least favourite chores. AJ opened her eyes and squinted at the bedside clock, its dim green LED numbers telling her it was 3:04am. She was instantly annoyed. 3:04am meant she had only been asleep for a few hours, and had to be up in a few more. Now she would fret over the urgency to get back to sleep, which naturally would stop her going back to sleep. Her boyfriend, Jackson, slept soundly next to her, making soft, restful breathing noises. She considered waking him to inform him that she couldn't sleep, but knew he would go straight back to sleep again, which would irritate her even more. She threw the covers back and slid out of bed, plodded the handful of steps across her tiny, studio-style cottage to the bathroom, and closed the door. A night light offered enough illumination for her to see Jackson had courteously left the toilet seat down.

He had finally made it to the island a few months back, after more than a year of their long-distance relationship while he worked for Sea Sentry, a marine conservation organisation, and then waiting for the Cayman Islands' borders to open for long-stay visitors. Her friend and mentor, Reg Moore, hired Jackson to work on his trio of dive boats, which created his work visa to enter and stay. These past few months had been the happiest for AJ. She had finally found a man who fitted perfectly into her life, and her soul. He was a calm, steadying influence that made her feel more confident in herself, and secure in their relationship. Her 31st birthday had just passed, and despite her loathing the attention of birthdays, his presence made it the most enjoyable party she had ever had. She smiled to herself as she thought about Jackson, and her eyelids felt heavy once again as the stress ebbed away.

AJ's head bobbed and she realised she ought to make it back to her bed if she was going to fall asleep, instead of collapsing off the toilet. She was about to stand up when something shook the cottage. At first she thought it might be a strong gust of wind, but the building shook again and she couldn't hear any wind blowing. So much for feeling sleepy, she thought, jolted wide awake by the strange, powerful rocking of the building. She stood and another wave ran through the cottage, rattling things in the kitchen and causing her to stagger towards the door. This time the movement didn't stop and she flung the bathroom door open.

"What on earth's going on?" she shouted towards the bed, a touch of panic in her English accent.

It felt like a giant hand had grabbed her little home in the grounds of a large vacation house on the famed Seven Mile Beach, and was violently shaking it in an attempt to rip it from its foundations. A clatter sounded as something flew from a shelf and hit the floor and AJ felt slightly nauseous from the unexpected swaying in the dark.

"It's an earthquake," she heard Jackson say calmly from across the room.

Born and raised in San Francisco, California, he would know, she thought. They had felt a few tremors on the island in the past, but she had been out on the ocean for the last big one. She had never felt anything as substantial as this. AJ clung to the door frame in an attempt to steady herself as the shaking began to subside and eventually petered out, returning the cottage to silence. She realised she had no idea what noise the earthquake had caused, but there was a notable quiet now it had stopped. Then she noticed the air conditioning wasn't running and looked over towards her bedside clock. She couldn't see it.

"Power's out," she said.

"Come back to bed," Jackson replied. "Nothing we can do until daylight."

AJ trudged over in the dark and slipped back under the sheet, throwing the lightweight duvet back.

"It's going to get steamy in here with no AC," she mumbled.

"Try and get back to sleep, you have your phone alarm set so it'll still wake you up on time," he said softly and kissed her forehead.

Two minutes later he returned to the slow rhythmic breathing of sleep and didn't wake when the air-conditioning kicked back on and AJ's bedside clock blinked annoyingly. She pushed the clock off the table where it continued strobing a faint green light across the corner of the bedroom nook. She pulled the duvet back over them both, turned on her side and wriggled backwards until she felt Jackson's warm body touching her. The next thing she knew there was a chicken clucking from the kitchen.

As she blinked herself awake she noticed she was alone. The empty bed next to her felt warm so Jackson couldn't have been up long. The room was dark and her mobile phone alarm hadn't gone off yet, but she figured it must be close to 6:00am if he had started the coffee maker. The aroma of the dark roast lured her from the covers and she walked the few steps to the kitchen and flicked the light switch on. The clucking sound came from the old coffee maker that gurgled and complained like a mother hen fussing about her brood. AJ pulled two cups from the cupboard and filled them with coffee, and when she returned the carafe to the coffee maker she noticed her stainless-steel travel mug on the floor. She picked it up and looked around her little cottage for other signs of carnage. Nothing else seemed too far out of place.

The front door opened and Jackson came in, turning off his torch as he closed the door behind him. He was dressed for the day in board shorts and a tee-shirt that nicely fitted his tall, lean frame. His long dark hair was tied back in a ponytail, and he smiled when he saw her in the kitchen.

"Where have you been?" AJ asked, handing him one of the coffee cups.

"Thanks," he said, taking a sip. "Just looking around outside to make sure there's no damage."

"The main house still standing over there?" she asked, referring to the large home, in the garden of which sat her rented cottage.

"No obvious problems, but I'll look again once it's light," he replied, leaving the torch on the two-person dining table near the door. "Power must still be out. I could hear the emergency generator running in the garage." He grinned as he looked her over. "I approve of the greeting outfit."

AJ blushed, standing in front of him naked apart from a coffee cup. Her shoulder-length, purple-streaked blonde hair messily falling around her face. "Don't get any ideas," she said, and shuffled over to the closet. "It's a work day."

At five foot three inches tall, AJ was no runway model, but her athletic physique and deeply tanned skin came from hard work running her dive boat. Her full-sleeve tattooed arms were toned, and her legs lean and strong from running five miles on the beach every other day. She put on her daily uniform of shorts and a 'Mermaid Divers'-emblazoned tank top over a two-piece bathing suit.

Her mobile burst into life, startling them both with Live's 'All Over You'.

"See. Time to get up," she declared unenthusiastically, and turned the alarm off.

Walking back towards the door, she reached under the table and retrieved a rarely used 24-inch LED television, wound the power cord clear of the chair, and sat the TV on the little table.

"I wonder what the news has to say about the earthquake," she said as she searched around the cottage for the remote control, checking near the sofa.

Jackson reached over and switched the TV on by the power button on the side. When AJ heard the device spring to life she turned around.

"Where was the remote?"

Jackson laughed. "I've no idea, but I found this strange button on the side and now there's small people trapped inside this flat box," he said, pointing to the newscasters on the screen.

AJ re-joined him and playfully punched his arm. "Smart-arse."

A dark-skinned Caymanian man on the television stared at them as he spoke. "Reports are still coming in as to the extent of the damage this morning from a 7.8 magnitude earthquake centred approximately 60 miles south-east of Grand Cayman, and 40 miles south of Little Cayman. The epicentre is where the Oriente fault zone on the northern side of the Cayman Trench is pulling away from the Walton fault zone, opening the trench wider every year. The trench separates the North American and Caribbean tectonic plates and according to the United States Geological Survey, the earthquake we experienced today came from more than six miles below the ocean's surface."

The man paused and a Caucasian lady sitting next to him took over in an English accent. "Several sinkholes have been reported as commuters start their daily drive. One we're hearing of in West Bay, is causing delays on West Bay Road, at the corner of West Church Street. A large hole has opened on the south side of the road, where police on the scene have closed the road to traffic in both directions, with fears the sinkhole may widen farther. We expect several after-shocks to be felt throughout the coming days, and a potential tsunami warning has been issued, although based upon the earthquake in January of this year from a similar location, with a magnitude of 7.7, concerns are low."

"Wow, that sinkhole is just over here," AJ said, pointing north. "We may have to sneak around the frontage road to get to the dock."

"Should we be going out this morning with a tsunami warning?" Jackson asked, as the reporters repeated the same snippets of news while they waited for fresh information to come in.

"Like she said, we were panicking back in January and it turned out to be a ripple. We'll keep an ear on the news and the Department of Environment or Marine Police will issue a warning if they're not letting boats go out," AJ replied, topping off her coffee in the kitchen. "I suppose the Metcalfs might cancel if they're worried about it. I'll text them before we leave."

She put a couple of cinnamon raisin bagels in the toaster and pushed the lever down. "Breakfast to go this morning," she declared as she picked up her mobile and began texting, "and I guess I won't be able to pick up ice as I can't get to the market. I'll see if Thomas can get some."

A few minutes later, with bagels and coffee in hand, they left the cottage as the first signs of dawn glowed in the eastern sky behind the island. Jackson took another quick look around the main house, before they exited the garden through a gate in the tall wooden fence, and walked to AJ's fifteen-passenger van parked on Boggy Sand Road. Her mobile chirped as she opened the driver's side door.

"Metcalfs are still on," she said, looking at the text, "I'll tell them to take the long way around the north side of West Bay."

She started the van and sent a reply on her mobile before pulling away along the narrow lane behind the large homes fronting the beach. As Boggy Sand Road curved left to meet the sea wall she waved out of the window at the ladies serving breakfast at a colourful little shack signed Heritage Kitchen. She could already see the sky was lit by red and blue flashing lights and at the junction she paused to look right towards the intersection where the sinkhole had been reported. Several police and government vehicles blocked the roads in all four directions and a series of bright orange traffic cones surrounded an area where tarmac used to be.

"Blimey, look at the size of that hole in the road," she exclaimed. "I was expecting an oversized pothole. You could fit this van in there."

"I bet it's not the only one either," Jackson commented. "Bound to be some more."

AJ eased the van forward down the tiny Mary Mollie Hyde road until it intersected with West Bay Road to the north of the closure. Commuters must have heard the news as traffic wasn't backed up, although it was still early. She turned left and drove a few hundred yards before making another left on North-West Point road where West Bay public dock was located immediately on the left, followed by Reg's small car park and dock. She parked the van as a bicycle whizzed by and skidded to a stop next to her door.

"Morning Thomas," AJ said to her friend, and only employee, as she stepped from the van.

"Good mornin', Boss," Thomas beamed back. "Gonna be a beautiful day too."

The lean, lanky young Caymanian stepped from the bike and held up a large bag of ice. "Got your message," he said, sweat already gleaming on his chestnut skin. "I'll paddle out and get the boat."

"Everything okay at home with the earthquake?" Jackson asked, coming around the van.

"Yes, sir. Just a little rockin' and rollin' is all," Thomas replied, and leaned his bicycle against the small hut they all used for storage and a makeshift office.

An old Land Rover pulled in and parked next to the van and an older man in his mid-sixties stepped out, his unruly salt-and-pepper hair blowing in the breeze off the ocean. His Cayman brown hound mutt, Coop, who was still less than a year old, leapt out of the vehicle behind him and enthusiastically ran around to everyone in turn.

"Hey Reg," AJ greeted her mentor, and the man scratched at his full, grey beard. "Cottage didn't fall down then?" he asked with a grin in a deep-toned London accent.

AJ unlocked the door to the hut and retrieved the key to her boat. "Threw some stuff around the place but otherwise alright, I think. Power's out though. Lucky we have the generator."

"Grab the key for Blue Pearl," Reg asked, and AJ picked another key from the hook inside the hut and threw it to Reg.

Reg turned and threw it straight to Thomas, who plucked it from the air.

"Sure thing, Big Boss," Thomas said and Reg nodded his thanks.

"Looks like we're both going," AJ said with a smile. "That's alright, I need the exercise."

AJ and Thomas sauntered towards the jetty where a pair of kayaks sat at the end, chained to a cleat. Morning light painted the Caribbean Sea in a warm hue as the sun steadily rose above the island and AJ smiled to herself as they untied the kayaks. It was easy to fall into her everyday routine and take her situation for granted, but lately she had reminded herself to pause for a minute and soak it all in. Her business was surviving, despite the crazy year, Jackson was here with her, and she was surrounded by wonderful friends on a gorgeous tropical island. As the two of them paddled out to the dive boats, a few hundred yards offshore at their overnight moorings, she thanked her lucky stars for the life she felt blessed to lead.

3

GRAND CAYMAN – FRIDAY

AJ and Jackson released the lines as Thomas idled the 36-foot Newton dive boat away from the dock. In normal times, the jetty would be a hive of activity with Reg's three boats, as well as AJ's 'Hazel's Odyssey', loading customers aboard for the morning dives. But with the island still restricting entry in the wake of the pandemic, business was slow and limited to Cayman residents and long-stay visitors. Reg was running one of his boats most days, and AJ had divers four or five days a week, usually taking out less than her eight-customer capacity. With very little debt, it was enough to keep the bills paid and Thomas's salary covered, so AJ had resigned herself to enjoying the slower pace while she could, and the time it afforded her to spend with Jackson.

They helped the Metcalfs set up their equipment and Thomas leaned over the railing at the back of the fly-bridge.

"Neptune's Wall, Boss?"

AJ looked at the daughter, Lindsey. "Fancy a deep wall dive now you're officially allowed, birthday girl?"

Lindsey, a slender girl with long auburn hair, lit up with a bright smile. "I think we should," she declared.

AJ gave Thomas the okay sign. "Neptune's Wall, Captain."

The Metcalfs had all learnt to dive with AJ shortly after they had arrived on Grand Cayman three years before. The father, David, worked for a property developer, a job that usually kept him busy six days a week. While building had stopped, and now returned at a slower pace, he had taken advantage of the time to dive once a week and move them all through advanced levels of certification. PADI, the largest training agency in the dive industry, restricted young divers to a maximum depth of 60 feet, which increased to 70 feet with a Junior Advanced Open Water course. At 15 years old, that certification rolled over to the adult limits, and Lindsey had just turned 15. She could now go as deep as 130 feet, although the Cayman Islands' recommended maximum was 100 feet, which AJ adhered to with her customers.

Once they reached the mooring buoy, Jackson tied the boat line in, while AJ began the dive briefing.

"As a special birthday treat for Lindsey, our first dive will be Neptune's Wall, so named because of the almost sheer drop-off into the depths where the legendary god from Roman mythology is said to reside. The top of the wall is already deep, around 70 feet, so this will be a shorter dive and our restriction will likely be our no-deco time rather than air remaining." She looked around and made sure everyone was paying attention. "Please keep a careful eye on both, and let me know if you reach half your tank, at 1500psi, or see less than ten minutes remaining of no-deco time."

The family all nodded. "Brilliant," AJ continued. "Keep a watch in the deep blue for sharks, eagle rays, jacks, and we often see ocean triggers here. The wall is spectacular and is covered in coral growth, where you're likely to find eels, some of the larger dog and mutton snappers, as well as the usual suspects you find on the reef. We'll drop down together, head straight to the drop-off and, if everyone is feeling comfortable, we'll descend to 100 feet. I don't expect any current but if there is, we'll head into the current, along the wall, and then we'll turn, moving up to the top of the wall at 65-70 feet, coming back to the line where we'll ascend to 15 feet for at least three minutes for our safety stop."

She looked around at the four faces carefully listening. "Any questions?"

The son, Andy, who was eighteen months older than his sister, raised a GoPro camera in an underwater housing. "Okay if I take my camera?"

"Of course," AJ replied, "and Jackson or I can film the four of you at some point if you like – he'll be diving with us."

The group geared up and one by one Thomas helped them waddle in their fins from the bench seats to the open stern of the Newton, before taking a giant stride into the gentle swells of the cobalt blue Caribbean Sea. Jackson was last into the water, and once he splashed in, they all began their descent towards the reef, visible far below them. Looking west, the end of the coral-covered sea floor could be seen as a hard edge giving way to the darker blue of the open ocean, where the side of the underwater mountain forming the island dropped abruptly away. AJ kept an eye on the family as they finned towards the wall. They were all competent divers with plenty of dives under their belts, mostly with her, but it was their first dive at this site, and Lindsey's first to these depths. They all seemed relaxed and at ease in the water, Andy playfully filming his sister, who struck various poses and removed her regulator to blow a kiss at the camera.

They reached the edge, where within a few feet the terrain changed from gently sloping to almost vertical. Beyond, the vastness of the open ocean stretched from the twinkling, sunlight-laced surface to the blackness of the depths. Farther offshore, the mountainside continued its way down to the bottom of the Cayman trench, the deepest part of the Caribbean Sea at 25,000 feet. Somewhere down there, the tectonic plates had shifted during the night, causing the island to shake, and the earthquake to be felt over 500 miles away. AJ felt a sense of awe, humbled by the power of nature and the sheer size of the terrain.

She heard a metallic tapping sound and turned to see Jackson signalling with a stainless-steel carabiner against his aluminium dive tank. He pointed with his other hand along the wall to the north, where AJ spotted a large loggerhead turtle slowly swimming towards the group. The largest of the three sea turtle species found in Cayman, the loggerhead was the least seen, preferring to stay away from the shallower reefs, apart from the females coming ashore to lay their eggs. Its shell alone was almost three feet long and AJ estimated this adult to weigh around 300 pounds. Andy patiently let the big reptile come to him, resisting the urge to swim towards it, which often scared the critters away. It cruised beneath them, and continued along the wall in search of the wide variety of food that made up its diet. Juveniles are omnivores, but move to a primarily carnivorous diet as they grow in size, preferring calorie-rich invertebrates.

After everyone had watched the loggerhead leave, AJ continued their descent, dropping down the face of the wall before levelling off at 100 feet. The water was still, without a trace of surge or current, and AJ chose to head south and follow the direction of the loggerhead for no other reason than the turtle had chosen that way. Unless the current dictated otherwise, she always went north, as there was a dramatic swim-through in that direction, but today she let the turtle guide her. She was happy to see Lindsey looked completely at home, shining her torch under coral heads and ridges in the wall, searching for interesting critters as they gently finned along. AJ continually switched between scanning the open water for larger pelagic fish, and studying the coral for smaller interesting life to point out. After a few minutes the wall softened its slope by a few degrees and more ravines and cuts appeared in the upper portion. She paused at a larger over-hang and peered underneath. A young nurse shark lay still, apart from its open mouth pumping water across its gills, making them flutter. AJ eased away and waved to the group, trying to avoid the need to tap against her tank, which might startle the resting shark. Rachel, the mother, made it over first, and once she saw the shark, stayed back and waved Andy over with his camera. Andy moved in closer, extended the collapsible stick his GoPro was mounted to, and began filming the brown, four-foot shark from a safe distance, while the group remained still in the water, watching.

Once he had finished shooting he turned and signalled okay to AJ, who held up her hand for him to stay still, then pointed below him. Andy looked down and jumped in surprise. A large green moray eel was free swimming along the wall below him, looking for a new crevice to wriggle into and hide. AJ watched as Andy swung his camera around to film the eel but, rushed and startled, he fumbled his grip and the GoPro along with its three-foot stick began dropping towards the depths. Andy's first reaction was to chase after his precious camera, but AJ quickly reached him, and holding his arm signalled for him to stay where he was. They all watched as the expensive little video camera descended towards the blackness below them. AJ checked her dive computer on her wrist. They were at 95 feet, had been under water for twenty-four minutes, and she had thirteen minutes of no-deco time left. The computer was telling her she could spend thirteen more minutes at 95 feet before she would need to make several decompression stops at shallower depths to allow excess nitrogen to dissipate from her body before surfacing. In recreational diving, avoiding decompression stops was considered mandatory to remain within safety margins.

She knew she couldn't catch up to the camera quickly enough to avoid going below 130 feet, so she watched to see if it would land on the steep slope, or if it would keep bouncing down to its demise hundreds of feet below. Two storeys below them, the long handle touched the wall and kicked the camera around where it landed on an odd-looking, silty debris field. The exact depth was hard to judge, but AJ decided she had time and margin to drop down and take a look. If the camera was below 130 feet, she would leave it. She turned to the group and signalled for them to stay with Jackson, who led them up the wall towards shallower water. They all acknowledged, and AJ held Jackson's stare for a moment. Behind his mask, his soft hazel eyes told her to be careful. She gave him an okay sign before turning and finning down. AJ covered the ground quickly, not wanting to spend any longer at depth than necessary, and kept a close eye on her computer. She reached the camera at 124 feet, perched on the pile of rock and sand debris covering the coral like a scree field. She scooped up the camera, collapsed the handle, and turned to swim back up, before stopping when she noticed a hole in the wall. Curious, she unclipped her torch from her BCD and shone the light inside the two-foot-long crack. It appeared that something had caused the face to blow out and reveal a cave. Peeking through the narrow fracture she shone the beam around and was surprised to see the cave, or cavern, was large. She estimated it to be tall enough to stand inside and about the same width. She looked back down at the fresh debris that had poured from the crack and realised it most likely happened in last night's earthquake.

AJ turned her light off. The crack was too small for her to crawl through, with or without her dive gear, but as she stared into the dark void, her eyes began to adjust to the darkness and she noticed a hint of light, way back inside. It was a cavern, and there was another entrance somewhere above. She shrugged her shoulders and reminded herself this was supposed to be a quick camera retrieval. There were hundreds of caves and caverns in the coral reefs; this one was no more interesting than any other, except that it had just been revealed. She looked at the camera. The power was still on and she pressed the record button on the top. Pointing the camera through the crevice, she shone her torch alongside and made a sweep of the interior. That'll give the Metcalfs something cool to talk about, she thought, pulling back from the wall and filming the opening and scree field. She stopped the camera and looked up. It felt like the wall towered over her, and the group were silhouetted figures against the bright surface above. She quickly filmed them as she started back up the wall. Turning off the camera, she glanced at her dive computer that told her she had only one more minute at that depth, which was now 117 feet. AJ finned firmly, careful not to ascend too quickly, and met the group at 70 feet where the reef met the wall. She handed Andy his camera to enthusiastic and thankful okay signs from the family.

Leading them up to 60 feet, she wasted no time heading back towards the boat, but couldn't help glancing down at the reef. Somewhere around there was the other entrance to the cavern. She laughed to herself. The last thing she needed was another crazy cavern adventure; she'd had enough of those in the past few years. She sure as hell wasn't venturing into a strange, empty cavern at 124 feet, but it did strike her as cool that fate had chosen to show her what the earthquake had revealed. Jackson was big on all things connected in nature, karma and ideology that she had felt, but never thought much about before meeting him. She couldn't wait to tell him how a turtle and a dropped camera had led her to a long hidden cavern that last night's earthquake had opened up.

4

GRAND CAYMAN – SEPTEMBER, 1986

If you're born in England and your last name is Jones, you will be called Jonesy. It's practically the law. Unless you have a lyrical first name that can be spun into something more comical or derogatory. Charles was not nearly interesting enough, so Charlie Jones had been known as Jonesy since he was a young lad in the West Midlands countryside. After six years on Grand Cayman, he and his wife Alison were familiar to most folks around Seven Mile Beach, and their well-used 1967 Bertram 25, 'Bottom Time', was a regular fixture running fishing and scuba diving trips. Jonesy enjoyed being out on the water, whatever they were doing, but his favourite activity of all was hunting for treasure. With that very much in mind, he pedalled his 10-speed Raleigh bicycle up to the post office in central George Town, where he had checked his mailbox every day for two weeks.

"Mr. Jones, sir," came a locally accented voice across the room, as Jonesy was about to put his key in the lock of his post box.

He turned from the wall of tiny metal doors and saw the postmaster waving to him from behind the counter.

"I have something for you, sir. Wouldn't fit in the box," the dark-skinned man in the postal uniform said.

Jonesy hurried over to the counter. He was more excited at 37 years old, waiting on this package, than he could ever remember being as a kid. Christmas, birthdays, none of them compared to his nervous anticipation for this bundle of papers.

The postmaster slid an overstuffed manila envelope across the counter and looked at Jonesy inquisitively.

"Been waiting on this, I'm guessing," he said, smiling. "Usually see Mrs. Jones in here but once a week, and you've been checking that box every day for a fortnight."

Jonesy barely heard the words. He stared at the scuffed and battered envelope that had made the journey from England in about the time he could have walked the same distance. He mumbled a thank you, grabbed the envelope and beelined for the door. The contents of this package were for his eyes only; he couldn't risk anyone else getting the slightest hint of what he was up to. That was the nature of tracking down things that had been lost, wrecked or discarded hundreds of years ago. They sat around in undisturbed solitude for centuries until someone found a clue or stumbled across them, and then everyone clamoured to snatch their piece of history.

Jonesy shoved the envelope into the top of his cargo shorts and pulled his faded multicoloured Benetton shirt over the package to hold it in place, before swinging his leg over the Raleigh. He plucked his headphones from where they hung on the bike frame and slipped the foam-covered speakers over his ears, hitting play on the Sony Walkman duct-taped to the handlebars. The guitar intro for Rainbow's 'Since You Been Gone' blasted from the headphones and if Jonesy's hands weren't occupied steering his bike, he would have air-guitared along with it.

As he rode north on Edward Street, his thoughts shifted to Alison. "Hey love, exciting news! I have a package full of information that will lead us to a fortune." He pictured her response, and his elation subsided a notch or two. His problem was, he had no idea if it would lead them anywhere. That, and the fact he had promised he would stop chasing lost treasure stories and focus on running the boat for paying customers. He knew she was right. If he didn't get more income rolling in they would lose their office, which happened to be attached to their home. It was also their best advertising, as the little building sat on the road out of town with the boat moored in the water outside the back door. The sign on the building brought in the majority of their clients.

He turned left on Fort Street and continued pedalling with sweat running down his forehead and his shirt soaking through, thinking about the words he would say when he walked through the door. With the small port in front of him, he turned right on North Church Street and continued north with the Caribbean Sea on his left. His eyes wandered to the calm blue water until a building blocked his view. His feet stopped pedalling, and before he made any conscious decision, he had braked and slowed to a stop outside the front door of the Hog Sty Bay Bar and Restaurant. Well, he thought, propping his bike against the wall by the door, might as well keep a bar stool pinned to the floor while I figure this out. He walked inside and squinted through the smoky haze wafting around the dimly lit room. Through the back of the restaurant section he could see a magnificent view of the ocean, but he turned to the right where a low-ceilinged bar was located. It was 4 o'clock in the afternoon, and the crowd was thin beyond a few regulars who nodded his way. He took a stool at the end of the bar by the wall dividing the drinking from the eating. A bleached blonde bartender had an Appleton and Coke on a coaster in front of him before his backside had settled on the seat. He nodded his thanks and tried not to look at her expansive chest, prominently displayed in a tip-inducing, form-fitting, v-neck tee-shirt. Sandy winked and walked away, her hips putting a little swagger to her denim shorts for good measure. Jonesy shook his head and took a hefty sip of his drink. The woman had to be pushing fifty, but Sandy could still put on a show, and she mixed a mean drink; the generous shot or three of rum hadn't spent long under the soda fountain.

He placed the envelope on the bar and sipped his drink

thoughtfully. He wanted to open it up and start poring over the contents, but what he needed to do was figure out how he was going to sell Ally on the whole matter. As the distilled sugar cane lubricated his thoughts and no obvious tact in handling his wife came to mind, his finger slipped under the sealed flap of the envelope and before long he had papers scattered on the bar top.

"Work or play, sugar?" came a southern American accent.

Jonesy looked up with a start as Sandy leaned over the bar and surveyed his jumble of papers. He awkwardly gathered them in.

"Just some old rubbish I've been meaning to sort out," he said, knowing the explanation sounded weak.

She swooped up his empty glass and grinned. "Whatever, sugar," she said, turning away. "Just cut me in on half if you hit big." In one fluid motion she picked a rum bottle up to shoulder height, spun around, tipped the bottle so the amber liquid poured like a fountain and landed in his glass, strategically held in front of her chest. "I'll make it worth your while," she added in a sultry tone, throwing one more wink at him for good measure.

Jonesy stared at the show and found himself in the rare position of being speechless. He nodded, and busied himself with the papers as Sandy dropped ice in the glass and gave the rum its courtesy moment under the soda fountain. She slid the glass towards him with a knowing grin and he felt like a boy caught with his face in a nudie magazine. Bloody hell, he thought, I bet she'd have half the money spent in two weeks, before taking off with the other half. Boy oh boy, what a two weeks it would be though. He blushed as thoughts of his wife shoved lewd ones of Sandy to the side. He had never been unfaithful, and never planned to be, but he guessed the bartender could test his resolve if she put her mind to it.

He looked back down at the papers and his mind refocused as he took a big sip of his drink. The pages were filled with photocopies of old letters, logs and reports with flourishing penmanship and old English spelling that was hard to follow. Jonesy had spent several years sending written requests to the Public Record Office in Kew, just outside London. With no success, he finally asked a cousin back in the UK, who was a school teacher, to request the copies he desired, and now every piece of written data from Sir Francis Drake's Caribbean Raid of 1585-86 lay before him. He thumbed through the pages, scanning the documents for specific dates or mentions of The Caymanes, the name given to the Cayman Islands at that time. He paused on a page showing a captain's log from April 1586. The following pages contained more log entries throughout the month and he searched for the 22nd. Jonesy rocked on his bar stool, his feet nervously tapping on the foot rail of the bar, and his eyes darting across the entries made by a man over 400 years ago. The cool rum was refreshing after an afternoon in the hot sun, and when his glass rattled with nothing left but ice, Sandy had it refilled by the time he reached for it again. He tapped a page and grunted in satisfaction. There it was, in Sir Francis Drake's own handwriting, the man's irritation clearly evident. Now, all Jonesy had to do was figure out where the Elizabeth Bonaventure had been at anchor, and he'd be diving for artefacts worth hundreds of thousands of pounds, maybe millions.

When the third glass was empty, he decided it was time to head home. Buoyed with the confidence of new information, he was sure Ally would be just as excited as he was. Jonesy looked at the bill tucked in a glass before him, slipped a Caymanian ten-dollar note back in the glass, and stood up. Sandy quickly swooped over, leaned over the bar and displayed her money makers.

"Leaving so soon?" she asked.

"Better be getting home," he replied.

"Too bad," she pouted, clutching the glass to her chest. "Need change?"

Jonesy laughed. "No, it's all yours, love."

"You're a doll," Sandy smiled. "Tell Ally I said hi," she added, and gave him another wink.

He left the bar, and through the large windows in the restaurant he noticed the sunset was in full glory over the water. He'd been there longer than he had thought, or planned. He hurried out to his bicycle and stuffed the envelope back in his shorts and under his shirt. It wasn't far to his house, but he put his headphones on anyway and hit play. He was in a great mood. Finally, he was bringing home the break they deserved. He pedalled away from the bar with Van Halen's 'Panama' lifting his spirits even higher. He had the answers to their problems, and if he timed things just right, he and Ally would be catching the end of a gorgeous sunset, drink in hand, before going upstairs and celebrating. Sandy had him all stirred up, and once his wife heard about the logs, she would be just as keen to spend the evening in bed, he was sure of it.

Jonesy swung around the small, two-storey wooden building signed 'Bottom Time Charters', hopped off his bike and leaned it against the back wall. Behind him their old Bertram bobbed alongside the short pier extending from the ironshore as he walked through the open door and called out to his wife.

"I'm home, love."

He strode through the back room where they kept their dive and fishing gear, past the bathroom, and the stairs leading up to their flat, and into the front office where he saw Ally sitting behind the desk.

"And where have you been, laddie?" came a male voice with a thick Scottish accent.

Jonesy turned to see the man standing on the opposite side of the office, blowing out a thick stream of cigarette smoke.

"Your lassie was getting worried about you," the man continued with a nod towards Alison.

He was a tall, thick-set man in his early sixties with close-cropped grey hair and a full beard. He wore jeans and a white singlet, displaying time-blurred navy tattoos on each thick, deeply tanned arm. Jonesy stopped in his tracks and looked from the man over to his wife. Ally looked scared; and pissed off. His optimism and glee evaporated under her glare, and he turned back to the man.

"How can I help you, Mr. McGinnis?"

5

GRAND CAYMAN – FRIDAY

The rest of the morning had been uneventful, their second dive a relaxing hour on the shallow reef with Thomas guiding, before they returned to the dock. The Metcalfs reserved another day the following week, and left AJ and Thomas an extra-nice tip for saving them the cost of a new camera. Thomas now sprayed down Hazel's Odyssey with the freshwater hose, while AJ and Jackson drove down the road to get them all lunch.

"I didn't want to say too much in front of the Metcalfs, in case the kids got any ideas," AJ said as she drove them south down West Bay Road, "but there was a bit of light in the back of that cave."

"Could you tell where from?" Jackson asked. "Are you thinking there's another way in?"

AJ shrugged her shoulders. "Maybe. I couldn't see much, but it's obviously above, and must be directly above for the light to reach the cave. The hole was at 124 feet and the top of the reef is at 70 feet so we're talking over 50 feet. That's a long way for a continuous chimney."

Jackson thought for a moment as AJ turned right at the crossroads onto Boggy Sand Road, which went a short distance towards the water before turning sharply left. She parked just after the corner and they both got out of the van and walked over to Heritage Kitchen, the local food shack they had passed that morning.

"There are several ravines and gullies where the reef meets the wall," Jackson said as they approached the counter in the brightly painted shack. "Could be it leads down from the base of one of them and isn't as tall as we think."

"Could be," AJ replied, as she studied the daily specials board. "We could have a look around next time we dive that buoy."

"Hi there, Miss AJ," a Caymanian lady with a big smile beamed from behind the counter.

"Hello, Miss Grece, how are you today, my dear?" AJ replied.

"Can't complain, sweetie," she said, laughing. "Ain't nobody gonna listen if I do."

AJ heard another woman's voice from the kitchen in the back. "That's right, Miss Grece."

Miss Grece smiled even wider and chuckled. "See now? Anyway, what can I get you today, sweetie?"

"I'll have that fish wrap you always make me, and let's get Thomas whatever your special is. You know him, he'll want whatever you tell him is good. Make that two of them – Reg will want something too once we show up with food." She turned to Jackson. "You want your veggie wrap?"

"I will, thank you," Jackson replied.

"Honey, when you gonna eat some meat? Get a little flesh on them skinny bones of yours," Miss Grece said, chuckling.

"You leave that boy alone, Miss Grece," came the voice from the kitchen. "AJ's man just fine the way he is."

Miss Grece waved a hand towards the kitchen and winked at Jackson, who smiled and stayed quiet. He was vegetarian and Miss Grece gave him a hard time, in good humour, every visit. AJ, who was pescatarian, was happy to have the lady's attention shift from her.

They took the sandwiches back to the dock and sat with their legs over the side in the bright sun and ate their lunch. Coop hovered near them, carefully watching every movement of every sandwich, willing a piece to fall his way. Thomas had already taken Hazel's Odyssey out to its mooring and AJ was correct in her assumption that Reg would join them. He brought the three of them ciders and for Thomas, who didn't drink alcohol, he brought a Coke from the fridge in the little hut.

AJ's mobile rang and she looked at the caller ID. It was David Metcalf and her first thought was they had left something on the boat.

"Hey David."

"Hi AJ, sorry to bother you," he said. "But Andy's been going through his video, and I think there's something you should see."

AJ was taken aback. The man didn't sound his jovial self, his voice laced with concern. "Okay, do you want to send it to me, or should I come by?"

"No, the file is too big to email, and I think it's best we show you in person," he replied. "Is there somewhere we can meet? I don't want to mess up your afternoon, just name a place that works for you."

"We're still at the dock if you'd like to meet here?" AJ suggested, and cringed when she looked at the drink in her hand. "We're just hanging out."

"Be there in ten minutes. Thanks," he said, and hung up.

AJ put her mobile down and took a swig of her cider, wondering what Andy could have shot on his camera that had David so worried.

"What was that about?" Jackson asked before taking another bite of his sandwich.

"I'm not really sure," AJ replied, honestly. "He's coming over. Apparently there's something weird on the video Andy filmed."

AJ finished her Strongbow and stood up. "I should probably ditch this though. Don't want customers thinking I'm in the habit of drinking at lunchtime."

Reg laughed and handed her his empty bottle. "Here, take this then, and bring me another one. I don't care what your customers think."

AJ shook her head and took Reg's empty from him as she walked up the jetty towards the refrigerator in the hut, Coop trotting along beside her.

A moment after she reached the hut, David and Andy arrived, and AJ walked over to meet them in the small car park. David smiled when he greeted her, but his expression still showed concern and Andy, who carried a laptop under his arm, looked pensive.

"We didn't know what you'd have to play this on so we brought Andy's laptop," David explained.

"Great. This is all very mysterious," AJ said, her concern growing. "We can step aboard Reg's boat at the dock and take a look in the shade. We already took my boat out to the mooring."

They walked down the dock in silence, and for the first time AJ wondered if she had done something wrong during their dives. She couldn't think of anything they would have had an issue with; they had seemed more than happy, so she pushed the thought aside.

"Reg, mind if we use your boat for a minute? We need some cover to look at the computer."

Reg waved a hand in the air. "Go ahead," he said and then continued under his breath. "Guess I'll get my own bloody drink."

AJ glared at him as she passed by and stepped aboard the *Newton* tied alongside the dock. The Metcalfs followed, and set the laptop up on the shelf at the front of the area covered by the flybridge. Andy woke the computer up and AJ saw the video player was paused on a blurry image of coral.

"Take a look and tell us if you see what we think we're seeing," David said, and Andy hit play.

The video rolled and AJ realised it was her shot of the cavern. The blurry coral was the wall as she had turned on record then the view moved inside the pitch-black crevice before her torch lit up a section of the interior. The camera panned around the inside of the cavern, which she could now see didn't go back as far as she had thought. The lens effect underwater explained why it had appeared larger to her, and now it was clear there was a back wall, but the ceiling ended before it met the wall. She knew she had seen a faint light in the back of the cavern so it made sense there was a chimney leading up towards the top of the reef, 50 feet above. As the image panned around, nothing about the cavern struck her as odd or particularly interesting. The floor was covered in a fine silt, crushed coral and lumps of debris which undoubtedly had fallen from the chimney above over time. The fracture, which she presumed was opened by the earthquake, was to the right side at the base of the cavern, which explained the amount of scree that had poured out when the coral face broke apart. Some of the accumulation across the floor had spilt out along with the thin, shattered wall. The camera finished its sweep inside with a pan across the left side before shakily pulling back from the hole.

"What was that?" AJ said, and looked at David.

Something caught her eye right before the image went blurry as the camera lost the torchlight and tried to adjust itself to the light outside. Andy carefully moved the cursor back on the play bar and hit pause.

"That was our question," David said quietly.

AJ stared at the screen. The image was far from crisp, half concealed in dark shadow. But something man-made was unmistakably in view. It had an unnaturally smooth edge and a dull brown colour. Andy moved the image frame by frame on the screen, but none were more revealing or clear.

"What do you think?" David asked.

AJ continued looking at the screen. "I think I know what it looks like, but it's hard to say for sure," she replied, "and why it would be in there I have no clue."

She turned to David, conscious of the fact the man's seventeen-year-old son was with them, "Can't think of a good scenario for a…" She stopped herself and thought for a second. "Mind if the guys take a look?"

"Of course not," David replied.

AJ turned around and looked over at the three men sitting on the side of the jetty chatting, Reg and Jackson with fresh Strongbows in hand.

"Hey, you lot. Come take a look at this, see what you think."

Jackson and Thomas got to their feet, but Reg turned slowly and looked at AJ with a grin. "Better be something good."

AJ rolled her eyes and waved at him. "Get in here, you grumpy old goat."

Reg got up and followed the other two onto the boat and they huddled around the screen. Andy played the video in real time from the beginning of the clip, and then found the best frame to pause on.

"Bloody hell," Reg mumbled under his breath.

AJ looked at him. "That is what I think it is, right?"

Reg nodded slowly. "If you're thinking that's a dive tank, I'd say you're right."

"It has the curvature at the top like a tank, but why would it be brown?" Jackson asked. "Surely coral wouldn't grow on the inside of that cave, there's no light in there."

"It's not coral, it's rust," Reg replied. "It must be a steel tank."

The group stood in silence for a minute, staring at the screen as Andy moved back and forth, frame by frame.

"So…" David finally said hesitantly, "if that's a dive tank, do we think the poor fellow that was using it is in there too?"

"Don't know why you'd leave a tank down there, especially at the end of a cave," Reg answered.

"Yeah, I suppose it was a cave until last night," AJ added. "The earthquake opened this end and made it a cavern."

"But this opening is way too small to enter through, how do we find the other entrance you talked about earlier?" Jackson asked.

AJ shrugged her shoulders. "Search around above, I guess."

"Don't need to if you just want to know what else is in der," Thomas said. "Go back down and stick the camera back tru da hole. Now you know what you're looking for you can try and get a better shot."

"We could reverse the camera on the stick too," Andy added enthusiastically. "Set it up like a selfie, so when you put it inside it would film the outside wall."

David held his hands up. "Wait a second everyone. Before we get too carried away, shouldn't we involve the authorities? Before we go rummaging around in what could be the scene of a fatality, we should probably inform the police."

"We can if you like," Reg replied. "They would likely send a diver down to take a look."

David nodded. "Then we better call them and give them the chance to do that."

AJ couldn't help but laugh, and Reg grinned at her.

"What am I missing?" David asked.

"The next person the police will call is likely to be me," Reg answered. "I'm their diver for stuff like this." He pointed to AJ. "And she's next in line."

David smiled. "Well, I guess you could see if there's anything in there to talk about before we call them."

"We'll likely see our police friend tonight anyway," AJ added. "We can tell him about it."

Reg nodded. "Yeah, Detective Whittaker will be at the pub tonight, we'll mention it to him."

"Dive again tomorrow then?" Jackson asked.

"Looks like it," AJ replied. "Want to come out with us?" she asked, looking at David and Andy.

"Hell yes," Andy answered immediately.

"Andy…" his father cautioned him.

"Sorry. Yes, I'd like to if you don't mind," Andy tried again.

AJ laughed. "No problem. Can't take you down to the cavern entrance, but you can watch from 100 feet. How about 8 o'clock tomorrow morning?"

"Thank you, AJ, we'll be here, just Andy and me," David said.

"Sounds good," AJ replied, as Andy closed the lid on his laptop and tucked it under his arm. "And just to be clear, this will be a fun dive with us – there's no charge."

Andy's smile got broader. "Cool, thanks."

"That's very kind of you, but maybe we can chip in for gas?" David added.

"No need," AJ responded. "It's a short run to Neptune's Wall. You've done more than enough to help us over the summer, David."

She turned to Reg. "You coming with us?"

Reg winked at Thomas. "Seeing as you're handing out free diving, I think I might."

AJ shoved him all the way off his own boat to the dock.

6

GRAND CAYMAN – FRIDAY

AJ followed West Bay Road around the north-west corner of the island and continued past Lighthouse Point for a few hundred yards before she turned into the busy car park of the Fox and Hare pub. It was a few minutes before 7 o'clock and the sun had long since set. She found an open spot, parked the van, stepped out and waited for Jackson to come around from the passenger side. They walked across the crushed coral car park towards the pub and Jackson leaned over and kissed the top of AJ's head.

"You look especially beautiful," he said softly.

AJ rarely wore make-up, but she had gone all out and put on eyeliner and a hint of blush for their date night. She had washed and blow-dried her shoulder-length blonde hair, and chosen a sleeveless floral summer dress which accented the creative artwork in her tattoos. As she smiled up at her boyfriend, towering over her by a foot, she wished she had worn heels instead of her Gumbies sandals.

The Fox and Hare was a plain, two-storey, stucco building from the outside, but once through the doors, the interior was a trip across the ocean to a traditional English village pub. Dining booths lined the right wall with the heavy oak wood bar on the left, lined with stools. A few tables and chairs were scattered along the centre of the room, leaving plenty of space for groups to stand and socialise near the bar. Three dartboards were constantly in use at the far end, with bathrooms to their left and the kitchen beyond that. In the front left corner was a small curved stage, and as AJ and Jackson entered to the sound of chatter, and music playing over the speakers, they waved to Reg's wife Pearl, who was setting up for her evening performance. Pearl was a good-looking, curvy blonde woman, a few years younger than Reg and the apple of his eye. Several Fridays a month, she played to a packed house, and since the island had opened back up internally after the pandemic restrictions, her gigs were more popular than ever.

The Cayman Islands had eradicated the COVID-19 virus from their shores over the summer, and with strict quarantine and border restrictions in place, the government had allowed the population to return to normal life. The tourist industry had taken a financial beating, but the government used its wisely accumulated financial stockpile to supply aid to resident workers and local businesses, keeping everyone solvent through the difficult months.

Reg was helping his wife get organised on the stage, but when he spotted AJ he pointed towards a long table he had commandeered for the group. AJ and Jackson made their way through the crowd and found Reg's table already filled with many of their friends. Everyone stood and AJ worked her way around, hugging everyone. After months of distancing, the physical contact of hugging the people she loved felt wonderful, and important somehow. She savoured each embrace and took her time greeting everyone in turn, although it had only been somewhere between hours and a few weeks since she had last seen them. When they all finally sat down, AJ looked around the table. Thomas was there with his girlfriend Jacqueline, who he had now been dating for most of the year – a new personal record for the lad. Next to them was Thomas's sister Sydney, and her boyfriend Carlos who she had met at university in Miami. He was a Cuban exile now working for Reg as a dive guide, and with most of Reg's crew heading back to their native lands when the pandemic hit, he was staying busy. Nora was a young woman from Norway who, along with her boyfriend, Ridley, had been granted amnesty to stay on the island after helping the authorities bring a couple of criminals to justice. Ridley now taught sailing lessons. The last person at the table was the youngest. Hallie Bodden was Thomas's second cousin but was being raised by his parents after her mother had died and she had fended for herself for a while. What a diverse and international group, AJ thought, looking from face to face. She had a connection to each of them in some special way that meant the world to her. Jackson squeezed her hand, and she grinned like a joyous child.

"Hi AJ, you need a drink, love?" the waitress asked.

"Strongbow, please," she replied, and looked over at the empty glass by Reg's seat. "Better bring Reg another too."

The waitress turned to Jackson. "What about you, dear?"

"Rum and Coke, please," he replied, and after checking with everyone else at the table, the waitress made her way back to the bar.

AJ looked across the table at Hallie, sitting next to Nora, and smiled. She was seventeen, but had already lived the life of a much older soul and was finally experiencing the world as a teenager should. She was doing well in school and making friends, but still preferred the company of people older than herself, and was closest to Nora. Nora was still only eighteen, and looked even younger, but spoke and acted with a maturity way beyond her years. She had started online college courses earlier in the summer, as she didn't have a work visa, and jobs providing one were currently non-existent.

"How are your studies going, Nora?" AJ asked.

"Okay," she replied in her accented English. "I'm trying to get through the requisite courses quickly. They're boring but I have to do them before I can begin classes in psychology."

"Wow," AJ said, and thought about it for a second. "I can see you being really good at that – you've certainly experienced some strange personalities in your life."

Nora grinned. "I suppose I have. I'd like to specialise in child psychology; maybe I can do some good with that."

Hallie leaned against her friend.

"I think you'll be brilliant," AJ replied, and thought how much the two seemed like sisters. One, a blonde, Nordic beauty with defined features and the other, a pretty, almond-skinned, dark-haired, soft-featured island girl.

The waitress returned with the drinks as Sydney leaned forward and spoke loudly to be heard over the crowd. "So what's new with you, AJ?"

AJ thought for a moment. "You know, apart from the earthquake last night, everything's actually been pretty quiet and… normal," she replied.

Carlos lifted his glass. "I say we drink to that," he announced.

They all raised their glasses. "To normal!"

"Normal?" Reg growled, arriving at the table. "There's nothing bloody normal about you lot."

The youthful group booed and groaned at the man in good spirits.

"Wait up," Jackson said, holding up a hand. "I like that better," he said raising his glass again. "Here's to never being normal."

The group enthusiastically agreed and loudly raised a toast to never being normal. Reg sat down, shaking his head, but AJ could see he was grinning behind his thick beard.

"Have you seen Whittaker here?" she asked when the noise settled.

Reg pointed a thumb over his shoulder. "Yeah, he's over there. Haven't talked to him yet, except to say hello."

The music over the speakers died down and the crowd began to quieten in anticipation.

AJ leaned over the table. "Maybe we'll go over and chat with him between sets," she said in a hushed tone as the opening guitar riff for Heart's 'Barracuda' boomed from the stage to a round of applause. Reg nodded to AJ as he clapped along with the crowd. She noticed him looking around the table at the group, and caught the glint in his eye. For Pearl and Reg, with no children of their own, the young people sitting around the table were the closest thing they had to offspring, and they cherished the time they spent with them. The couple had taken AJ under their wing over ten years ago when she moved to Grand Cayman, and with her parents thousands of miles away in England, they had become her extended family. His gaze met hers and he gave her a wink.

Pearl ran through her first set, her gritty and powerful voice covering classic rock tunes by Janis Joplin and Melissa Etheridge and finishing with Sass Jordan's 'You Don't Have to Remind Me'. She made her way over to the table as the applause died down and Reg stood and held her chair while she sat. Her forehead glowed with perspiration and she took a long drink of cold water while everyone complimented her on the great music.

"Thank you, my dears," she said in her London accent, putting the glass down on the table. "This old broad's got a few tunes left in her."

Reg leaned over and kissed her cheek. "I'd say."

AJ stood up. "Sorry to run off just when you come over, but we need to talk to Whittaker for a minute."

"What are you up to now?" Pearl asked, eyeing her suspiciously.

Reg stood up as well, and Pearl looked up at him. "The pair of you, huh? I don't like the look of this."

Reg laughed. "How come you think we're up to no good?"

Pearl rolled her eyes and grinned, "Because that's what you two are always up to. And, why else would you be off to talk to a detective?"

AJ realised everyone at the table was staring at them, waiting for an answer. "It's probably nothing," she said, trying to sound casual. "We found a cavern opened up by the earthquake, and maybe there's something inside it."

Everyone started asking questions at the same time and AJ threw her hands in the air. "Jackson and Thomas can tell you about it. We'll be right back."

Reg squeezed Pearl's shoulder and he and AJ quickly escaped through the crowd.

Born and raised on Grand Cayman, Detective Roy Whittaker was a slim man, five-ten with skin the colour of milky coffee. He had a friendly face and an easy manner, especially out on a Friday night with his wife, listening to their favourite music. He peered over his glasses at the two as they approached, and smiled.

"Good evening, Reg. Pearl is wonderful tonight, as always." He stood and surprised AJ by greeting her with a hug. "Hello, AJ."

His wife shook their hands and they all sat.

"She'll come by and say hello at some point," Reg said, "but we had something to talk to you about, if you don't mind?"

Whittaker's expression tightened a little. "You're not going to ruin my evening, are you?"

Reg laughed. "No, it's nothing that serious."

"We were diving off the west side today, and we found a cavern that seemed to have been opened up by the earthquake last night," AJ started. "I couldn't see much inside but I shot some video, and when we looked back at the film, well, it was the Metcalfs that actually saw it first, but anyway, we noticed what looks like an old scuba tank."

Whittaker listened carefully until she finished. "Inside this cavern?"

"Yeah, it's at what would have been the back of the cave," AJ explained, "but the earthquake popped a piece of the wall out so now you can see in there."

"I see," Whittaker said thoughtfully. "And you're concerned about how it got there?"

"Well, most times, scuba tanks are attached to humans," Reg said with a grin. "We are wondering how this tank got to the bottom of a cave."

"And if the human is still with it," Whittaker finished for him.

"Exactly," AJ said.

"Did you see any evidence of human remains?" the detective asked.

"No, but the opening is really small, much too small for me to fit through, and I only did a quick sweep around the inside with the camera, shining my torch in there," AJ explained. "We thought we'd go back and try filming a bit more, see if I can get a clearer shot."

"Okay, well that seems like a good plan. I'm sure there's a few explanations why the tank could be in there," Whittaker said, with little conviction. "Was the rig with it or just a tank?"

"Can't tell from what we have," Reg replied. "There's a chance it's not even a scuba tank to be honest, but it definitely looks like one."

"Sounds like getting better video is the best way to move forward – why don't you do that and let me know what you find," Whittaker said, sitting back in his chair.

"Great," AJ said, getting to her feet. "We're going back out tomorrow, so we'll give you a bell once we look at the film."

Whittaker nodded. "Thank you." He looked at Reg. "Could you tell how long it's been there? Did it look in good shape, like it might be recent?"

Reg shook his head. "It's old is my guess. It's rusty, which means it's a steel tank, and we haven't used steels on the island for donkey's years." He scratched his beard for a moment. "Everything's been aluminium since the late eighties."

Whittaker looked thoughtful. "Really? That might be interesting."

"What are you thinking?" AJ asked.

The detective smiled. "Let me know when you get the new film and if you can see something more," he said, clearly choosing not to elaborate.

The house music stopped and AJ heard the stage microphone come on.

"Before I play this next song, I'd like to sing happy birthday to somebody very special," Pearl's voice echoed around the room and the crowd went quiet. "Where's Reg then?" she asked, and the crowd parted until she could see her husband standing by Whittaker's table.

"There's that wonderful old fella of mine," Pearl said, trying not to laugh.

She strummed her guitar and began singing happy birthday with the crowd loudly, and untunefully, joining in.

Whittaker shouted to be heard. "I didn't know it was your birthday, Reg. Happy birthday, my friend."

Reg shook his head and AJ sang as loudly as she could, a huge smile on her face. As the song came to an end and the crowd's cheers and applause subsided, Pearl began the intro to Guns N' Roses' 'Sweet Child O' Mine'.

"It's not actually his birthday, but look how embarrassed the old bugger is," Pearl said, and the crowd cheered even louder.

The place began to shake and the aftershock rattled every bottle and glass in the room, spilling drinks and rocking the pictures on the walls. Pearl never stopped playing and didn't miss a beat.

"That's what Reg does to my world, ladies and gentlemen," she said, smiling at her husband.

7

GRAND CAYMAN – SEPTEMBER 1986

Given more time to reflect, and considerably less of Sandy's rum in his system, Jonesy might have been better equipped to handle a conversation with his landlord. But just as fate is misguidedly blamed for poor decisions, he forged ahead with the commitment of a man convinced his standing had merit.

"I'll be able to pay you, no problem."

"'I'll be able' works before the due date," Torsten McGinnis explained calmly. "Able is the only thing that matters now."

The man took another draw on his hand-rolled cigarette and squinted at Jonesy through the hazy smoke that hung around his side of the room.

"We don't allow smoking in our office, Mr. McGinnis," Jonesy said, and couldn't believe the words left his lips.

Ally rolled her eyes and cringed from behind the desk.

"Do you not, now?" McGinnis replied with a hint of a smirk. "Well if this building belonged to you, that would mean something, wouldn't it?" he said quietly, before his booming voice escalated. "But as I own the bloody building, and you're about to be kicked out on your arse, I don't give a damn what your bloody rules are."

Alison stood up. "I'm sorry Mr. McGinnis, he just means we do take great care of your building…"

"You can call me Torsten," he interrupted her in a pleasant tone.

"Oh, okay, thank you, Torsten," Ally bumbled, clearly rattled by his uncomfortably charming manner towards her. "Well, the point is, we've been good tenants, we've made many upgrades to the premises since we've been here, and we have a charter in the next few days that will allow us to pay our rent to you."

McGinnis smiled at Ally before turning to Jonesy, who felt one step behind the whole situation. He didn't know about this new charter they had.

"I think I've been a very patient man," McGinnis said. "You're late paying every month, and I've given you plenty of time to get your business in order. I have someone with a real business, who actually takes paying customers out on his boats. Aye, I said boats. Not one crappy little piece of junk like you're running, Jones. So this month, I'm giving you until the 11th, as the lease clearly states, and if you dinnae pay in full, you're oot. That clear, Jones?"

"But that's only four days from now," Jonesy mumbled.

McGinnis shook his head and smiled sympathetically at Ally.

"Today's the 8th," Ally corrected her husband. "We have three days, if you include today."

Jonesy looked over at Ally. "Good job we've got that charter."

Her shoulders sank and he saw a look on her face he couldn't fathom.

"Until the 11th," McGinnis reiterated, as he headed for the door. He paused next to Jonesy. "What's under there?" he asked, pointing to his brightly coloured shirt.

Jonesy quickly wrapped his hands over the thick envelope. "Just our post, I went by the post office earlier."

McGinnis stared down at him, towering over the smaller man. "Three days, Jones," he finally said, and walked out.

The evening had derailed in Jonesy's eyes about as badly as he could have imagined. He'd left the bar full of hope, excitement and dopamine, but now he sat in their flat above the office, staring at his wife, who had not stopped crying since the Scotsman left. The sun had set, and so had any chance of romance. He had tried consoling Ally, but she had pushed him away, so he poured them both a drink and sat waiting for whatever was coming next. He held little hope for it being pleasant.

Jonesy realised he still had the envelope tucked under his shirt so he sat forward on the sofa, removed it and placed it on the coffee table. Ally looked up from the chair across the coffee table from where he sat. He figured she had taken the chair to stop him sitting near her.

"What is that?" she asked sternly between sniffles.

Well, he thought hazily through the alcohol-induced fog that continued to descend upon him, this is probably not the best time to enter into this conversation, but surely this will cheer her up. He pondered for a moment on the words he should choose. On the way from the bar he'd had it all planned out, but now he couldn't remember any of the smooth presentation he was sure he had conjured up. Winging it had always been his best approach, so with a surge of confidence, he put his best foot forward.

"This, my love, is the answer to everything."

Ally stared at him in the same way she had in the office earlier. Perhaps it was confusion on her part, he decided.

"This pile of paper will lead us to one of the greatest treasure discoveries of this century," Jonesy said, leaning farther forward, hoping he had cleared up any misunderstanding.

Silence rained down upon the room, the subtle rustling of net curtains fluttering in the breeze through the open windows providing the only break in the awkwardness.

Ally's jaw appeared to grind several times before she spoke. "You're seriously going to tell me that your best plan for the next three days, to save our home, our business, our whole existence here, is to go on some wild goose chase hunting long-lost sunken treasure?"

Bloody hell, he thought, running back through the words in his mind, maybe I said it wrong.

"But you said we have a charter," he mumbled. "That should get us through the rent and buy us a whole month to find this," he declared, holding up the envelope.

"Bugger me, Charlie," she said, throwing her arms in the air. "There's no charter, you idiot. I told the Scottish bastard that to make him think we could come up with the money."

Jonesy sat back on the sofa with all the wind knocked out of his sails one more time. "Oh," he said quietly.

The gravity of the situation sneaked up and rested itself squarely on his shoulders, before reaching down and tying his stomach in a knot. Three days to come up with all the rent money was a mountain he didn't know how to climb. If they scrounged every penny they had, he guessed they could come up with a tenth of what they needed. The bank wouldn't touch them, and the only loan shark he knew on the island was the man who was threatening them with eviction. He did the math in his head and realised even if they did drum up a charter, it was unlikely to bring in enough to cover the whole rent at this point. He didn't think he could get any more despondent. Until Alison spoke again.

"I followed you here on this adventure, because I thought it would be a brilliant experience, and it could work. It all sounded exciting, but I didn't ever consider it would come to this." Her voice gained strength as she continued. "We knew it wouldn't be a walk in the park, but we'd get to live in paradise, we'd be together every day, and the work would be enjoyable. But you'd rather sit in a bar than do the little work we do get, leaving me trying to figure out how to make this all work. Now we could lose our home, and our business, and all you want to do is chase pie-in-the-sky ideas of lost treasure." She stood up. "Aargh! How did you let it come to this?"

He adored his wife, and while they'd had an argument or two over the years, it had always been over something silly and been put behind them. Or so he thought. Now she sounded like a woman with years of pent-up anger and frustration, a person he didn't recognise. The hurt surged through him like blades in his bloodstream, pricking and poking at every nerve in his body. The pain drove the anger, and he too stood up.

"Just because you're trapped inside your tiny mind that can't see the opportunities I've worked bloody hard to create doesn't mean I'm not pulling my weight around here," he bellowed, words tumbling from his lips in an alcohol-fuelled fountain, void of any logic, contemplation or filter. "Right here," he held the envelope aloft, "I have the key to finding Sir Francis bloody Drake's missing chest from his visit to this island, exactly 400 years ago. Sod McGinnis and his rent, we're talking about a piece of history worth a fortune." He managed to calm his voice and take a few breaths, while Ally stared at him with a look he didn't have the wherewithal to process. "Let me show you what I have here, and once you've seen the evidence, you can judge for yourself. Three days isn't much time, but even if we ran a fishing charter for three days straight, at the locals' rate, we wouldn't have enough to meet the rent. You heard the arsehole, he already has someone he wants in here; we're done either way whether we pay him or not – he'll find a way to kick us out. We need another plan." He shook the envelope in his hand. "This is it, I swear to you."

Jonesy held his breath and waited. He was unsure exactly what he had just said, it had happened so fast he couldn't keep up with himself, but he felt the last part had been a compelling argument. He sensed Ally was chewing it over, but her expression hadn't changed, at least as far as he could tell in the dimly lit room, and he couldn't judge which way she was leaning. The thought of a life without her had never crossed his mind, until this moment. From her outburst, he realised she might be done with him. Surely not, he thought. He vaguely remembered using some words and phrases he didn't mean just now, and she probably had done the same. His devoted, loving wife had portrayed him as a worthless drunk, but they were the words of a woman scared, and worried about the days ahead. She had never talked to him like that before. Well, he foggily recalled, she has been on to me lately about the booze, but that wasn't a *problem*. They both enjoyed a tipple occasionally. She let out a long sigh, which he hoped was the steam leaving the pressure cooker.

"Tiny mind?" she said between gritted teeth.

"What?" he replied, confused at why she was still insulting him. Apparently, more steam needed releasing.

"You said I have a tiny mind," she reiterated.

"I did?" he replied, searching his memory for when that happened.

"You don't even know what you're saying," she said quietly, shaking her head.

"I'm sorry," he blurted, still unclear what he had done, but guessing he had screwed up. "I was mad and I probably said some stuff I didn't mean, love. You know I think you're the smartest woman I've ever known."

She scoffed. "That ain't saying much. I'm the only woman you've ever known."

"You know what I'm saying, Ally," he pleaded. "I'm sorry if I said something dumb, but I truly believe what I have here will save our bacon. Let me show you."

"I don't want to be homeless, Charlie," she replied quietly.

"Neither do I, love. Neither do I," he reassured her. "Worse case, we live on the boat for a night or two."

"What about all our belongings?" she replied. "Where do we put all this?" She looked around them at the small one-bedroom flat. "I know it ain't much, but it's everything we have."

"I have a friend with some room in his garage, Ally, don't worry about it," he said, feeling like he was finally getting ahead of the game. He didn't know what friend he was referring to, but he could deal with that later. "We might not even need to move out. We could get lucky and find what we're looking for in the next few days."

Ally sat back down and stared at the envelope Jonesy placed back on the coffee table. He slipped the papers from the pale brown cover and shuffled through the sheets until he found the copy of the log from 22 April, 1586. He handed it to her. She looked at him a long moment before taking the piece of A4 paper.

"Read that," he whispered.

Ally sighed again and looked at the paper, squinting in the low light to read the old script. She took her time and appeared to read it a second time.

"Is this the ship's log?" she asked.

"It's not just the ship's log, it's the captain's log. And that captain was none other than Sir Francis Drake," he answered keenly.

"And you think this rowboat that sank with his things on it is still out there somewhere?" she asked, looking at the window facing the water.

"No one's ever found it," he retorted, his confidence growing.

"Maybe 'cos it's beyond the wall, in thousands of feet of water," she said, and put the paper down on the coffee table.

He took a long sip of his drink, put the glass down and leaned forward. He was ready for this question.

"All the ships in the fleet were at anchor, right?"

She shrugged her shoulders. "If you say so."

"Of course they were, they were sailing ships. If they didn't anchor they'd drift about and it would have been a pain in the arse to put up the sails and manoeuvre them back into position," he explained. "Not like they had motors to zip about where they wanted. So to drop anchor, they had to be inshore of the drop-off, which puts them 90 feet or shallower. We know they launched a rowboat," he said, pointing to the paper she had just read, "so they had to be close enough in to make the shore."

"But we don't know which shore they were facing, do we?" Ally said. "And even if we did, it could be anywhere littered on the sea floor over miles of shoreline. That's a needle in a haystack and you think we'll get lucky in a few days of looking?"

Jonesy rummaged through the stack of papers again until he found the one he was looking for.

"We know it was what we now call Seven Mile Beach," he

replied, handing her the paper. "And this photo of a wood block print from a sketch the artist aboard made shows exactly where they were at anchor."

Ally took the paper, showing water stretching away to a beach lined with trees and many ships at anchor. She studied it a moment. "I guess this narrows it down a bit, it's still a big area to search."

"Not if we put ourselves in the exact spot this sketch was made," Jonesy said triumphantly. "We line up the north-west point and move around until the curvature of the beach matches the sketch. From there we know Drake's flagship was anchored deeper than the rest of the fleet, and the rowboat didn't make it far. It's not sitting in plain sight, 'cos no one's found it yet. We'll be searching a much smaller area looking for somewhere the remains of a rowboat, and the captain's chest, could have stayed hidden for 400 years."

Ally looked up at him and her expression had finally softened. "Easy as that, huh?" she said, the venom not entirely absent in her tone.

"Easy as that, love," he replied.

8

GRAND CAYMAN – SATURDAY

AJ stood on the deck of Hazel's Odyssey and stared thoughtfully off the stern at the deep blue water, rolling in light, gentle swells beneath the Newton. For the second day in a row they were tied into the buoy at Neptune's Wall, and she paid attention to the boat's movement in the water. She turned around and faced the group on the boat.

"Okay, looks like there's no surface current, so let's gear up," she announced, and the divers began slipping into their equipment.

David and Andy Metcalf were eager to get back in the water after their discovery, and Reg planned to dive deep with AJ to the cavern.

"I have my camera, Andy, so you can keep yours with you," AJ said. "Maybe film us down there so we get video evidence of where we were."

Andy nodded. "Will do, miss."

"And try not to drop it again, 'cos it might hit me on the head this time," AJ added, grinning at the lad.

Andy held up his camera and telescopic stick with a new safety strap to loop around his wrist. "Learnt that lesson, Miss Bailey. We bought a strap yesterday afternoon."

"Blimey, Andy, don't call me Miss Bailey. You're making me feel like an old boarding school teacher. Please call me AJ," she said and looked at Jackson and Thomas.

"One of you has to stay on the boat, I'm afraid; we have to have someone aboard," she said, not wanting to pick one of them to miss out.

"I was down there yesterday, so you go ahead Thomas," Jackson offered.

"Are you sure, man?" Thomas replied.

"Hey, whoever goes is hanging with David and Andy at a hundred feet, and there's a good chance we'll make a second dive," AJ reminded them.

"From a hundred feet I'll be able to see your face, Boss, and dat's all dat matters," Thomas said with a grin.

"Huh?" AJ replied, looking puzzled.

Thomas leaned in closer. "'Cos if there's some-body, attached to the some-thing, your face is gonna be a sight to see."

AJ punched him on the arm as Thomas hopped around laughing and high-fived with Jackson.

"Stop buggering about and let's get in the water," AJ said, trying not to laugh herself.

The five divers descended towards the reef where a nurse shark circled a coral head before cruising away towards the shallower waters. AJ finned west to the drop-off, staying well above the reef at 60 feet to save air and available bottom time. They needed to find the spot where Andy had dropped his camera, which was south of the buoy, so she turned that way, staying above the edge of the wall. They had turned around immediately after finding the cavern so it was at the far extent of their previous dive, and AJ wished there was a closer buoy. Slaughterhouse Wall was the next one along, but she estimated Neptune's was still closer, as they had cruised slowly and not covered that much distance. After less than 10 minutes, she stopped kicking when she spotted the pile of debris on the steep slope below. She signalled to David and Andy and they both gave her the okay sign, confirming they also recognised the terrain. As they had been above it the whole time, she figured their memory of the area was likely to be better than hers. She signalled for Thomas, David and Andy to stay together as a buddy team, and checked that Reg was ready to go.

The two descended the steep slope and AJ found her heart rate rising as she approached the pile of silt and broken coral. What if there is a body inside there, she thought? They arrived at the narrow crack in the wall and AJ pulled her camera from her BCD pocket and unclipped her torch. Without being able to see much to the side of the crack, she realised it was unlikely they would know what was there until they looked at the film she was about to shoot. She wasn't sure if that made it more creepy, or less. She extended the camera stick and turned her GoPro around to face back towards her, slightly off to her left. She eased it through the narrow gap and shone her torch after it to see if the angle was right. Reg added his torchlight and the inside of the cavern brightened considerably. They both peeked through the crack and tried to look to the left where the film from yesterday had flashed across what they thought was a dive tank. The outer wall was too thick to see much and AJ pulled the camera back out and adjusted the angle to point farther left and up a bit more. She nodded to Reg and hit the record button, sliding the camera back inside the small entry to the cavern. Reg reached his arm through the crack and pointed his torch back towards the outer wall to light the shot. AJ tried to pan the camera around but being backwards and on the end of a long stick, she found herself wobbling it around more than making panning sweeps. She pulled the camera back out and hit the button to stop the recording.

Reg nudged her out the way and reached his big hand back inside the cavern, feeling around as far as he could to the left. AJ watched in amazement as he groped about, bare handed, inside a pitch-black hole, 130 feet underwater. She turned the camera back around on its mount and filmed her friend armpit deep in the crevice. Reg pulled back and AJ held her breath when she saw he held something in his hand. He shook the silt off the object and AJ kept filming for a few moments as Reg studied his find. She stopped recording and moved closer to see what appeared to be a metal buckle. Reg looked at AJ and she saw a worried look in his eyes. He put the buckle in his BCD pocket and AJ moved back to the cavern entry. She hit record, poked the camera through once more and shone her torch inside, making a slow sweep around the room, carefully panning across the sandy floor before retrieving the camera.

AJ looked at her dive computer. They had been at the cavern for five minutes and needed to ascend. She cursed herself for not organising a different breathing gas the afternoon before, when she had the time. If they were to spend more time investigating the cavern, they needed a custom nitrox mix to give them more bottom time. Their bodies were taking in nitrogen from the compressed air they were breathing at a highly increased rate in balance with the water pressure applied to their bodies at this depth. Nitrox breathing gas was mixed with a lower nitrogen content by increasing the oxygen in the blend, giving them more time before their bodies became saturated. She pointed a thumb towards the surface and Reg nodded.

Back aboard Hazel's Odyssey, the group gathered around the Metcalfs' laptop and Andy put the memory card from AJ's camera into a card reader and plugged the reader into a USB port. They waited while he copied over the file and they occupied themselves looking at the buckle Reg had brought up.

"What do you think, Reg? Looks like a BCD buckle or maybe a weight belt?" AJ suggested.

The buckle was tarnished and showed signs of rust around its edges but the stainless steel had held up well. It didn't have any brand engraving or stamping they could see.

"Probably a weight belt, be my guess," Reg replied. "BCD buckles have been plastic for a long time now. Mind you, that tank is most likely old, so perhaps this stuff has been in there longer than we're thinking."

"Is it a tank?" Thomas asked, "Could you feel it when you put your hand in there?"

Reg nodded. "Reckon it is. I could feel it alright, but I couldn't reach the top to see if there was a first stage attached. See what the film shows."

A video player opened on the laptop screen and after the image bounced and jarred around for a moment, it settled and the inside of the cavern came into focus. For a moment the camera struggled with the outside light from the crack overexposing the shot, but once it was tilted up, the cavern wall could be clearly seen. Resting upright against the wall was a rusty scuba diving tank. On top of the tank was a regulator first stage, the hoses long since rotted away. AJ held her breath a moment as the camera moved around the area, and half expected to see the skeletal remains of the tank's owner resting next to it, like a set from Disney's Pirates of the Caribbean ride. But there was no other evidence on the screen.

"That's a tank alright," Thomas said quietly.

"I don't see anything else though, do you guys?" Jackson asked.

"I don't either," AJ said as the image went wild when the camera was pulled back out of the cavern and turned off. "If there was a BCD attached to the tank, I would have thought there would still be parts of it around."

"Might be," Reg pointed out. "I found the buckle in the silt and sand. Could be more metal parts buried nearby. This stuff has to have been down there for at least twenty years or more to have rotted all the fabric and rubber away. Anything metal will have dropped to the floor."

"We need to get inside that cavern," AJ quickly replied.

"Isn't that rather dangerous?" David said, looking worried. "Besides, I thought you said the opening was too small?"

"It is," AJ said. "But this guy got in there from somewhere else. Best we know, the crack wasn't even there until the other night."

"A lot could have changed over the years," Reg added, "and we still don't know for sure there's a 'someone' in there."

"Had to be someone in there at some point," Jackson said. "The tank didn't get there by itself."

Reg laughed. "Well, that's certainly true."

Andy opened the second video file and they all looked at the screen. The camera panned slowly around the inside of the cavern with the torchlight clearly illuminating the rough interior of the rock walls.

"Pause it a moment, Andy," AJ asked, and she leaned in closer to the screen as Andy froze the image. "Can you go back about a second?"

He moved back frame by frame until AJ said stop.

"Look," she said, pointing to the back of the cavern on the screen. "See where the ceiling opens up at the back?"

Reg leaned in closer with her. "Hard to tell the ceiling from the end of the cavern, but I see the bright area you're talking about; could be a chimney. If it is it looks pretty big."

"That's where I saw the light coming from, so it leads out," AJ explained. "And it must have a fairly direct route as the light makes it into the cavern."

Reg stood up straight. "Alright, first things first, let's call Whittaker and tell him we've verified the tank and found evidence of more equipment in there. Then we'll dive again and search the top of the reef and the ravines to see if we can find the entry point."

"That sounds like a plan. I'll ring Whittaker," AJ said, and reached for her rucksack to retrieve her mobile.

"Is there more film?" Jackson asked Andy, who nodded and hit play on the laptop.

"There's another fifteen seconds."

"Sorry, Andy," AJ apologised. "I was getting a little ahead of myself."

They moved in closer as the camera shot tilted down and panned across the floor of the room. The sand and silt appeared flat and evenly distributed across the room, well protected from the ebb and flow of the surface waves and deeper current. The view was from a low perspective as the crack was close to the bottom of the cavern, and the sand closest to the camera was out of focus. Mid way across the floor, something dark and unnatural looking protruded a few inches from the sand, distinct amongst the coral debris scattered about.

"What is that?" David asked.

Andy paused the video and rolled back several frames to the best image of the object. It was still indistinct apart from its dark brown, almost black colouring.

"Hard to say," Reg said, squinting at the screen.

AJ gave him a nudge. "One more reason to find our way inside there, I reckon."

9

────────

GRAND CAYMAN – SATURDAY

AJ reached Whittaker's voicemail, which felt slightly anti-climactic after watching their new video. She left him a message telling him what they had found, and that they were diving again to look for a way into the cavern. She stuffed her mobile back into her rucksack and joined the others on the deck. They had been out of the water almost an hour, which was enough time for their bodies to dissipate much of the excess nitrogen in their systems, and were ready to get back in.

"We can gear up," AJ said. "We'll have been up an hour by the time we splash."

They slipped into their BCDs, which they had all moved to fresh tanks during their surface interval, and prepared to dive again.

"We'll stay in two groups, but everyone can help search," AJ briefed the group as she checked over her rig. "Jackson, David and Andy will work on top of the reef, and Reg and I will start looking in the larger, deeper ravines."

"What should we be looking for exactly? A hole in the coral obviously, but I assume it won't be that obvious," David asked.

"Divers have combed these reefs for years now, so no, I doubt it'll be obvious," AJ replied as she walked upfront to the door leading to the cabin below the bow, "Look under overhangs, coral heads and in the smaller gullies and cuts in the reef," she called back as she stepped below and rummaged amongst the diving gear stored below. "Light is reaching the cavern so it can't be completely covered over."

She came back out of the cabin with a penetration reel and line in her hand.

"Who knows what's moved over the years, through all the storms and hurricanes," Reg added. "We're expecting to find a big hole a diver could fit through, but that might not be the case now." He looked at the reel in AJ's hand as she sat down on the bench and clipped it to a D-ring on her BCD. "What are you bringing that for, missy?"

AJ turned and grinned at him. "Be prepared, scout leader."

"Don't give me that bollocks, you're not going inside anything on this dive," he growled back at her.

AJ frowned, "Of course not," she said, slipping into her BCD. "I wouldn't blindly stick my arm inside an unexplored cave either."

Reg shook his head and stood up, ready to go. AJ poked her tongue at him.

"Are you going diving, or are you two going to stand there and argue all morning?" Thomas asked, standing by the open stern, grinning.

"Diving," AJ declared, standing up.

"Then how about you get off dis boat?" Thomas added and checked each of their tank valves were on, as they filed by and took a giant stride into the ocean.

They followed the same course south for eight minutes, and with the terrain becoming more familiar, AJ quickly recognised the top of the wall where the cavern lay below. She surveyed the reef, and pointed out details to Reg who hung close by. There were two deep ravines that cut through the corner of the wall from a hundred feet back on the reef, forming a gully that looked like a deepening drainage ditch running off the wall. She looked up and checked on the others who had already spread out and were slowly making a run over the reef. She turned back to Reg who signalled that he would start from the deeper side of the first ravine, off the wall, and for AJ to start from the shallow end. She gave him the okay sign, and their search began.

The ravine dropped steadily from the top of the reef, like a stream cutting a gully in a dirt embankment leading to a river. The closer it reached towards the wall, the deeper and wider it became. AJ was able to quickly cover the first twenty feet, but as the cut became more than four feet deep she had to float upside down and lower her head into the narrow opening to see what lay below. Which could be any number of critters that might be upset by her presence. As the ravine widened she was able to lower herself down in a normal diving position and felt more comfortable as she hunted for any kind of opening. About the time Reg and AJ met along their ravine, she heard the familiar clanking of a carabiner against a tank. She looked over the reef and saw Jackson waving to her from thirty feet away to the south near the edge of the wall.

Reg and AJ both finned over to see what Jackson had found, following his finger pointing to a narrow split in the top of the reef. AJ shone her torch inside. The crack remained tight for quite a distance but then appeared to open up, but by how much she couldn't tell. She pulled her torch away and let her eyes adapt to the darkness inside. Somewhere, quite far below, there was another light source. She wondered if this small fracture could be the light she had seen in the back of the cavern. Swimming gently forward, she peered over the wall and sure enough they were slightly south of the debris field outside the cavern below. If the chimney angled a few degrees it could easily meet the cavern. She presumed the light she had seen down the chimney must be the new crack in the wall fifty feet below. But if this fracture up top was the only other entrance, how did the scuba tank get inside? She swam back to the opening and looked at the coral growth all around the slim hole. Could the coral have filled in that much over the years since the tank was left there? Coral didn't grow that fast, especially hard coral that formed all the reef structure. She looked at Reg, who appeared lost in thought himself.

He finally looked back at her and signalled he was dropping down the wall to the cavern. He pointed and signalled for her to cover the crack in the top of the reef. It took a moment, but she realised he wanted to look inside the cavern and have her take away the ambient light from the surface and he would see if it shaded the cavern. If it did, they had their chimney. She gave him the okay sign and watched him ease over the drop-off and descend. She checked her dive computer. They had been underwater for twenty-two minutes, most of that time at 70 feet. Reg would only have a few minutes at 124 feet before he needed to go shallower.

Reg reached the debris field below them and signalled up to AJ. She went to move back towards the opening in the top but Jackson had figured out what they were doing and moved his body over the crack, staying a few inches off of the delicate coral. This allowed her to stay at the edge and signal between the two men. Reg waved his hand and she signalled for Jackson to move away from the opening. He did and Reg immediately signalled okay. AJ tapped on her dive torch and Jackson switched his on and shone the beam down the chimney. AJ looked down and Reg signalled okay again. Well, she thought, we've found the chimney that reaches all the way down the wall to the cavern, but we're no closer to figuring out how the gear got in there. AJ looked down and saw Reg starting back up, but an idea hit her. She signalled for Reg to stop and cover the opening below. He hesitated, but then seemed to get the idea and shielded the light from the fracture in the wall with his body. AJ kicked over to the other opening and covered it as much as she could and still look down the hole. Bingo, she thought, there was still some light in the chimney. There had to be a third way in.

She moved back to the wall and signalled for Reg to come up. She then looked at the other three, who were all curiously watching, and signalled for them to stay where they were. A few fin kicks farther south was the second ravine they had planned to explore, and AJ dropped straight into the gully in a line with the top crack.

She immediately met a coral outcrop that reached halfway across the ravine, blocking her descent. She looked behind her and saw it extended well up the gully; ahead, towards the drop-off, the overhang seemed to meld into the ravine walls and block the gully altogether. She finned towards shallower water where the beginning of the ravine formed and turned around to see if she could fit below the start of the overhang. It was tight and she was careful not to break off the many protrusions of coral and beautiful fans. With her torch held out before her she ducked under the overhang and most of the living coral disappeared. Hidden from the surface light where nothing could grow, the space quickly opened up. Antennae probed the water from nooks and crannies where lobsters spent their days, waiting for nightfall. A small school of glassy sweepers moved around the dark space as though they were one fluid creature, wrapping and twisting itself away from the intruder. AJ carefully finned forward, staying on the right under the overhang to avoid the sparse growth on the left side, fed by the sunlight squeezing between the wall of the ravine and the overhang. The glassy sweepers parted and swam behind her, leaving the view ahead clear in the beam of her torch. Except it wasn't clear. It was blocked by a pile of rock and coral debris stacked up against the end of the ravine where the overhang had grown back into the reef. Bugger, she thought, surely the third light source had to be down here somewhere. She slowly shone her torch from the left side to the right, where it illuminated the dark corner of the rubble. And an opening. Narrower than her shoulders and only a foot tall, the opening wasn't big enough for a diver to fit through, but may well have been at one time before the rocks and debris filled the end of the ravine in.

AJ shone her torch down the opening, flashing it around vigorously, and hoped Jackson was still looking down the crack from above. She turned to leave but quickly checked her dive computer. It showed 95 feet. She had been down for twenty-eight minutes and needed to ascend to a shallower depth, which meant Reg, who had been down even deeper, was probably out of no-deco time. She turned around in the tight space that she guessed was five feet wide, and finned back up the ravine. It tapered until the overhang disappeared completely and she slipped out into the brighter light. The group were waiting close by and she saw Reg had ascended above them 20 feet or so. She signalled for everyone to head towards the boat and they all steadily kicked up to join Reg at 50 feet for the return trip.

Back on the boat, they stowed their gear and bobbed on the mooring while they all debriefed about the dive and what they had learnt. AJ and Thomas made sure everyone had cool water to drink and passed around a Tupperware container of fruit pastries Thomas's mother had made for them.

"Could you see my light inside the chimney? I was trying to signal you from inside the ravine," AJ asked.

"I saw it," Andy replied. "We took turns watching down the hole in case you showed up down there."

Reg frowned at AJ. "What?" she asked, pretending to be offended. "I would never have gone inside."

"Like hell you wouldn't," he grunted in reply.

"Okay, we know there are three access points, but none of them are currently passable by a diver," Jackson summarised. "So how did the gear get inside there."

"My bet is from the ravine," AJ replied. "There's a pile of debris that has been shoved down the gully over the years and almost completely blocked that entrance. It's hard to tell how big the opening used to be, but unless there's another way in we haven't found yet, that has to be it."

"If I'm right and the tank is older, then you could be looking at twenty, thirty years or more of movement down there," Reg added. "A lot happens in the ocean over that period of time."

"Could we move some of the rocks and debris?" Andy asked. "You know, without hurting any coral."

AJ thought for a moment before replying. She pictured her torch running over the debris and tried to recall what it had looked like. She kicked herself for not shooting a quick video. "Hard to say, there's a lot of sand and smaller debris piled up but the real blockage is bigger pieces of rock or dead coral. It's all in the shade so there's no living growth but until we move the rubbish out the way we won't know if the larger obstructions are movable by hand or not."

"It's a much bigger problem if it requires equipment to move stuff," Reg said. "Be difficult to use lift bags as it's covered overhead."

"Not much room to put large bits aside either, once you pull them out," AJ added. "But it's worth another look to see. Two of us could fit down there, so why don't we head in and get some lunch, off-gas for a few hours and go back out and dive on nitrox?"

Reg nodded. "Sure, we could do that."

Jackson smiled. "If Reg doesn't need me on his boats and you'll take me, I'm in."

"We'll have to bow out I'm afraid," David said, and Andy looked like he'd been sucker punched. "You have schoolwork, Andy, and I have a videoconference meeting I can't miss."

"I can catch up the schoolwork, Dad, I promise, I'll do double tomorrow until I'm caught up," Andy pleaded.

"You're supposed to be doing it today because we went diving yesterday, Andy; you're going to run out of tomorrows to catch up," David said with lessening resolve. "Besides, I can't ask these guys to buddy with you without me here."

"Why not?" Jackson said with a grin. "He can be my dive buddy."

"Dat's settled den," Thomas exclaimed and climbed the ladder to the fly-bridge. "Now somebody cast us off, I heard talk of lunch, and I'm starving."

AJ headed to the bow, leaving Andy with a broad smile on his face.

10

GRAND CAYMAN – SEPTEMBER, 1986

Jonesy stirred awake with the first light of dawn breathing life into the flat, and reminding him he was on the sofa. Ally had softened, but had not been ready to forgive him. For which part of his failings he wasn't sure; he had accumulated a few, according to her. Perhaps his inability to provide financial stability, but he preferred to think it was his slip of the tongue during their argument. He felt that would be easier to move past, although he had come to realise he had no idea what his wife was thinking.

His mouth felt like it had spent the night stuffed with cotton wool, the work of a devious spectre who had removed it just before he awoke. The insides of his cheeks and gums seemed to be a different size from what he remembered, and he kept running his tongue around his mouth in an attempt to pull it all back into shape. He sat up and his head reluctantly followed. There was a dullness and a pressure behind his eyes which he attributed to the emotional turmoil started by that bastard McGinnis. He scooped up the empty glass from the coffee table, and the near-empty rum bottle, then walked to the kitchen. He put his head under the tap and took a drink of water. His mouth still felt dry and somehow foreign, although he had experienced this feeling more often recently, now he thought about it. As he poured cheap coffee grounds into the paper filter of the coffee maker, his excitement began to build and push the events of last night from his mind.

Half an hour later, when Ally emerged from the bedroom, Jonesy was dressed in yesterday's shorts and shirt, had the picture of the sketch, a bag of snacks and a large bottle of water ready to go. He patiently waited while she made herself coffee, poured cereal into a bowl and sat at the dining table to eat.

"I'm ready whenever you are, dear," he finally said, unable to stay silent.

She glanced his way. "I see that."

His enthusiasm had removed the predictable scenario of her still being chilly about this 'losing their home' business from his thoughts, but they flooded back with her look of disdain. That's the look she had last night, he realised. He felt ill-equipped to handle their new state of affairs and decided avoidance was far better than digging a bigger hole.

"I'll go get the boat ready," he said and made for the stairs.

Frosty silence accompanied him out of the flat.

It was a beautiful morning with calm seas, a handful of wispy clouds and a soft, steady breeze to knock the edge from the building heat. Jonesy walked down the jetty, passing a friend's 12-foot inflatable dinghy that shared the dock. The rubber pontoons were sun faded, but the little boat had a reliable 15-horsepower outboard and was perfect for quick snorkelling trips, or runs to the sandy beaches. Their friends rarely took it out, so Jonesy kept it clean and topped with petrol in exchange for using it whenever they needed. He stepped aboard Bottom Time and immediately felt closer to holding Sir Francis Drake's possessions in his hand. He wasn't fool enough to believe the search would be easy, but surely his desperate need would be met with the solution he had put so much effort into. He carefully stowed the sketch away in a cupboard under the pilot seat, and the snacks and water in the cuddy cabin sink, before heading up to the building and dragging two sets of scuba gear back down to the boat.

He had bought Seaquest Advanced Design Vests for them both when they became available the year before. The new design revolutionised the diving industry with its comfortable jacket style, under-arm wrap, shoulder buckles, cummerbund, and almost exclusive use of plastic buckles and straps. Ally had complained about him spending the money, but had soon forgotten about the cost once she had dived in the new gear and fell in love with it.

He made one more trip to bring two steel 72 cubic foot tanks to the boat and slipped a BCD on each and then a regulator first stage. All their tanks had J-valves, which were fast becoming obsolete with reliable modern submersible pressure gauges. The J-valves had a spring-loaded mechanism that closed the air supply off when the tank got down to the last 300psi. The diver pulled a lever on the valve that opened the supply back up to use the final 300psi of air. Before submersible pressure gauges were available, this was how a diver knew their tank was low and they needed to surface. Jonesy set the valves open as they both had pressure gauges on stainless-steel braided lines from their regulator first stages. He didn't like using the high-pressure rubber lines the gauges came with, so he had substituted them for flexible braided lines from brake systems on automobiles. He checked both tanks were full at 2400psi, then used a couple of bungee straps to secure them against the gunwales. Next, he turned the ignition on and looked at the petrol gauge. It read a little under a quarter of a tank. He ought to fill it up, but that required money he didn't have, and they didn't plan to go far today. He decided to kick that can down the road a day. One by one, he started the two inboard-outboard Mercruiser 292s and let them gently idle and warm up. He could feel more than hear the slight roughness from one of the straight six-cylinder motors, both well overdue for a service. In a few days, he thought, all these problems will be a thing of the past, and servicing the engines will be a phone call away. Heck, he wouldn't bother servicing Bottom Time; he'd be trading her in for something bigger and better.

The boat rocked as Ally stepped aboard and surprised Jonesy.

"Oh, hey dear, ready?"

She was wearing a two-piece bikini, covered by a tee-shirt, with her hair in a ponytail and dark sunglasses hiding her eyes. She stared blankly at her husband as she dropped a canvas bag at her feet.

"Just to be clear," she started. "I still believe this is a hare-brained scheme that has no chance of working, and you are well and truly on my shit-list."

"Okay," he mumbled.

"I'm only coming out this morning to make sure you don't screw around while we only have a few days to fix this mess you've put us in," she announced.

Jonesy scratched his head and shuffled about nervously. "That's a bit harsh, my love…"

"Harsh? I'll give you bloody harsh," she barked back, cutting him off. "You better cast off and get on with this before I head back in, pack, and take a taxi to the sodding airport."

"Right," he managed to say with all the steam knocked out of him.

He leapt to the dock and threw the lines off, stepped back aboard and eased the little Bertram away from shore. He felt nauseous. The reality that she was contemplating leaving him was another gut punch that had him wishing he had brought his flask along. She sat silently in the other seat, and he realised he preferred her screaming and shouting at him. At least that would suggest she hadn't given up completely.

Jonesy pushed the throttles forward and brought the boat up on plane to make the run north. Their dock was south of the rather ambitiously named Seven Mile Beach, which really measured closer to six miles in length, and was crescent shaped, concavely curving into the island. He set a course across the open water, taking the shortest route to start their search towards the north end. The sketch appeared to have been made facing east-north-east as the north-west corner of the island was in view. Jonesy figured the ship was anchored well out by the drop-off, as the log mentioned the rowboat was lost in deep water, yet they knew it was between the ship and the shore. He guessed the artist had orientated himself facing the nearest stretch of beach so when he spotted the large cemetery on the south side of West Bay, he eased back the throttles and coasted to a rest, picking a spot to start.

Jonesy pulled the sketch from the plastic bag and stepped out clear of the covered helm to the deck. He held the piece of paper out in front of him and lined it up with the coastline. Right away, he realised the black-and-white drawing of an uninhabited tree and mangrove-covered island did not resemble the condo-littered view before him. This would be harder than he imagined. Ally stayed in her seat while he turned, twisted and lined up the paper with nothing much he found of reference except the corner of the island. The problem was he needed at least one more landmark to align them with, and the sketch didn't extend to the other side of George Town where the shoreline turned again. It didn't extend much past half the length of the beach, he guessed. After several more minutes, Ally spoke up.

"Got it all figured out?" she said, with a touch more sarcasm than he would have liked.

"Well, it's a bit tricky, as this picture is full of trees and ships, which are no longer here," he replied, holding up the paper. "And this view," he continued, pointing to the shoreline, "is full of buildings and new things. Be handy if the island had a mountain, or a cliff, or a river estuary. You know, something more distinctive."

Ally left the seat, picked up the canvas bag, and joined her husband on the deck.

"This was your whole plan, I take it?" she asked, but didn't wait for a response. "Stand here with the picture, and think you could match it all up. In 400 years, you didn't think things might have changed a bit?"

"Well, you know, of course I knew it had changed, but…" He stopped babbling when she reached into the canvas bag and pulled out a Polaroid camera.

Ally looked at the sketch on the paper, then through the viewfinder of the camera, then back at the sketch again.

"Move us farther north," she said and went back to her seat.

Jonesy fired the motors back up and did as she suggested, moving slowly as he had no idea how far he was supposed to go. He noticed her looking over at the shoreline for points of reference and after a minute she told him to stop. He took the motors out of gear and shut them down, letting the Bertram drift in the gentle swell. They walked back to the deck and Ally followed the same procedure again, looking from the sketch, which he held for her to see, to the viewfinder, with the camera aimed towards the island. She hit the button and the camera whirred loudly as the picture peeled out of the front of the casing. She removed the picture and went back to her seat while she waited for it to develop. Jonesy, unsure once again of what he was supposed to do, followed and sat in the pilot's seat.

"I forgot we had that camera," he said, breaking the uncomfortable silence.

Ally waved the picture in the air, attempting to speed up the developer, and ignored the comment. The picture finally became clear and she held out her hand for the paper. Jonesy gave it to her and she compared the two.

"Where's the drop-off from here?" she asked, looking to the deeper water.

Jonesy turned the ignition back on so the simple fathometer lit up and displayed their depth. It read 400 feet.

"We were over it when we stopped but we've drifted deeper. I'd say we're no more than a hundred yards beyond it," he replied. "I can make a run back and forth to find it, if you want?"

She shook her head. "No, we're still too far south. Move north about the same amount again, and make sure we're inside the drop-off."

He went to start the motors but paused for a moment. "How are you figuring that out?" he asked.

Ally looked at him and he guessed she was deciding whether to acknowledge his question or not, as she took a while to reply.

"Here," she said, holding up the Polaroid and the paper for him to see. He stepped closer and she pointed to the north-west point in the sketch. "See the point?"

He nodded. "Sure."

She pointed a finger out of the front window towards the land to the north. "You can see the land runs straight for a bit before the corner itself, right?"

He nodded again. "Okay, yeah, I can see the curve of Seven Mile Beach ends and the shoreline goes straight north-west for a while before the point."

She held up the paper. "So look here, the artist doesn't show that. The shoreline curves and then ends. He couldn't see the flat part towards the point which means he was either farther inside, or looking straight down the line at it." She pointed to the beach directly in front of the artist's perspective. "Here, he's drawn the beach running straight for a while either side of his view and then curving after that. To the north, it meets the point, and to the south it extends out of the view of the sketch."

Once more she pointed out of the window towards the island. "That's exactly how the shape of the shoreline still is. From West Bay public dock to about the cemetery, the beach is relatively straight. It curves in both directions after that. Assuming your anchorage theory is correct, we're looking to position ourselves in line with the flat shoreline running to the point, about halfway between the dock and the cemetery, and just inside the wall. Can't be much farther north as the wall begins to curve somewhat parallel with the beach, which will have us looking at the trees all along the flat section, like we are now. The Polaroid gives a snap-shot of the view, similar to what the artist saw. It cuts out all the other stuff we don't need to look at. When the Polaroid matches the sketch we'll be in the right spot."

She put the sketch and the Polaroid down in her lap and stared out of the window, waiting for him to move the boat.

"Bloody hell, Ally," he said slowly, trying to understand everything she had just told him. "That's brilliant."

"Brilliant?" she said calmly. "Couldn't be, could it? You know, me having a tiny mind and all."

11

GRAND CAYMAN – SATURDAY

Reg had set up a breathing quality air compressor at his West Bay dock, but it would only fill tanks with regular air. For nitrox, they loaded ten empty nitrox tanks in AJ's van, pulled out of the car park and headed for Island Air in George Town. David had reluctantly left Andy with them before he headed home, giving his son some cash to pay for his lunch and whatever else he needed. AJ had just turned right on West Bay Road when her mobile rang. She saw it was Roy Whittaker and answered the call using the hands-free system in the van.

"Hi Roy, did you get my message?"

"I did, thank you. Did you dive the site again?" he asked.

"We did and we think we may have found an entrance, but it looks like it's been blocked for some time," AJ replied.

There was silence for a moment before the detective responded. "Where are you now?"

"We're heading into town to fill tanks," AJ replied. "We were planning to go back out this afternoon."

"Is Reg with you?" Whittaker asked.

"I am," Reg answered from the passenger seat.

"Could you two meet me for a few minutes?" Whittaker asked. "If you haven't eaten lunch yet, perhaps we could grab something and chat for a bit before you go back out on the water?"

AJ looked at Reg, who shrugged his shoulders.

"We'll get the tanks filled," Thomas said from the back, "just get us something to go."

"Okay, Roy, we can do that," AJ responded. "Where do you want to meet?"

"I'll be at My Bar in ten minutes," Whittaker replied. "Thank you."

"Sounds good," AJ said, and hung up the phone.

She looked at Reg again. "Wonder what that's all about."

"Dunno," Reg grunted and turned to look at the others in the back seat. "But we'll be having a nice lunch in a few minutes."

Thomas rubbed his tummy. "That's harsh, Big Boss, you know this machine needs fuel to burn. You better scratch dat to go order, Boss, I can't be waitin' dat long."

"Don't worry," Jackson added. "We'll get Thomas fed before he falls over."

Ten minutes later AJ and Reg stepped from the van in the car park at Sunset House Dive Resort. Before them a large, thatched roof covered the open bar and restaurant area, facing the ocean. My Bar was always popular with locals as well as visiting guests, and while border restrictions were still in place, they relied solely on the local clientele. AJ spotted Whittaker at a table in the shade, away from the other patrons. He stood when they approached.

"Thank you for joining me. I hope this didn't disrupt your plans."

AJ shook his hand. "Not at all, got us out of getting the tanks filled, and probably a better lunch than we had planned."

She felt a little guilty leaving the guys to do the work, but as she sat and took in the view, she began to relax and enjoy the rare opportunity to slow down for a few minutes. Reg greeted Whittaker and the two men sat. A waitress came by right away and they all ordered water to drink, and their food, as they knew the menu well.

"So, sounded like you had something on your mind," Reg said, never one for small talk.

The detective took off his glasses and cleaned them with a cloth he pulled from his pocket. "I do," he said, taking his time. "It may be nothing, but I thought it was worth bringing up in case you find more evidence in this cavern you've discovered."

He slipped his glasses back on his face. "Let me ask you this. In your opinion, how old could that tank be?"

AJ kept quiet, deferring to Reg's experience to answer more accurately than she could, and Reg thought for a moment while the waitress set large cups of ice water in front of them.

"Like I said before, it's steel, and there's some places and people using steel tanks today, but not many here on the island." He scratched his beard and paused a moment. "That likely narrows it down to at least twenty years old, I'd say. But it could be a lot older than that."

"If we can get to the tank and see the first stage, that would help, wouldn't it?" AJ asked.

"It would certainly give us the oldest time it could be, if we could identify the brand and model of the regulator," Reg agreed.

Whittaker nodded. "You mentioned you found a buckle – could that help us with the timeline?"

Reg shrugged his shoulders. "Maybe. It doesn't appear to have any manufacturer markings on it so it would be hard to trace and identify. Stainless-steel buckles like that have been used for years. It was most likely from a weight belt rather than a BCD, but if it's older than the mid to late 80s it could be from a BCD."

"Or from a technical rig," AJ suggested.

"True," Reg agreed. "So, there's a lot of variables. We really need more evidence to get a better idea."

"I see," Whittaker responded, and paused while the waitress put their plates on the table.

"Can I get you anything else?" she asked, and when they all declined, she left them alone to continue their conversation.

"But the buckle suggests the tank was indeed attached to diving gear, when it originally made its way into the cavern," Whittaker said, and looked up at them. "Would you agree?"

Reg nodded, and AJ replied, "You would assume so. You'd also assume there was someone attached to the rig."

Whittaker chewed on a bite of his lunch and waited until he had finished to respond. "Yes, well that's where I have a thought."

"You mean, you know who this belonged to?" AJ asked in surprise.

Whittaker held up a hand. "I wouldn't say I know anything, but there's a chance this might be linked to an unsolved case from 1986."

"Really?" AJ said, and felt a bit guilty when she realised the idea of discovering something to do with a criminal case excited her. After all, she was expecting to find a body if they ever got inside the cavern.

"A murder case?" Reg asked.

Whittaker again took his time, carefully constructing his reply. "We don't know. It was listed as a missing persons case for several years and eventually closed as missing, presumed dead. No one was ever charged and a body never found. It was filed as most likely being a diving accident."

"Was it considered suspicious at the time?" AJ asked, still in awe and leaving her lunch untouched.

"It was," Whittaker replied cautiously. "Only reason I recall anything about the case was because I was new on the job when it happened. I was a regular bobby, and I had some contact with the person that went missing."

"Who was it?" Reg asked, between bites of his lunch that he had no problem tucking into.

"I don't want to get ahead of ourselves," Whittaker replied. "It's unlikely this is related, but I thought it best to mention it as the cavern may turn out to be a crime scene. Or the site of an accident.

Either way, we need to preserve as much integrity in the location as we can."

"If we get in there," AJ pointed out.

"Of course," Whittaker agreed. "And I don't want you taking any undue risk in doing so."

"Don't worry, I won't let her," Reg said with a chuckle.

AJ was about to take her first bite of her fish but stopped and frowned at Reg. "What do you mean? I'm not the one who already stuck my bloody great big paw in the crime scene and stirred it all up."

That made Reg chuckle even more.

"You've both helped before with underwater crime scenes, so we all know how difficult they are to work with," Whittaker said, grinning at their banter. "Especially if the gear has been in there for thirty-four years. I'm just asking that we treat it carefully and film every step of the process for me if you would."

"No problem, Roy," AJ answered, giving Reg one last glare before she finally started her lunch.

"Keep a log for me as well, please," the detective added. "List each dive, who was present, what you found, et cetera."

"This afternoon we'll have an idea whether it's likely, or even possible, to access the cavern," Reg commented. "Three decades is enough time for coral growth, hurricanes and high seas to have changed the landscape enough that what might have been accessible back then, isn't now without damaging living reef."

"Yeah, and we can't do that," AJ added.

"No, no, I wouldn't want you to," Whittaker agreed. "Just take it one step at a time and keep me informed. If the police had discovered the site we would likely have called you two in to help with the dives, so we're not going about this any differently really. I'm just waiting to bring in my scene-of-crime officer until we know it's a scene of anything other than a rusty old tank."

"And a buckle," AJ reminded him.

"Indeed, that does add an increased level of interest," Whittaker admitted.

"You folks still enjoying your nice lunch in front of da water here?" Thomas said playfully, walking up to the table. "Tanks are filled and we're ready any time."

AJ quickly stuffed a few more bites in her mouth and Reg reached for his wallet. Whittaker held up a hand.

"The Royal Cayman Islands Police Service can take care of this, I appreciate you joining me." He looked up at Thomas. "How are you, young Bodden?"

Thomas beamed. "Couldn't be better, sir, thank you."

"Please pass my regards on to your parents."

"I will do that, sir," Thomas replied.

"We'll call you this afternoon after we dive again," Reg said, standing and shaking hands with the policeman.

"And thank you for lunch," AJ added, shaking his hand in turn.

The ride back to the dock was a chaotic mess of babbling. The three lads excitedly grilled and questioned AJ and Reg about their lunch conversation once they heard there may be a possible link to an old cold case. AJ and Reg told them very little, as they knew very little, but it didn't stop the questions flying. Andy seemed to be coming out of his shell and fitting in perfectly with the group, which didn't surprise AJ, having left him with Thomas and Jackson for an hour. If there were two people who could make anyone feel comfortable and welcome it was those two. She smiled as she listened to the three chatter in the back seat. Once back to the car park by Reg's dock, they unloaded all the tanks and Thomas pointed out what they had.

"I had dem fill two tanks with 28% O_2, like we do for da submarine wreck, Boss. In case you need to go back down to the cavern or we get inside."

"Good thinking, Thomas, thank you," AJ said, grabbing one heavy tank in each hand by the valve. "The rest are regular 32%?"

"Yes, Boss," Thomas replied, taking two tanks himself and starting towards the pier. "Eight tanks regular and two with 28%."

"Save them two for the second dive then," Reg added, carrying a couple of tanks as though they weighed nothing.

They dropped the tanks into empty holders behind the bench seats along either side of the Newton's deck, and AJ went up the ladder to the fly-bridge to start the motors. With lines cast off, she idled the boat clear of the dock and pointed it back towards the buoy on Neptune's Wall.

12

GRAND CAYMAN – SATURDAY

Thomas lost the game of rock, paper, scissors to see who would stay on the boat first, so he stood at the stern and helped the other four get in the water. He hung his head forlornly when Reg told him he planned to wrap this business up this dive, so don't expect a second. AJ swore she could still hear Reg laughing after he had stepped in the water and submerged.

"Don't worry, we'll be diving again," she told Thomas before she followed the others in.

The four divers were now familiar with the routine, and kept to 30 feet depth as they followed the drop-off, saving gas and bottom time. Life on the reef went about its business below them, and it struck AJ as amusing that they passed over a turtle, a nurse shark and a large school of horse-eyed jacks without pause. All three sightings would bring a normal recreational dive to an excited stop, but they were on a mission, and the fish were casually observed with little more than a glance. Once they reached the second ravine, all four descended and AJ pointed to the tight entry below the over-hang where they would enter the gully. Reg dropped down and took a look at the low gap. There was plenty of width but not much height, especially for a barrel-chested man and his dive tank. He carefully eased his way into the slot, angling his body to present the narrowest form. He slipped past the bottleneck with an inch or two to spare, and once through he straightened up and finned forward towards the rock pile.

AJ signalled for the other two to stay above the ravine and followed Reg through the gap, clearing the restriction with a lot more margin than the big fella. She met him at the end of the overhang, where he knelt on the sandy bottom and was shining his torch into the opening she had found that morning. He pointed into the hole and held both hands wide apart, signalling he thought it opened up to a large tunnel beyond the blockage. They both looked at the pile of debris before them. AJ figured there were larger rocks and broken chunks of coral below, but the face was mainly sand mixed with smaller pieces of debris. They had worn gloves for this dive and she began clawing at the sloped face, shovelling the loose material away and to the side. Reg joined her and they were soon lost in a cloud of silt and fine detritus. Using both hands they weren't able to hold their torches, so the dimly lit overhang quickly became a cloudy darkness. They kept digging at the slope until AJ felt the hard surface of something bigger below the loose particulate. She assumed Reg had reached the same point as he stopped digging beside her and they sat still, waiting for the fog to clear.

It took several minutes until they could see much at all around them and their torch beams illuminated the grit in the water more than the end of the ravine, but slowly they could see what they had revealed. It was indeed larger chunks of coral piled in a heap covering the entrance. They had cleared two small sections down to the rocks but the rest of the pile was still covered in sand and debris. AJ realised what a task they had ahead to clear the entire stack. Reg pointed at the area closest to the small opening and she figured out he was indicating they should focus on this section. That made sense, she thought; they didn't have to clear the entire end of the ravine, just a space big enough to fit through. She checked the dive computer on her wrist while she could see it and noted they had been underwater for eighteen minutes, but almost half of that had been on the shallow swim out. They placed their torches off to the side, shining into the corner and set about clearing more of the debris, using more care and focusing on the smaller area. Silt still billowed as they brushed and scraped, but didn't create the total blackout they had experienced before. They were shoulder to shoulder for them both to reach the section near the hole, which made discarding what they pulled out much harder. Reg swung his handfuls to the right, being careful not to dump any into the hole they were attempting to clear, and AJ shovelled hers to the left.

After what felt like ten minutes, Reg put a hand on AJ's arm and they both stopped and allowed the fog to clear once again. AJ wondered what it looked like to Jackson and Andy hovering somewhere above them over the reef. Probably like Pigpen from the Peanuts cartoons was running amok in the ravine, she decided with a smile. The haze cleared and AJ could see several smaller rocks about the size of footballs in front of a much larger chunk of coral. Reg pulled the first rock away which dislodged a second, smaller one, and AJ grabbed it. They were heavy, but not the unmanageable weight they would be if they were solid rock. The coral was porous and far less dense. Reg took hold of the edge of the larger piece and gave it a good tug. It didn't budge. AJ pointed to the top where it appeared to be trapped under more chunks of coral and wedged into the wall of the ravine itself. They needed tools. Their torches were starting to fade as the batteries drained from constant use, but there was still enough light for her to signal Reg that they needed a pry bar. He nodded and checked his own computer. He pointed a thumb towards the ceiling and she gave him an okay sign; they had been down long enough.

Emerging from the ravine through the bottleneck, AJ looked around for the other two. She spotted Andy, filming her and Reg as they finned their way out of the gully, and then spotted Jackson near a cloudy haze above where they had been working. In and around the wafting debris was a myriad of fish life. Their disturbance had apparently caused a stir in the reef community as well as the sea floor, with the locals swooping in to see if there was an easy meal to be had. Parrotfish of varying colours and sizes were in abundance. They fed on hard coral with their incredibly strong, parrot-like beaks, grinding the coral down into a granular substance which they excreted, making sand. AJ signalled to Andy and Jackson to head back towards the boat and the group steadily ascended as they made their way north to the mooring.

AJ sprayed herself from the freshwater shower back on the Newton, trying to get the grit and sand from her hair while Reg rummaged around in the cabin looking for useful tools.

"Reg, I don't have anything sturdy enough down there, we need to go back in," she called over.

Reg stuck his head back out, his scraggly hair dripping wet from the dive. "Who doesn't carry a crowbar aboard?"

"Why would I have a bloody crowbar on my boat?" AJ protested.

"For moments just like this," Reg retorted.

"Back to the dock, Boss?" Thomas asked, already climbing the ladder to the fly-bridge.

"Yes please," AJ replied, giving up on getting her hair clean and turning the water off.

She started towards the bow to release the line, but Jackson beat her to it, so she switched her gear over to the fresh nitrox tank and Andy did the same.

"Sorry to leave you two up top, but there's not much room below the overhang," she said.

"That's okay, I was filming almost the whole time," he answered. "Once you began stirring up the bottom, the fish came straight over to see what was going on. I hope I got some good shots."

AJ paused a moment. "You know what I forgot? Detective Whittaker asked for us to film as much of the process as possible. I should have had you film a bit before we started. That was silly of me. I had my GoPro in my BCD pocket, too. I could have filmed it myself, come to think of it."

"I did lower the camera down the edge of the overhang a few times while you were working, but I don't know if I got a clear shot," Andy replied. "I reached as far down as I could and had the stick extended all the way."

Thomas eased the throttles forward and pointed Hazel's Odyssey towards the shore, a quarter of a mile away. AJ finished her switch-over and reset her computer for the 28% nitrox mix she would use for the next dive.

"We'll take you under the overhang next dive," AJ said, looking at Andy he as readied his gear. "Get some footage of what we've cleared before we fog it all up again."

She noticed Andy couldn't stop grinning the whole way back to the dock.

Forty minutes later they were back at the dive site, tied in and ready to make another dive. Reg wielded a large crowbar and Thomas insisted on carrying the four-foot-long steel bar they had found behind the hut, so AJ didn't have to. She watched the other three step into the water and paused to give Jackson a quick kiss.

"Be careful, don't do anything crazy," he said softly and smiled.

She kissed him again. "Why does everyone think I do crazy things?"

"Be careful of anything crazy happening in your presence," he said, still smiling. "Is that better?"

"Much," she replied, then put her regulator in her mouth, and strode from the swim step into the Caribbean Sea.

AJ knew Jackson's words were from the worry of someone who loved her deeply, but it weighed heavily on her mind as she led the group towards the dive site one more time. His concern didn't bother her. If anything it strengthened her belief in his commitment to her, but the idea that she might be reckless did. Was she foolhardy? She had been in more scrapes than the average dive boat operator in the past few years, but was that circumstances, or poor decision-making on her part? Her natural reaction to her own question was the defensive stance that she had no control over other people's actions; which was true. But her concern rested on her reaction to those situations. Was she doing what needed to be done, or was she impetuously audacious? Diving alone, twelve miles offshore, in search of a long-lost submarine would fall under the latter; three years of reflection had cemented that in her mind. Reg certainly considered her willingness to help a cave-diving drunk on several escapades to be ill-advised. Her various exploits and adventures had turned out okay, to date, so did that justify her actions? It gave her a knot in her stomach thinking about it. She hated to think of herself as reckless and, more so, she couldn't abide the thought she was frivolous in risking other people's lives. As they arrived at the ravine, she shook the negative thoughts from her mind and descended to the entrance of the overhang, signalling for Andy to follow her. Before entering she paused for a moment, and then felt annoyed. Bugger it, she berated herself; the kid is more than capable of diving into the ravine. It's wide inside, has some light throughout, the exit is 30 feet away, and she would be right next to him. Her self-doubt felt like treacle bogging her down until every decision became a stand-off with her own demons. One thing she knew for sure was that inaction never made anything happen. She finned carefully through the low opening and checked Andy was safely through behind her.

The glassy sweepers had returned to the dark shadows of the overhang and Andy filmed them brushing by as they approached the end of the ravine. In the beam of her torch, with the silt and debris settled, AJ could clearly make out the progress they had made earlier. If they could shift the larger boulder, they would open up the entrance hole a significant amount, possibly enough for her to enter through. Andy methodically filmed the surroundings as AJ brushed her torch light around and finished by aiming down the small opening they hoped to widen. Once done, AJ turned and saw Reg and Thomas had both squeezed into the ravine behind them. There was enough room for everybody, but the extra bodies blocked much of the meagre natural light. AJ directed Andy off to the side and back, to allow room for Reg to take his place upfront. Thomas handed AJ the long steel bar. Reg played around with the crowbar, seeing where he could gain leverage to move the boulder. Several times he traded with AJ for the steel bar and back again, testing what would work best. Eventually he directed her to move to his right and wedge the steel bar into the rock pile. Using the steel bar as a fulcrum, he dug the crowbar in behind the boulder and heaved with all his might. Reg moved, but the boulder stayed put. Gravity was negated by his buoyancy in the water, so his body mass, which he could usually use to great advantage, was of no use at all. He looked around for something to push against with his feet, and found a large rock sticking up through the sandy floor. He tried again, and AJ let her end of the steel bar rest against the wall of the ravine as Reg's powerful legs jammed the crowbar against the steel rod and pried the boulder free of the hole in a burst of debris and wafting silt. Reg's effort sent him into the pile of rocks with both tools tumbling to the floor and AJ falling over backwards.

It took a minute for the cloud to clear, but finally revealed the boulder was now turned sideways to the entrance, more than doubling the size of the opening. Some of the debris and smaller rocks had cascaded down and Reg and AJ carefully scooped them away, trying not to stir up any more mess in the water. AJ glanced back and saw Andy was filming every step, with Thomas keeping his dive torch trained on the end of the ravine. She looked at the opening. It was roughly the shape of an obtuse triangle, with the tall side being the edge of the boulder. Pointing her torch through the hole, she peered into the tunnel. It widened much more than the space they had opened up and she estimated most of the rock pile was covering the remainder of the entrance. Twenty feet in, she could see where the tunnel met the chimney between the cavern and the top of the reef. She eased farther forward to see if she could fit through the hole. Her shoulders and tank all brushed against rock, but she figured it was possible to wriggle through. She felt a big hand on her leg which tugged firmly several times, so she shimmied out of the gap and sat back, looking at Reg. He signalled that the hole was too small. AJ shook her head, pointed to herself and then made an okay sign. He shook his head and frowned, signalling that he couldn't fit and held two fingers next to each other in the dive buddy sign. She knew he didn't want her going in there alone, but she was the only one who could fit, except perhaps Andy, and there was no way they were letting him go in there. She was trained for cave and cavern diving, as was Reg, but unless they could move the rocks some more, he wasn't going in.

AJ unclipped the penetration reel from her BCD, pointed to herself and then the entrance. She tapped two fingers against her mask, pointed again to the entrance and then made the shooting movie sign. Reg sat still and looked at her, his eyes full of concern. She looked around and grabbed the steel bar sitting in the sand. She looped the end of her reel line around it and placed it across the base of the opening, which it easily spanned. She noticed it was slightly bent from Reg's efforts. She looked back at Reg and held up an okay sign again. He shrugged his shoulders, tapped his dive computer, then held up two fingers. He was telling her she had two minutes to search the cavern. What he could do after two minutes she didn't know, as it wasn't like he could come and get her, but he had given her the go ahead so she checked her own computer then ducked her head back into the opening.

As she wriggled through the tight entrance and crawled into the dark tunnel, it dawned on her that this might be one of those moments that others classified as crazy.

13

GRAND CAYMAN – SEPTEMBER, 1986

It had taken another hour of shuffling the boat around in the water, snapping Polaroids and comparing the view, the sketch, and the pictures, until Ally announced they were as close as she could figure to the artist's perspective. Jonesy dropped the anchor in the sandy area between the deep reef leading to the wall and the shallower reef farther towards the shore. He figured anything in the sand would have been spotted years ago, found on magnetometer scans, or buried to the point it couldn't be discovered, so he decided to focus on the deep reef. That gave them a strip which averaged a hundred feet across, from wall to sand, and a quarter mile long by Ally's estimation. Once he was sure the anchor was secure, Jonesy took the bungee cords off their dive gear and prepared to get in the water. Ally watched him from her seat under the covered helm.

"You're not diving with me?" he asked, surprised she wasn't getting ready.

"I'm not sure you can trust me," she replied, her expression hidden behind her sunglasses.

Jonesy paused and looked up. "What the bloody hell does that mean?"

Ally slipped from the seat and took off her tee-shirt and sunglasses. "Nothing," she said, and joined him on the deck. "I've no idea why I let you talk me into this, is all. We should be trying to get a charter to take out; even if it didn't make enough, we could pay the bastard something. Maybe it would buy time," she finished, and started putting on her gear.

His wife had become a foreign entity to him, he decided, a mystical being he couldn't fathom. She had always been such an easy-going, fun-loving woman, but now, he couldn't tell if he was on foot or horseback around her. He knew he had screwed up, but surely she could see he was trying to get them out of their predicament. She's out here, on the boat with me, he decided, so she must think there's some chance this could work. He took a deep breath, sat on the gunwale, buckled into his BCD, strapped his depth gauge to his wrist, and put his fins on his feet.

"Let's head north from here," he said. "We'll stay about 20 feet apart from each other and go until we're down to almost half a tank, then we'll turn around and move over west to come back. We should cover the whole north segment in one dive."

Ally didn't respond, but pulled her mask over her face and back-rolled into the water, which he took as an acknowledgement of the plan. He followed her in and they descended to the reef 55 feet below. He realised right away his plan was flawed. He had them starting the dive at the shallowest depth and returning at the deepest, out by the wall. They should be doing it the other way around. He noticed Ally kept finning towards the wall, so he followed her. She took up position close to the drop-off in 70 feet of water and pointed for him to start 20 feet farther over the reef. He felt like an idiot. This was the woman he had apparently called simple minded, or something along those lines. He couldn't recall what he had said, but she sure did, and he wished he hadn't been so stupid. He was glad they couldn't talk underwater – maybe it would save him from putting his foot in his mouth again.

They began their search. Looking for what, Jonesy realised, he had no real idea. Anything organic would have long since rotted away, leaving only metal, glass or ceramics, which would only have been a small part of the missing chest's contents. The rowboat was most likely to have been constructed completely of wood and rotted to dust over time. If anything came to rest on the top of the reef, then coral would have covered them in the 400 years since their demise, if they had been wedged in well enough not to be swept off the wall during a storm. As he swam along, peering into every nook and cranny, he became more pessimistic about their chances of finding anything. He looked over and saw Ally was upside down inside a small gully with just her finned feet visible above the reef. His hopes briefly surged until she reappeared and continued along the edge of the wall.

Ten minutes later, Jonesy checked his pressure gauge, which showed his tank was slightly below half. He waved to his wife and signalled he was turning around. They both moved away from the wall and the reef gently sloped shallower. He positioned himself along the inner edge, where the coral protruded in short fingers reaching into the sand flats, creating a series of ravines between each finger. This terrain would take a lot longer to search and meant dropping to the sand at 65 feet, then returning to the top of the reef at 50 feet. Somewhere on the boat, Jonesy had a set of US Navy dive tables to reference how long it was safe to stay at a given depth during a dive, but he couldn't remember where. The customers he took out usually burned through their air so fast they were back on the boat in half an hour. He always took them to the shallow reef where the light was better anyway, so it wasn't an issue. He found the tables confusing, and they calculated the bottom time based on one depth, as though you dived down to that depth and stayed there until you ascended to the boat. They never dived that way, and he'd never had a problem, so he relied on his pressure gauge. If he had air left, he kept diving.

Looking in the ravines, he found a lot of natural debris and realised they were great gathering spots for anything floating around near the bottom. He pulled the broken pieces of sea fan and coral aside to see if anything interesting hid beneath, but so far all he had found was a couple of cans and a rusty piece of pipe. By the third ravine, he had used up most of his remaining air and found nothing of use or interest. He waved to Ally, who looked up. He held up his pressure gauge and pointed in the direction of the boat. She looked at her own gauge then kicked south so he guessed she was ready to go up as well. Before he followed her, he took three pieces of coral rock lying in the sand and set them together forming a triangle. He found one more football-sized piece and stacked it on top.

As he made his way towards the Bertram, pessimism shoved his usually optimistic nature aside, and he wondered if he was witnessing his whole world collapsing around him. In a few days he could be homeless, penniless and left alone to face the consequences. He clambered back aboard Bottom Time and helped Ally drag her gear into the boat. He wished he had put more tanks aboard, but he had just brought the two with them. They were supposed to stay out of the water for a while between dives, according to the Navy, but he would rather stay out on the ocean than run back to the dock. Petrol cost money they didn't have. He started the motors and eased forward, relieving the strain on the anchor, before slipping them into neutral. He walked around the cabin to the bow and heaved on the line to free the anchor from the sand. It took a strong pull, but after a minute of huffing and puffing, he broke it from the grasp of the sea floor and hauled the line up. Back at the helm, he put the boat in gear and was about to push the throttles forward when he heard Ally speak. He was getting used to her not talking to him so it took him by surprise.

"I'm sorry?" he said.

"Do you know where to come back to?" she repeated, over emphasising each word.

He looked at her, puzzled. "How do you mean, love?"

Ally let out a long sigh. "We just searched an area of the reef that we don't want to search again. So, do you know where you dropped the anchor so we can come back to exactly the same spot to start over?"

"Yeah, of course," he started, embarrassed and completely off guard. "We're where you lined us up, so we just do that again, right?"

She shook her head. "It took us over an hour to figure out that spot. So your plan is to come back out with more tanks, because you didn't think to put extras aboard this morning, and motor around for an hour again to find what we hope is the same place?"

He opened his mouth, but this time he made sure nothing came out. One thing he was slowly learning: if you're digging yourself into a hole, the first trick to getting out was to stop making the hole deeper. He resembled a goldfish opening and closing its mouth, but at least he was a goldfish who had put his spade down.

"Exactly," she said. "Head back. I did bother to take a set of references from the shoreline. My tiny mind managed that much."

"Bloody hell, love," he reacted, before he could stop himself. "I've said I'm sorry, can we leave that alone now?"

Ally took off her sunglasses and glared at him. "You've spent sixteen years deciding I'm an idiot, and you want me to forget about that epiphany of yours in a matter of hours? You ain't getting off that bloody easy."

Jonesy pushed the throttles gently forward and turned the wheel to aim them towards home. Why, oh why, he asked himself, did I pick up the spade again.

Back at the dock, Ally stomped off the boat and up to their flat without a word. Jonesy carried the heavy steel tanks up to the gear room, and brought two more down to the boat. He then went back up and got two more; he wasn't giving her that bullet to use again. He turned the ignition on and looked at the petrol gauge. It was now below an eighth full and the gauge was notoriously unreliable when it showed that low. He opened a cabinet beneath the passenger pilot seat and pulled out a two-gallon emergency petrol can. It was empty. Perfect, he thought, and cursed himself for not refilling it the last time he had used the contents. He trudged back up to the building and grabbed his bicycle from against the wall where he had left it. He slipped the headphones on and hit play on the Walkman. Bon Jovi blasted into his ears explaining why 'You Give Love a Bad Name'. He smiled for the first time since he last sat on his bike, hooked the petrol can over the end of the handlebars, took off around the building and turned north towards the petrol station.

Fifteen minutes later, the ride back was a little trickier with the petrol can full. Jonesy slowed as he approached the office but his feet never actually stopped pedalling. The Scorpions were now telling him there's 'No One Like You' and he felt his spirits nudging him back towards his jovial self. He was also incredibly thirsty. His bicycle finally came to a stop outside the Hog Sty Bay Bar and Restaurant, and he chuckled at the idea that the bike knew its own way to his favourite bar. He leaned the Raleigh against the wall, put the petrol can on the ground next to it, and walked inside.

The place hadn't been long open for the day, and he was the only patron as the staff began setting the restaurant tables for lunch. Sandy greeted him at the bar with a smile and an off-the-shoulder, over-sized neon pink tee-shirt. The wide scoop neck advertised the lack of bra straps and the bobbling movement below the fabric provided further evidence that the woman's impressive chest was unrestrained. While Jonesy found himself mesmerised, a glass magically appeared in front of him. He took a long drink of the cool rum and Coke, to ease his thirst, then thanked Sandy very much.

"What have you been up to this morning?" she asked, wiping down the already spotless bar and sending Jonesy cross-eyed as her breasts fought each other for space beneath the light fabric.

"Been out on the water," he managed to piece together in reply. "Diving on the deep reef with… Ally."

He trailed off the sentence with the mention of his wife, and realised he was hesitating to mention her name in front of the bartender. His enjoyment of Sandy's shows and her flirtatious ways had been going on as long as he could remember coming to Hog Sty's. Ally was usually the first to point out when Sandy was offering a better view than normal. But somehow it felt different today. Ally was thinking of leaving him. Was he really contemplating his chances with the bartender, he asked himself? Sandy, who winked at every man who stood before her bar. She was legendary for never leaving the bar with a customer; nobody knew anything about her private life and the chatter was rife with tall stories and rumours. But Sandy and her availability wasn't the real question, he contemplated as he made quick work of his second drink. Keeping Ally was all he really wanted.

Lost in his dilemma, and sipping the cool drinks that remained topped up before him, time once again evaporated from his day. Jonesy looked around the bar and then the restaurant. The place had filled up, and was bustling with customers. Most of the stools were now occupied at the bar which had somehow completely escaped his notice. An empty plate sat before him so he must have finished the food he couldn't recall ordering. He had recounted the past 24 hours again and again in his mind, and so far it still ended up with him about to lose his wife, along with his home and business. His head sank slowly down until his forehead rested against the bar.

"You alright there, sugar?" Sandy asked softly.

He picked his head up, and forced his eyes all the way up to hers, pausing only momentarily on the way.

"I don't know what to do," he said, and was surprised his voice sounded slurred.

Sandy smiled. "I'm guessing a good start will be to get yourself home, sweetie."

"Yeah," he mumbled. "I should talk to her, you know? Sort all this out."

"Or maybe take the afternoon to yourself, sugar, sleep this off first," she suggested.

Jonesy reached for the jar containing the bill and managed to wrangle it towards him on the second try. He took his wallet from his pocket and hunted all around the singular, ten Caymanian dollar note inside until he was convinced it was alone. He took out the note and stuffed it into the jar.

"Keep the change, Sandy," he said. "And thanks for, you know… Being you."

"Well sugar, I don't know how to be anyone else," she beamed. "Now you get yourself home, and you can settle the balance next time you're in."

The last part made no sense to him, but he smiled, held up a hand, checked out the duelling twins one more time, and headed towards the door. Between the bar and the front door he apologised to three other patrons he bumped into, as well as the wall he ricocheted off several times. The outside world hit him with the full force of the early afternoon sun. Squinting, he pointed himself in the general direction of his flat, and started walking with the confusing sounds of passing cars whirling around his head. Someone was blasting a horn loudly, which made him squeeze his eyes closed even tighter and then the car sounds stopped. Much better, he thought, and opened his eyes. Someone had pinched the pavement and moved it somewhere was all he could fathom.

"Let's get you out of the road, sir," came a pleasant, yet firm, Caymanian man's voice.

Jonesy had no idea what was happening, but he let his new friend steer him away and he heard the cars begin making their driving noises again.

"I'm guessing you've had a drink or two for lunch, sir," the man said, and for the first time Jonesy noticed the uniform.

"You the old bill?" he asked.

"I am indeed, sir," the policeman replied. "How about I help you get home?"

"That'd be great, mate," Jonesy enthused. "That's exactly where I was just going."

"Wonderful, and where is home, sir?" the man asked.

"It's down there a bit," Jonesy replied, pointing approximately north.

"Let's walk that way then, sir," the policeman directed.

"You can walk if yer like. I'm riding my bike," Jonesy pointed out.

"I see," the man answered, looking around. "Would that be your bicycle over by the entrance to the bar, sir?"

Jonsey peered over at the Raleigh. "How'd it end up there?" he mumbled. "I was riding it just a minute ago."

The policeman retrieved the bicycle, and the petrol can. "This yours too, Mr…?"

"Jonesy, mate, everybody calls me Jonesy. Yeah, don't forget the petrol, boat won't go far without that."

"I have to caution you against operating either the bicycle or a boat in your condition, sir," the man said politely.

Jonesy laughed. "You're alright, you are, mate. What's your name anyway?"

"Officer Whittaker," the man replied. "And it's a pleasure to meet you, Mr. Jones."

14

GRAND CAYMAN – SATURDAY

AJ was surprised how roomy the tunnel was, relatively speaking. She could just touch each wall with outstretched arms and she guessed it was over four feet high. It angled down gently, leading deeper to the junction with the chimney, which she quickly reached, playing out line from her reel. She held her torch on top of the reel handle, using her index finger to keep tension on the reel spool leaving her right hand free, which she now used to turn the torch off. Her eyes took a moment to adjust, but the tunnel was far from pitch black. Natural light filtered in from the crack above, Reg's torch beam from the entrance behind her, and below she could see a faint glow from the fracture opened by the earthquake, where the chimney met the cavern. She switched her torch back on and shone the light around her. It quickly became apparent that the tunnel down to the cavern was a continuation of the one she entered through. It turned almost vertically downward and the chimney above was much smaller, leading from the ceiling up to the reef.

AJ let more line play out from the reel as she eased head first into the vertical shaft towards the cavern below. She had decided to survey the layout first, and film on her exit, keeping her focus on where she was going and a hand free in case it was needed. As she approached the top of the cavern she hesitated and paused for a second. Maybe I should be filming, she wondered nervously; if I see something awful, I may turn tail and scoot back out. She fumbled with her BCD pocket to retrieve the camera, struggling to free the Velcro flap and then careful not to drop the GoPro as she hung inverted in the water. She pressed the power button, waited for the camera to come to life, checked it was on video and not still pictures or set-up mode, then hit the record button on the top of the housing. Their video from the outside hadn't shown anything by the tank, but she was still half expecting to see the remnants of the owner somewhere in the cavern, and had to will herself to exhale the air from her lungs in order to descend.

She turned around to face the outer wall as she lowered her upper torso into the cavern and tentatively swept her torch beam around the room. The cavern was taller than the tunnel, perhaps 6 feet from the sand covered floor to the ceiling, and about the same width. From where she dropped in it was no more than 12 feet to the outer wall and the fracture just above the sand. The tank stood upright against the outer wall, and she noted right away it clearly had a first stage attached to the top. Next to the tank, on the darker side, away from the crack in the wall, was… nothing. AJ continued down and into the cavern as she finally exhaled all the way. She couldn't decide if she was wholly relieved or slightly disappointed at not finding Whittaker's missing person. She had kept the video running so she continued to film the cavern, finning carefully closer to the tank and getting a clear shot of the valve and first stage. She noticed a single line running from the first stage and hanging down into the sand, and presumed any other lines had rotted away. It all had a dark brown hue and rough texture, but she couldn't tell if it was deeply rusted or superficially oxidised. The top of everything was covered with a fine layer of silt and she considered using her regulator to blow a little air over it, but decided to leave it untouched. She had visions of prodding the tank and the whole thing disintegrating in a wafting cloud of rusty particles. Even if there wasn't a body in the cavern, she didn't want to explain to Whittaker how she had destroyed all the evidence that was there.

AJ turned and was about to switch off the camera when she realised she hadn't filmed the sandy floor. She kept the camera on and moved her torch beam around, capturing the base of the room. She paused when she saw the dark piece of debris they had noticed from the outside. She moved closer, keeping her fins well above the sand so she didn't stir up the silt. It looked metal but certainly didn't appear to be anything from a BCD or a piece of normal dive gear. AJ stopped the recording and placed the camera on the sand to free up a hand. She took the opportunity to wind the excess line back into the reel, using her fingers to keep tension on the line. She locked the reel and placed it down on the sand, keeping her torch in her left hand. She gently reached down with her right hand and touched the object. It was firm and didn't move, indicating there was more of it below the sand. She held the end of it between two fingers and gave it a wiggle. The sand around it moved and the piece came free. It definitely felt like metal, was roughly 4 inches long, 2 inches wide and perhaps an eighth of an inch thick, with a slotted hole towards one end. Beyond that she had no clue what she was holding. She rested it back on the sand and retrieved the camera, hitting the record button with her finger and taking a quick shot of the object and the divot in the sand where she had pulled it from.

Slipping the piece of metal into her BCD pocket, she carefully secured the flap and glanced at her computer. She had been inside for four minutes. She clamped the GoPro stick on the reel handle with her left hand, instead of the torch, which she switched to her right hand so she could use her fingers to turn the reel. It made the light beam jump round as she wound the reel, but without a third appendage with an opposable thumb, it was the best she could do. Gently finning, she made the turn at the end of the cavern and headed up the tunnel, filming the passageway as she went. Once she turned the corner towards the entrance she was hit by Reg's torch beam, which he quickly turned off and replaced with his big head sticking in the entrance hole. AJ chuckled to herself. She had been scared of what she might find in the cavern, but the shaggy-haired, scruffy-bearded monster above was a far more fearful sight. As she wriggled back through the tight opening, Reg tapped his dive computer and waggled a finger at her. She looked over at Andy, filming her exit, and held up an okay sign for the camera, before giving Reg a friendly punch on the arm.

AJ thought about showing the group her find, but as they couldn't discuss it until they were on the boat, she decided against it. Reg signalled that he wanted to work on the opening some more, as they hadn't been down very long this dive, and he pointed to AJ's computer, indicating she should let him know when it was time for her ascent, as she had gone deeper than the rest of them. She nodded and tried to position herself to help with the steel bar again. Reg waved her back and Thomas came over instead. She soon realised they had been scheming while she had been in the cavern and now wanted to try their plan. Both of them had removed their fins so they could use their feet more effectively. She guessed they had waited until she returned in case it went wrong and filled the hole instead of clearing it. She knew Reg wanted to be able to go inside with her, and the more she thought about it, the more she realised she would like him to as well. She didn't fancy the idea of moving the tank on her own if Whittaker wanted it brought up.

The two men positioned the steel rod and the crowbar, before wedging themselves against something solid, and levering the boulder. This time it slowly moved a few inches before grinding to a halt. They repositioned themselves and tried again, heaving, pulling and shoving, but the boulder wouldn't budge again. It appeared to be firmly wedged into the opening from years of storm surge and rocks beating into the wall. Reg took another careful look and had Thomas reposition for one more attempt. AJ tapped Reg on the shoulder and held up two fingers, signifying he had two minutes left before they should leave. He nodded and she slid back out of the way, keeping her torch pointed at the corner so they could see. Reg heaved again, jamming his feet against the rock in the floor to get all the power he could behind his leverage. The boulder held fast, and she saw Reg wrench even harder. She was worried if he slipped he might go careening into Thomas but the boulder began to move and finally shuddered as it broke free of the opening. They all tumbled down in a heap in the sand while another cloud of silt and debris engulfed everyone.

When the mess settled enough for them to see, Reg looked pleased with himself. The opening had increased by more than enough for the big man to fit through and he turned to AJ and gave her an okay sign. She took great pleasure in waggling her finger at him and tapping her computer, letting him know he'd exceeded his two minutes. He shoved her towards the front of the ravine and her mask leaked water as her face contorted in laughter.

Back on the boat, they stowed their gear and towelled off before sitting on the benches under the fly-bridge with water to drink and AJ produced a packet of bourbon biscuits to snack on. She partially filled a bucket with sea water, and slipped the piece of metal into the container. She had watched a show about treasure hunters and they had kept the artefacts in sea water until they began the restoration process, so she figured she would do the same. At least for now.

"What have you got there then?" Reg queried, as she brought the bucket over.

AJ slid the bucket under the bench and ignored his question. "So the tunnel from the ravine is actually what we thought was the chimney. It takes a turn down, and enters the top of the cavern. It stays quite roomy all the way. The chimney is a lot smaller and reaches up to the top of the reef where we saw the opening."

Reg couldn't stop looking at the bucket and AJ was doing her best not to grin.

"Was there... you know..." Andy struggled to ask.

"There was no one inside the cavern to greet me, if that's what you're wondering," AJ said, helping him out, and she saw an expression on his face that matched how she had felt when she'd entered the cavern.

"What was in der den?" Thomas asked.

"Definitely a scuba tank," AJ replied. "It does have a first stage on the valve but it's all corroded pretty badly. I took some video so maybe we can decipher something from that."

"Nothing else in there?" Jackson asked.

"I didn't see any other scuba gear," AJ replied.

Reg couldn't stand it any longer. "What's in the bloody bucket?"

AJ burst out laughing. "I really wish it was nothing, 'cos I got you all wound up fussing about it!"

Reg stomped over and pulled the bucket out. "You cheeky bloody wench."

He picked the piece of metal up out of the water and looked at it. "What is it?"

AJ managed to stop laughing enough to speak. "I was hoping you'd tell me – you're the old one who's been around since the earth cooled."

The others got up and huddled around to look at the object in Reg's hand. "It's a lump of scrap metal," Reg said. "Could have fallen down the hole any old time."

"It don't look like no scuba diving part now, does it?" Thomas asked.

"Nah," Reg replied. "Could be something a fisherman tossed over the side, could be rubbish blown around in a hurricane, who knows what."

Jackson looked at it carefully. "It looks like it's at an advanced stage of corrosion. It could be older than everything else you've found down there."

Reg looked at him and frowned. "Bollocks."

"Pretty sure it's not bollocks, Reg," he replied and grinned at the big fella.

Reg laughed. "Don't you start on me." He nodded towards AJ. "Got enough with that one."

They heard Andy chuckling behind them and realised he was filming them.

"Best we do some editing before we show the detective our footage," AJ said, laughing.

She turned back to Reg. "Could we get it carbon dated?"

"No," Reg replied. "First of all, it's probably a lump of scrap from an anchor or an engine block someone used as a mooring. Secondly, you can't carbon date anything non-organic, doesn't work that way."

"Shame it's not bollocks den, huh?" Thomas said and they all laughed.

Reg dropped the metal piece back in the bucket and handed it to AJ. "Make you a paperweight if nothing else," he said with a grin.

She took the bucket. "Tell you what though, I think the sand in the bottom of the cavern is pretty deep, there might be more stuff buried I couldn't see. I didn't want to stir it all up and make a mess until Whittaker tells us what he wants to do, but it would be worth digging around in there I reckon."

"All right, well let's head in," Reg said. "We'll give him a call and see what he wants to do now. We don't really know much more about his missing person than we did already."

"Except the tank had a first stage on it," AJ reminded him. "That plus the buckle suggests it was a rig, not just a tank on its own."

Reg nodded. "Let's see what he says."

15

GRAND CAYMAN – SATURDAY

On the run back to the dock, AJ called Andy's father David and let him know they were on their way, and then Detective Whittaker, who said he would meet them in a few minutes. True to his word, Whittaker was standing on Reg's dock when AJ pulled the Newton up and Thomas and Jackson tied the boat into the cleats. With the detective was a woman in her mid-thirties whom AJ had met once before.

"Hello Roy," AJ called down from the fly-bridge. "Why don't you come aboard and we can tell you what we found."

"Good evening," Roy replied, looking up. "I brought my scene-of-crime officer along. I hope you don't mind?"

"Hi Rasha," AJ said, smiling. "Nice to see you again."

The woman waved. "Hello. Bit better circumstance this time I'm happy to say," she said with an English accent.

The first time AJ had met her was when they fished a young woman's body from the ocean outside the North Sound, so she agreed this was certainly more pleasant.

The two boarded the boat and everyone gathered under the shelter of the fly-bridge where Andy set up his laptop and plugged in the memory card from AJ's camera.

"We've cleared the entry enough for divers to go inside the cavern," Reg began. "It was blocked by large pieces of coral that appear to have broken away from the surrounding reef over time."

Andy hit play and the group studied the eerie view of AJ entering the main cave for the first time.

"You can see the crack in the outer wall we first spotted yesterday," AJ commentated as the film ran. "And there you can clearly see the dive tank with a first stage attached."

"Pause there," Reg asked, and Andy stopped the film.

Reg leaned in closer. "Can you zoom in a bit?"

Andy did as requested and zoomed in closer to the image of the dive tank paused on the screen. The picture became blurrier in the low light recording and Andy moved back and forth through frames to find a clearer image where the light from AJ's torch produced a crisper recording.

"That's an old tank," Reg said, pointing at the screen. "See, it has a J-valve on it."

Everyone looked at him.

Jackson asked the question the whole group were pondering. "What's a J-valve?"

Reg stood back and looked at AJ. "You bloody kids," he said, laughing. "A J-valve is the old style of tank valve we used before we had pressure gauges we could take underwater with us."

"I've heard the term, but I don't think I've ever seen one," AJ said.

"In the old days," Reg explained, "you used to have a pressure gauge on the boat you'd use to check the tank, and back then we'd fill them to 2400psi. This was before aluminium tanks. During the dive you had no way of knowing how much air you had left until you either surfaced, and checked the tank again, or ran out of air down there."

"Bloody hell, that's a bit dodgy," AJ said.

"Too right," Reg agreed. "So the J-valve had a spring-loaded mechanism and would shut off when you were down to 300psi, then you'd open the valve, which had a little lever on it, and you'd get the rest of the air. Gave you time to finish the dive and come up to the surface."

"Not much time for a safety stop," Thomas commented.

Reg laughed. "There was no such thing in those days. Same as there were no back-up regulators, and this tank was probably attached to a horse collar-style adjustable buoyancy life jacket. We didn't have BCDs like you know today. You'll occasionally see a J-valve today. Divers working in zero visibility use them as they can't see their pressure gauge."

"What era would you guess this is from then, Reg?" Whittaker asked.

Reg thought a moment. "Fifties through seventies most likely, but we'd have a better idea if we could bring it up and have a better look."

Whittaker nodded, slowly. "Interesting," he said quietly.

"Does that timeline fit?" Rasha asked him.

"No. No it doesn't," Whittaker replied.

"Hang on though," Reg said, leaning in closer to the screen again. "What do we have here?" He pointed to the line from the first stage. "That must be a steel-braided line. See how it's the only hose or line from the first stage?"

"Should be several lines, right?" AJ said. "Regulator and inflation line at least, plus a gauge of some sort."

"Not on an old rig from the sixties," Reg corrected. "There'd be one line, just the regulator hose, that's it, but it wouldn't be steel-braided. My guess is any rubber hoses are rotted away. That line we're seeing must be for an SPG."

"What's an SPG?" Whittaker asked.

"Submersible pressure gauge," Reg replied.

"But didn't you say you didn't have those in the day of the J-valve?" Whittaker questioned.

"Exactly," Reg replied, thinking. "Might be newer than I'm thinking. If that is a steel-braided line, it could mean the tanks and valves were older, but still being used. There was a long crossover when K-valves were introduced, which is what we use today."

"What time period would you estimate that to be?" Whittaker asked.

Reg scratched his beard. "SPGs came into use in the seventies, and by the time aluminium tanks became the norm in the Caribbean, no one was putting J-valves on them. That was late eighties and through the nineties. So, I'd say seventies or eighties." He tapped a finger on the screen. "We need to pull that up so we can get a good look at the first stage; that will help us."

"Eighties is right, isn't it, sir?" Rasha asked Whittaker.

The detective nodded. "Yes, that puts it in the window. But until we can define the time more accurately, it's all speculation."

"You mean about your missing person?" AJ asked.

"Correct," Whittaker confirmed. "It happened in 1986. Is there anything else on the video that might provide a clue?"

"Not really," AJ said. "I didn't want to disturb the scene until we spoke to you, so I didn't dig around." She reached under the bench and pulled out the bucket. "This was sitting in the sand around the middle of the cave though. The next part of the video will show where."

Andy hit play on the video and Rasha took the piece of metal from the bucket to examine it. Whittaker watched the screen as AJ picked up the object from the sand and held it clearly in her torch-light, before putting it in her pocket and leaving the cavern.

"That doesn't look like any piece of dive gear I've ever seen," Whittaker said, looking at the piece of metal in Rasha's hand.

"It's not," Reg confirmed. "Could just be some scrap that made its way down there over the years."

"Or not," Rasha said. "I'd like to take this to show a friend of mine at the museum, if you don't mind?"

"Of course not," AJ replied. "What do you think it might be?"

Rasha shrugged her shoulders. "I've no idea, really, but going by the corrosion, and the shape of the piece, this looks a lot older to me. Rates of corrosion vary greatly upon location, exposure, and many other influences, but my guess is this doesn't come close to the timeline we've been talking about."

"Ha!" AJ said, and smacked Reg on the arm. "Piece of scrap he says."

Rasha laughed. "It may be nothing more than a piece of scrap. I'm just saying my guess is it's been down there longer than the tank has. Which probably makes it nothing to do with our missing persons case."

Whittaker smiled. "Maybe not."

Rasha placed the object back into the salt water. "Really?"

"Our missing person was looking for artefacts last seen in the late 1500s," Whittaker replied.

"Blimey," AJ spluttered, staring in the bucket at the piece of metal. "That could be from the 16th century?"

Whittaker held his hands up. "Let's not get ahead of ourselves. We have no evidence he ever found anything, and we're still not sure we've found evidence linked to that case."

"Who was this bloke?" Reg asked.

"His name was Charlie Jones," Whittaker replied. "Went by Jonesy. I met him briefly. I had just joined the force at the time. It was the first serious case I was involved with, although I was hardly part of the investigation."

"He went missing on the water?" Jackson asked.

"So we believe," Whittaker said. "While diving we suspected, as neither he nor his gear were ever found. Just his boat, drifting off the west side."

"Any suspects?" Reg asked.

"I dug out the file today and refamiliarised myself with the case," Whittaker replied. "As you can imagine it was a while back and I couldn't recall the details. At the time, the investigator treated it as a potential accident. There was little evidence beyond hearsay and suspicions to prove otherwise. If foul play was involved, the two parties they interviewed at length were his wife and their landlord. A man named Torsten McGinnis."

"McGinnis?" AJ said abruptly. "Any relation to Brenda?"

Whittaker nodded. "Her father."

"Bugger," AJ muttered. "Well if he was anything like Brenda, he should have been a top suspect."

AJ had crossed paths with Brenda through a mutual acquaintance; Jonty Gladstone, a treasure hunter on the island AJ had helped with a couple of projects. Brenda McGinnis had left a lasting impression, and not for good reasons.

"They were behind on their rent and were about to be evicted by McGinnis, which would have ruined them." Whittaker added.

"Doesn't make much sense though, does it?" Reg said.

"Not on the face of it, no," Whittaker agreed.

"Why's that?" Thomas asked.

"Makes it much harder to evict someone who just died," Reg answered. "Police, estate settlement, all kinds of red tape. Would have delayed the eviction."

"So what about the wife?" AJ asked.

"Well, times were hard, obviously, as they were about to lose their home and place of business, so according to her, they had been having disagreements," Whittaker explained. "He was also known to be overindulging at the bar, which is how our paths crossed at the time."

"So that doesn't make much sense either, does it?" Reg pointed out. "Divorce is a lot easier than murder, and doesn't seem like there's a motive there if they were broke."

Whittaker chuckled. "You're thinking like a policeman now, Reg."

AJ shook her head. "Sleeping policeman maybe."

The group laughed, except Andy, until AJ explained a sleeping policeman is the term used for a speed bump on the road in England.

The boat began to rock and AJ looked to see who had caused a wake this close to shore, but didn't see any boats. She then noticed the jetty was shaking, the boards creaking and groaning and the water around them had turned choppy.

"Aftershock," Reg said.

They all stayed quiet until after the disturbance settled down.

"That's the third one I've felt since the big shaker," Rasha commented.

"Probably be one or two more before it's done," Whittaker added.

Andy raised his hand. "May I ask a question, sir?"

"Of course, young fella, and you don't have to ask for permission to speak," Whittaker replied.

"Thank you, sir," Andy said nervously. "But I was wondering. If that's Mr. Jones's dive gear, then where is Mr. Jones? If it was a diving accident, then surely he'd still be with his tank."

AJ looked at Whittaker, curious to hear his reply, as she couldn't think of a good reason for them to be separated either.

"That's a valid point," Whittaker replied cautiously. "Of course we don't know that the tank you have found ever belonged to Jonesy, but let's say it did." He looked back at Reg, then AJ. "You folks are the divers. Why would someone leave their dive gear behind? Would he do that if he ran out of air?"

Reg shook his head. "If he ran out of air, he wouldn't take the time to remove his BCD before trying to get out. He'd have bolted as fast as he could; 124 feet is a long way to go with nothing to breathe from, especially starting inside a cave."

AJ agreed. "Yeah, I agree, only way would be if the BCD and tank were caught up on something and he had to get out of it. But the tank is just sitting in there against the back wall."

"Are we sure he's not still in der?" Thomas said. "Buried in the sand."

"Ooooh," AJ replied, wriggling about. "That gives me the willies. I was much happier thinking I was alone in there."

"We have enough evidence to pursue this further, and more questions than answers," Whittaker stated, "so I'm declaring the cave a police investigation site. Rasha will work with you on procedures moving forward. You'll be paid by the RCIPS for subsequent dives. If of course you're willing to continue helping with the investigation?"

Reg nodded. "Of course."

AJ was still getting over the idea that this Jones fellow may be under the sand she was just kneeling on, but she agreed as well.

"Yes, I'd like to see this through."

"Excellent," Whittaker said, rubbing his hands together. "Can I get a copy of the video footage you've shot so far?"

Andy closed his laptop. "I can make copies of both memory cards and put them on a thumb drive for you, sir."

Whittaker smiled. "Thank you." He turned to Rasha. "Can you organise to get those for us?"

Rasha nodded. "Yup, and I'll chat with Reg and AJ about mapping out the cave. When can you two dive the site again?"

Reg thought a moment. "We'll need to put some gear together if we plan to go through all that sand, and I have boats running each morning I need to see off the dock. But Monday should work. What about you?" he asked, looking at AJ.

"What's today?" she asked, looking at the date on her watch which didn't help her figure out the day of the week.

"It's Saturday," Jackson said.

"Okay, yeah. I have customers tomorrow morning but I can help prep whatever we need in the afternoon, and then I'm open Monday," AJ replied.

"Hi guys, how was the diving?" came a voice from the dock, and they looked up to see David arriving to pick up his son.

"Incredible," Andy blurted with a big grin on his face.

"Hello David," AJ replied, smiling at Andy's enthusiasm. "We're just wrapping up here, we'll be up in a sec."

"Okay then," Whittaker said. "Thank you all for your help. I'll try and speak with Mrs. Jones on Monday."

"Oh wow," AJ said in surprise. "She's still here?"

Whittaker nodded. "She is. She left after the accident for a few years, but returned to the island and has lived here since."

"And then there's Brenda…" AJ said tentatively.

Whittaker raised his eyebrows. "Yes. And then there's Miss McGinnis. I plan to speak with her too."

16

GRAND CAYMAN – SEPTEMBER, 1986

Ally alternated between thanking and apologising to the policeman as he left the office. She could hear her husband stumbling around upstairs in the flat, but couldn't bring herself to walk up there and deal with him. She locked the office front door, walked out the back through the gear room, and sat on the edge of the concrete deck. She stared across the sun-bathed Caribbean Sea and fought back the tears that welled from deep inside. Fancy houses, money and expensive jewellery had never been of much interest to her, and she knew marrying Jonesy was a sure way to avoid them. She had been twenty years old when they married, and he was two years older. It was the early seventies, flower power, sex, drugs and rock 'n' roll. They had both dressed the part and listened to the music, but the wild parties, hallucinogenic drugs and promiscuous sex never made it to their little farming village of Helmdon. Well, there were a couple of girls at school who did their best on the sleeping around front, but Ally could never throw caution to the wind in quite that way, or risk her mother ever finding out. In a village with a few hundred residents, if you included the neighbouring hamlets and scattered farms, nothing made it past the housewife rumour mill of which her mother was a major contributor. Ally's biggest rebellious gesture was ditching her bras, which her mother only noticed when she realised the laundry was short on one of her daughter's undergarments. Ally's slender figure had little to hide until it finally bloomed in her late teens and her figure filled out. She had known Jonesy since childhood, as they both lived in Helmdon and went to the same school, but she was in the same year as his younger brother, creatively named 'Little Jonesy'. It wasn't until she was eighteen that they began socialising at the King's Head in nearby Syresham and he became her one and only serious boyfriend.

She was finishing her A-levels, and he had been working on his family farm since he had left school after his O-levels. He hated the farm and talked endlessly of travelling the world, living off their wits and seeking adventure at every turn. Ally loved the idea of taking off in a Volkswagen van and stopping wherever they chose, leaving anywhere they didn't like, and staying places they fell in love with. For the next ten years the closest they came was a week away in Torquay. Jonesy had left the family farm and worked for a man with a small repair garage in Sulgrave. It was the owner, Jonesy, and one other mechanic, who happened to be an avid scuba diver. The man took Jonesy to the local quarry where they blindly swam around in the murky, frigid water on Sunday mornings, which Ally had no desire for and couldn't understand her husband's interest. He told her he loved the Jacques Cousteau undersea world shows on television and could picture himself on a coral reef in warm, clear water. When the mechanic said he was leaving the job at the garage and moving to the Caribbean, both Ally and Jonesy were awestruck. The man told them as soon as he got himself squared away, he would write to them and see if he could line them up with some work. He had landed a job as a dive guide and was sure they would need others.

Ally allowed her hopes to rise, but after three months without a word, they had both given up hope. She had been working as a secretary in an estate agent's office in Brackley since school and resigned herself to saving for the occasional holiday abroad. They had become stuck in the regular, everyday life, paying rent on their little terraced cottage and splurging on a night out at the pub on a Friday. Ally came home from work one evening and an international air mail letter sat on the floor below the letterbox. She paced around the kitchen waiting for Jonesy to come home and barely gave him time to change out of his dirty work clothes before opening the envelope and handing him the letter to read. His mate apologised for the delay, but they had a job for Jonesy if he could get to a place called Grand Cayman in the next month. If he couldn't, let them know right away, as they needed to find someone else. They scrambled to find an atlas and looked up where this place was that they had never heard of. It was a tiny dot in the middle of the Caribbean Sea, west of Jamaica and south of Cuba. Jonesy looked at Ally and asked what she thought they should do.

As Ally sat out the back of their office, and gazed at the paradise they had called home for the past six years, she clearly remembered that moment and the excitement mixed with trepidation she felt when she told him they should go.

She couldn't put her feelings about her husband in any order that made sense to her at the moment, but she knew she didn't want to leave this place. Her anger, disappointment and frustration all channelled themselves into a determination, and she stood up. She could sit here and feel sorry for herself while Jonesy slept off his liquid lunch, she decided, or she could try and do something about their mess. She looked north along the ironshore coast and saw Torsten McGinnis's 41-foot Viking Sport fishing boat tied alongside his dock. His house, with several other buildings he used for storage, was a few hundred yards away and she could see movement in the cockpit of the expensive boat. She set off at a brisk pace with a new-found confidence that something could be arranged. McGinnis had been respectful and polite with her, although less so with her husband, but surely they could have a sensible conversation between two responsible adults, and find an amicable solution. When she returned, with a reasonable extension negotiated, she would sober up Jonesy and they would focus on filling charters to cover the rent.

Torsten was indeed aboard his boat, and he looked her way as she marched down the concrete jetty and stopped by the stern. Ally noticed a woman about her own age standing on the fly-bridge looking down at her. The woman was short with a sturdy build and a severe expression on her face. Ally had no idea if Torsten was married, had family, or even how long he had been on the island, but her guess was the woman was his daughter.

"Can I help you Mrs. Jones?" Torsten asked politely, wiping his hands on a rag.

He was shirtless, and his broad shoulders and barrel chest were surprisingly firm for a man of his age. Sweat beaded on his forehead and glistened on his tanned, leathery skin.

"Please, it's Ally, and I was wondering if we could have a chat for a few minutes?" she replied, some of her gusto escaping her now she stood before the man.

He lowered the engine bay cover before extending a hand to help her come aboard. She accepted the help and stepped from the dock to the gunwale where he took her by the waist and effortlessly lifted her gently down to the deck, much to her surprise and embarrassment.

"Oh my, well, thank you," she bumbled.

Without a word he stepped to the sliding door leading into the salon and pulled it aside, then waited for Ally to walk inside. As she moved across the cockpit she noticed a couple of dive tanks with horse-collar style life jackets attached, against the port gunwale before she went inside the salon. The room was cool and she heard the low drone of an air conditioner and the rush of air through the vent system. If the vessel wasn't gently rocking on the water she wouldn't know she was on a boat – it seemed like she had entered an expensive hotel room. The salon was elegantly appointed in fine varnished wood and soft carpet under foot. A comfortable sofa was positioned against the starboard side and a low cabinet opposite. A short step dropped down to the galley and a dining area, and beyond she could make out a berth through the partially open door. Torsten held a hand out towards the sofa, and she nervously sat. He stepped down through the galley and grabbed a towel from the head which was tucked away by the vee-berth. He wiped himself down as he opened the refrigerator door and pulled out a bottle of beer. He held it up towards Ally.

"Beer?"

"No thanks," she replied.

The more polite and accommodating he was, the more uncomfortable she became, and she wondered what the daughter was up to above them. Her father, presuming he was her father, she reminded herself, had just disappeared inside with a strange woman. Maybe that's something that happened often, but it felt rather awkward to Ally, and she cursed herself for not thinking this through a little more. She should have stayed on the dock and talked to him outside. Torsten opened his beer and took a long pull, then came back up the step and looked at Ally.

"So, what did you wish to talk about?"

Her bold idea of an amicable solution had not come with a 'how to start this conversation' plan, and she stumbled over her opening words with another blush of embarrassment.

"I was just thinking that, well perhaps there was a…"

"A way to come to an alternative agreement?" he said, helping her out.

"Exactly," she replied, relieved it seemed to have been on his mind as well. Maybe he wasn't the tyrant he came across as being after all.

"You're looking for a wee bit of extra time, I presume?" he continued in a helpful manner.

"That would be incredibly generous of you, Torsten, it would help us out immensely," she said, wondering why she had got herself all worked up. He was really quite a charming man, and despite being old enough to be her father, he wasn't bad to look at either.

"Okay, I think we can work that oot," he said and took a swig of the beer. "How long were you thinking, Ally?"

She thought about that a moment. For someone who prided herself on being organised and prepared she realised she had walked into this emotionally charged and logistically lacking. She thought about asking for two weeks, but that would put them close to the end of the month when rent would be due again. She doubted he would go for that and wasn't sure how they were going to swing October anyway. But first things first.

"Would a week be acceptable?"

Torsten nodded. "I dare say I can work with that."

He took a long pull and finished his beer, stepped back down to the galley and dropped the empty bottle into a rubbish bin beneath the sink cabinet. He turned and looked back at Ally who sat on the sofa wondering how this had been so easy.

"Let's go," he said.

"Excuse me?" she asked politely, confused and unsure where she was supposed to go.

"I've agreed, and I'll take my payment now if you don't mind," he said.

"Payment?" she said slowly, as the situation finally dawned on her. "Oh no! You've misunderstood me, Mr. McGinnis. I didn't intend to… do what you think I was willing to do. I was hoping you'd just be kind enough to give us more time."

"Why would I do that?" he said, frowning at her.

"Because… Because, we're good people and we've been good tenants, and we deserve a little kindness," she said, her voice breaking and tears welling in her eyes.

Torsten laughed. "Deserving, kindness, or any of that crap has nothing to do with it. This is business, lassie, you pay or you're oot. I already told you I have another tenant lined up. I figured I'd be nice and give ye the best shag of your life, but that's as nice as I get. You're a fair-looking lass and that useless husband of yours couldnae been keepin' you happy, so it's worth a week to me I reckon."

Ally jumped up and bolted for the door, scratching and clawing at the slider before noticing the catch and managing to open it. She scrambled across the cockpit to the sound of Torsten belly laughing behind her. She jumped from the gunwale to the dock and strutted away, tears streaming down her cheeks. She glanced back and saw the daughter watching her leave. The woman had a broad smile on her face.

17

GRAND CAYMAN – SUNDAY

Their Sunday morning dives went without incident. AJ had a group of six, who were all friends and newer divers, so she took them to the shallow reef for both dives. Back at the dock, they washed the boat down and refilled the tanks before sitting down to enjoy sandwiches they had made that morning for lunch. Under the fly-bridge of the Newton, AJ, Jackson and Thomas sat on the benches and idly chatted.

"I don't think the sand is deep enough in the cave to hide a body," AJ declared.

"You just don't want to think you was in der with der ghost of Jonesy," Thomas said, laughing.

"That's not it," AJ replied indignantly.

Jackson grinned at her. "I think that's partly it."

"Okay, maybe a little bit," she confessed and the two men laughed some more.

"Wait, but I still think the sand isn't deep enough," she said, pleading her case.

"Based on what?" Jackson asked. "Did you stick your hand through the sand to the rock?"

"No. But it just doesn't look that deep," AJ replied. "And did

you notice how the surface is smooth? You can see it in the video –
it's not in waves or shoved up against the sides. The surge and
movement in the water must be dissipated before reaching the
cave."

Jackson finished chewing a bite of his sandwich before speaking. "Did you see any life in there? Fish, lobsters, anything?"

AJ shook her head. "Nope. Nothing after I left the overhang.
The tunnel is smoother than most of the swim-throughs we find in
the reef, so there wasn't much in the way of nooks and crannies
that lobsters and crabs like. Plus there's no food in there."

"Not since dey gobbled up Mr. Jones, anyway," Thomas said,
trying to keep a straight face.

AJ looked around for something to throw at him, but all she had
at hand was her lunch or a spanner she had been using earlier. She
decided she was too hungry to waste her food, and the spanner
might damage the boat.

"He's not in there," she said, and Jackson and Thomas grinned
at each other like schoolboys.

There weren't many reasons to take your BCD and tank off
during a dive, she knew; it was tricky to do and not something
anyone did frequently. She considered the few times she had done
it herself, outside of training. The only circumstances she could
recall were to fix a problem she couldn't reach, or squeezing
through a tight space in a wreck or a cavern system.

"Maybe he had a problem with his gear," she said, continuing
her thought out loud. "Took off the rig, couldn't fix the issue and
tried to swim out."

Jackson nodded. "That's a plausible theory. It would explain the
tank neatly parked by the wall, and no body."

"Assuming der's no body," Thomas said with a beaming smile.
"But say dat so, what kinda problem gonna make him take off dat
tank and try to fix it? If he ain't getting air, he gonna start swimming I reckon."

"Good point," AJ replied. "Maybe we'll find something more
when we search the sand. Although it would be really odd if we

don't find evidence of a BCD. That would mean the only thing in there was the tank and first stage."

"Maybe it's a back-up tank," Thomas suggested. "Or da primary tank and he switched to da back-up. That explain why there'd be no BCD in der."

Jackson pointed at Thomas. "Now that's a good theory."

AJ agreed. "That is. Nice work, Detective Bodden. If we don't find evidence of a BCD, you might be right."

"Which means our man Jonesy may have swam out of that cavern in perfect health," Jackson added, "and made himself disappear."

AJ jumped to her feet and hurriedly swallowed her last bite of sandwich. "Whittaker said he was looking for something from the sixteenth century, remember? Maybe he found it!"

"And took off with der treasure," Thomas finished for her.

"Barely worth diving again, I'd say," Jackson said with a grin. "Looks like you sleuths have it all figured out. Case closed."

They laughed and gathered up their lunch tins, putting them in their rucksacks to take home later.

"You just don't want me diving the cave anymore," AJ said, smiling at Jackson, "in case I do anything crazy."

Jackson's shoulders sank and he looked over at her. "I worded that poorly – you know I trust you."

AJ wanted to believe he trusted her decision making, but she couldn't shake the fact that he had mentioned something. It had weighed on her mind since yesterday. Normally, it wouldn't bother her, and she would have taken it in the humorous light he had said it, but his comment stacked on her own concern.

"I suppose, but something made you say it," she said, her uneasiness about the subject coming out as frustration.

Thomas looked uncomfortable and Jackson calmly took a few breaths before responding.

"What I said came from my natural instinct to worry about someone I love," he said softly. "I certainly should have expressed that differently, and I'm sorry for my choice of words. I'm not sorry for caring what happens to you."

She smiled at her boyfriend, and felt like hell. Now she had made him feel guilty, and it wasn't about him, it was her issue.

"You didn't do anything wrong, it's me," she admitted. "Seems like crazy shit keeps happening and I do end up doing something reckless."

Jackson went to reply but Thomas surprised them both by beating him to it. "It's none of my business, Boss, and I probably shouldn't say nuttin', but best I know, reckless mean doing something without thinking or caring about the consequences. I don't think dat's what you do. I think you've had to make some tough decisions, and not had no time to consider all der consequences. That's just da way of things sometimes. You had to pick a direction and do it right den. I don't see dat as reckless. You care about what happens to you, but you care more about what happen to da udder people. Dat brave, not reckless."

AJ sat with her mouth slightly opened, stunned.

"Dude, that's perfect," Jackson said quietly.

AJ walked over and hugged her friend. "Thank you," she whispered in his ear, trying to keep from crying.

She released him and sat back down on the bench. "You're too kind. I don't feel in the least bit brave, but truthfully I don't feel reckless either. I do care about what happens to me, and quite honestly I think I'm a bit of a chicken sometimes. I'm glad Reg will be with me when we dive the cave again, I don't want to go in there alone."

Jackson laughed. "That doesn't make you a chicken, it makes you sensible and cautious. Which reinforces Thomas's comments."

AJ had never been comfortable receiving compliments and felt awkward now her concern had turned into a shower of praise. She tried to sense how their words fit with how she felt inside and struggled to align them.

"I feel like I've been lucky," she said tentatively, trying to find the right words. "There's been a few occasions when I did make poor decisions that I think were reckless. But I hope I've learnt something each time and I'm getting better at choosing what I should do."

"When do you think you were reckless?" Jackson asked.

"Diving the submarine on my own would be a stand-out example," she replied quickly.

Thomas laughed. "I must agree with dat, I was mad about it too."

AJ had taken her boat out alone, tied it to a submerged buoy they had set up, and dived in search of the wreck on her own when Thomas and Reg weren't available to go with her. She discovered the wreck and beat a ruthless treasure hunter to the find, which ultimately saved the war wreck from being destroyed for its cargo, but she almost lost her life.

"Okay, so that was years ago now," Jackson said. "What lately?"

AJ shrugged her shoulders. "I don't know. Reg would say anything I've done with Jonty Gladstone would be considered reckless."

"Dat man be reckless – Mr. Gladstone I mean – Big Boss be right about dat," Thomas said, "but don't mean you reckless to help da man."

"I suppose," AJ admitted.

"Don't mention that bloody name on my dock," Reg's voice bellowed from nearby.

He peered at the group from the jetty. "And who's reckless?"

They all laughed. "None of your beeswax," AJ ribbed him, "ear-wigging over there."

"Well I was up there working away," he retorted, "and I thought to myself, hey, there were three other people gonna help me with this, but they don't seem to be here."

"My fault, Mr. Big Boss," Thomas said, throwing his hands in the air. "I got carried away with theories all about Mr. Jones and his mysterious whereabouts."

"Well, if you're done with your three martini lunch and bullshit session," Reg growled with a big grin behind his beard, "there's work being done up here."

Reg turned and walked back up the jetty and Thomas hurried after him. Jackson turned to AJ and took her in his arms.

"I love my brave girl," he said and kissed her forehead, her head fitting neatly under his chin.

"I love you too, and I'm sorry I get all bothered about things sometimes," she said into his chest.

He gently lifted her face with his hands until she looked into his eyes. "That's part of what makes you so wonderful."

She shook her head and smiled. "You're a barmy yank."

18

GRAND CAYMAN – SUNDAY

Reg had parts and tools strewn about the concrete deck next to his little storage hut by the dock. AJ always reckoned the hut, which was eight feet square, was akin to Doctor Who's TARDIS. She was constantly amazed by the amount of gear that appeared from the tiny space yet still had room for a small desk and a stool where Reg or Pearl checked divers in and out. Coop excitedly greeted everyone and assisted where he deemed appropriate. Mainly by standing on whatever they were trying to work with and wagging his tail.

Reg held up the one 18-inch metal sifting pan he had. "I forgot this old thing is a bit worse for wear, so we need to fix it up."

The perforated base had separated from the stainless-steel band, around part of the circle, which would allow the sand to slide through the break, instead of filtering through the tiny holes. Sifting sand underwater was no easy task, as the finer particles wafted in a cloud before slowly settling back down all around. The cave would quickly become a white out with zero visibility, but the heavier debris, and hopefully any artefacts, would remain in the pan. They may not be able to see what they had at the time, but they could collect them to examine later. Professional treasure hunters used powerful vacuums to suck all the sand to a barge at the surface and sort through the findings there. They didn't have such equipment at their disposal but the depth and narrow access would make a vacuum system trickier to use anyway.

"Did Rasha give you the plan on how we need to work in the cave?" AJ asked.

"Yeah," Reg replied, putting the pan aside. "She came by this morning and we talked for a while. She's coming out with us too. She said she'll probably stay on the boat most of the time, and sort through what we bring up."

Reg picked up an old roll of reel line. "First, we have to mark out the floor into segments using the line. Then we assign a letter and number system to the segments. You know, A1, A2, et cetera."

AJ held up her hand as though she was in class. "How big should each segment be?" she asked.

"Rasha said no larger than three foot square, and two foot is about ideal," Reg replied.

"What do we tie the line around," she asked. "Do we put stakes in the sand?"

"If the sand is deep and dense enough, we can use stakes," Reg said, picking up a wood stake from a pile he had next to him.

"We decided the sand is deep enough for a body," Thomas said, and this time AJ grabbed one of Reg's stakes and flung it at the young Caymanian.

"Hey now!" he yelped, laughing and dodging the projectile.

"Settle down, children," Reg barked. "This isn't Sunday bloody school."

"Well," Jackson said, "it sort of is."

Once the laughter died down, Reg held up a three-pound dive weight, and Thomas looked worried.

"This is a trick Rasha told me about, so we're going to rig these up," Reg explained, putting a stake through one of the slots in the dive weight. "We'll use zip ties to hold the stake to the weight and then you push the stake into the sand but the weight sits on top. Have half the stake above, and half below the weight, then we wrap the line around the bit sticking up. She says it keeps them in place in fine sand."

AJ picked up a bag of zip ties she spotted amongst the gear. "Want me to start on them?" she asked.

"Nah," Reg said. "Them two can put the stakes together, you can come help me weld up this pan. I have a welder at the house."

"How many, Big Boss?" Thomas asked.

"What d'yer reckon that cave is? Six by ten?" Reg asked, looking at AJ.

"About that, I'd guess," she replied. "There's no sand under the entry tunnel as the floor slopes up slightly, so the cave is more like twelve or fourteen feet long, but the sand is six by eight or ten. It's also wider out by the wall than under the tunnel."

"Figure out how many we need for a grid six by ten in two-foot sections. That should give us more than we'll need," Reg told them. "The outsides won't use stakes as the sand will be thin, we'll just use weights." He pointed to a folded bag with a clip and a pull string lying near Jackson. "That's a lift bag; we'll use it to float all the weights and staked weights to get them down there. So figure out how many we'll need of everything, and we'll put them in that heavy duty mesh bag and tie it to the lift bag," he continued, pointing to a black bag. "And put it all on the boat. We'll bring the tank up using the same method."

"Sounds good," Jackson said and he and Thomas began gathering what they needed and looked for a shady spot to work.

"Right," Reg said, picking up the broken pan. "We'll be back in an hour or so."

AJ followed Reg over to his Land Rover with Coop trotting along at their heels.

"Will we have time to get tanks filled in the morning, Reg?" AJ asked as they climbed into the vehicle.

"Yeah. I told Rasha we'd push off at nine," he replied. "That gives us time to get them filled first thing."

Reg fired up the old Land Rover and pulled up to the road.

"You want to keep diving on nitrox or switch to trimix at that depth?" she asked.

Reg turned right out of the car park, drove to the junction with West Bay Road, then turned left towards his house.

"I've been thinking about that," he replied, taking his time. "Ideally we'd dive trimix so we could work for longer in there, but there's not much room with two of us in the cave. If we kept the three tanks each we'd need with us, it'll be cumbersome and hard to work. We could stage the nitrox and oxygen tanks outside the cave, but that always makes me nervous."

Reg made a left on Hell Road and continued talking. "The other problem will be our safety diver. I planned to place someone under the overhang, but they wouldn't be able to stay down as long as us, so we'd be rotating them out, which isn't ideal."

AJ kept a hand out of the open window directing the air towards her face as the old Land Rover bounced along the road. "So, should we stick to nitrox then? Get them filled to 28%?"

Reg nodded as he made a right turn onto his street, a narrow lane lined with small trees, shrubs and the occasional home. "That's what I reckon, at least to start tomorrow. Should give us twenty minutes in the cave each time with an hour break between dives."

Reg reached his bungalow on the right and parked in front of the garage, hitting the remote opener so the door began rising. They hopped out and Coop rushed over to his favourite tree in the front garden to lift his leg and reclaim his home. Reg's garage was another marvel of fitting a warehouse worth of stuff in a residential double garage. Somehow he still had room for Pearl's Jeep. Reg reversed the Jeep out, clearing their way to reach the workbench at the back. He put the pan down on the bench and turned on a small MIG welder sitting on a rolling cart parked next to the bench. From the bottom drawer of a cabinet under the bench he pulled out an angle grinder and two pairs of clear safety glasses. He handed AJ a pair.

"Hold the pan still for me and watch your eyes," he instructed and plugged the grinder into the outlet.

Sparks flew across the garage as he cleaned the area he planned to weld, and AJ flinched as streams of red-hot flecks of metal hit her bare arms. Reg turned off the grinder, set it down on the bench and inspected his handiwork. The door from the house opened and Pearl walked into the garage. Without a word, she put two opened bottles of Strongbow cider on the bench, lifted up on her tippy toes and kissed Reg, then went back in the house. They picked up the drinks and clinked the bottles together.

"I'd keep her around if I were you," AJ said with a grin, before taking a swig of the cold drink.

"Better than I deserve," Reg replied.

AJ laughed. "That's the truth."

Reg laughed with her. "Make yourself useful for once, put those gloves on and hold the base steady so I can tack it back down."

He adjusted a few settings on the welder, clipped the ground to a vice bolted to the metal bench, and donned a welding helmet.

"I don't have another welding helmet so make sure you don't look at the light," he told her. "But hold it still."

AJ looked away as the corner of the garage lit up from the bright white light of the welder, and the tip sparked and buzzed as the welder fed wire into the molten joint it formed. Reg had AJ rotate the pan around until he had reattached the perforated base to his satisfaction. He shut the welder down, put his tools away and leaned against the bench while they finished their drinks.

"I know this looks like a straightforward job inside that cave," he said after a few minutes. "But we need to be careful."

AJ looked at her mentor and wondered if he had heard more of their conversation on the boat than she had thought. Her first reaction was to feel defensive.

"How do you mean? We're always careful, right?"

Reg nodded. "Sure. I'm just saying it won't be a no-brainer. Once we start sifting sand the cave is going to white out and we won't be able to see a thing."

AJ settled down and realised Reg was just being his over-protective self. Reg had done plenty of dangerous dives in his day, but he was sensibly cautious these days and especially so when he dived with AJ. Was that because he thought she wasn't? She cursed herself for worrying about it again, and tried to focus on their dive plan.

"We should set our computers' alarms to sound in case we can't see them," she said.

They both had the audible alarms turned off on their dive computers as nothing was more annoying than electronic beeps sounding underwater. The sound travelled farther and in a group it was hard to tell whose computer was beeping. They were trained to constantly monitor their computers so in normal conditions the alarms were redundant.

"Good thinking," Reg agreed. "Just set an alarm for 800psi and five minutes no-deco time left. That way, if you hear an alarm, it's time to ascend. Won't matter who's alarm it is, we'll both hear it, and we'll both need to go up."

AJ finished her drink and dropped the bottle into a blue recycle bin by the door to the house. "I'm glad you'll be in there with me," she said, taking Reg's empty bottle from him and throwing it in the same bin. "It's a bit creepy in that cave alone."

"We need to stay together in a buddy team the whole time," he reiterated. "We won't have back-up tanks in there, so we enter together and leave together."

"How about staging a spare tank under the overhang?" she suggested. "Just for emergencies. Are we having one or two safety divers out there? Could be a back-up for them too."

Reg thought a moment as he carefully checked to see if the metal had cooled down enough to carry the pan.

"Guess we should use two, so they're in a buddy team as well," he replied. "Thomas and Jackson can handle it. We'll put them on 32% nitrox; they won't need to use 28% at their depth. They could have a spare tank with them as well – it can stay down there the whole time."

AJ thought through the numbers for a moment. Nitrox was a gas mix with a higher ratio of oxygen versus nitrogen compared to the 21% in the air we all breathe. Nitrogen delivered in its compressed state, equalised against the surrounding water pressure which increases with depth, needed to be dissipated through the body's tissues. There was only so much that the body could process until it became saturated. When that happened, the diver had to stay under water at a shallower depth to allow their body to 'off-gas' the nitrogen before surfacing. Their computer calculated their time until that point of saturation, known as 'no-deco' time, taking into account the dive profile, gas consumed and duration. On the flip side, the additional oxygen received by the body could cause problems the deeper the diver went, so each nitrox mix had a maximum safe depth according to the percentage of oxygen, known as MOD (Maximum Operating Depth). At 32%, the maximum standard MOD was 111 feet, with a contingency – meaning an absolute maximum never to be exceeded – of 132 feet. The safety divers would be within the standard MOD under the overhang, and if they had to descend into the cave for any reason, they would still stay within the absolute maximum. It was a lot of numbers to remember and there were charts to consult if needed, but after years of working with the mixed gases, AJ and Reg were all too familiar with them.

"Perfect," she said. "And we could actually use 29% nitrox – that'll give us an MOD of 126 feet. I saw max 124 feet inside there and we can't go any deeper without drilling rock."

They walked back to the Land Rover and Coop came running around to join them from the side of the house.

"Alright," Reg agreed, and then he paused before opening the driver's door. "Just remember, we stay together regardless of what happens."

"Of course," AJ replied, and wondered why Reg felt the need to reiterate that.

19

GRAND CAYMAN – SEPTEMBER, 1986

Jonesy groaned and rolled over in bed, but whatever was jolting him didn't stop. His head throbbed and he guessed opening his eyes would not make it feel any better. He was right, but now at least he could see in the dimly lit room that his wife was the cause of the motion.

"Wake up, Charlie," she was saying, in a less than encouraging tone. "Come on, we need to go."

"Alright, alright," he mumbled and rubbed the sleep from his eyes. "What time is it?"

"It's six-thirty," she replied, standing over him with her hands on her hips.

"Blimey," he said, sitting up. "It's dinnertime already?"

"Bloody hell, Charlie," she replied and stomped towards the door.

"I'm not saying you gotta fix me nothing," he said, confused.

She paused at the doorway. "It's six-thirty in the bloody morning."

"Oh," he replied, but it was drowned out by the door being slammed.

He got up, splashed some water around his face and found a

pair of shorts and a shirt that appeared clean enough. He tentatively made his way out of the bedroom in search of coffee, bracing himself for the next round of Ally's wrath. She was shoving a few bags of crisps and biscuits into a bag, which seemed to be taking the brunt of her anger. He guessed the biscuits would be crumbs by the time she was finished.

"I'm sorry, love," he started, unsure how long his list of offences for the prior eighteen hours might be. He certainly had no clear recollection of anything after leaving the bar. "I know I screwed up, but I'll make it right today, I promise."

Ally paused the punishment she was doling out to the snacks and looked up at him. That expression was back again, the one he didn't care for one bit.

"Oh yeah? And how are you going to do that?"

"We're gonna find that chest," he replied with less conviction than he hoped he would muster.

Ally drew in a long breath and appeared to be holding back tears. He noticed her eyes looked red and a little puffy as though she may have been crying already.

"Your stupid idea has no chance of working," she barked, but her voice began to break, "and it's the only chance we have left. We have no choice but to try until he kicks us out."

Jonesy took a step towards his wife, his arms outstretched to take her in an embrace, but she turned quickly away. "Just get yourself ready. I'm going down to the boat."

He stopped and hung his head as she made for the stairs. He felt like a fool. More than a fool, he felt like a failure. He had let her down and then compounded the problem by getting drunk and losing a precious half day they could have spent on their last option. He poured himself a coffee then headed down the stairs after her. In the gear room he noticed the petrol can and picked it up, pleased to find it was full. He looked around for anything else he should take. Two spearguns leaned against the wall by their fishing rods, but he knew they wouldn't have time for either. At the boat, he noticed there were four dive tanks already aboard and recalled he had prepared the boat to go back out. It was the petrol run that had started his slippery slope, not helped by Sandy's cleavage, or her fine drink-pouring skills. A stab of guilt stopped him looking over at Ally. His conscience was well aware that petrol runs, buxom bartenders and strong liquor had never hurt a man who didn't allow them. His hangover combined with his shame left a pit in his stomach and a bad taste in his mouth.

He stepped aboard and opened the petrol cap, pouring the meagre two gallons in the tank. The potent smell of the petrol did nothing to help his less than stellar condition. He hoped they could quickly line themselves up at the dive site with Ally's markers, and not burn too much petrol. The twin engines would devour the two gallons in a hurry.

"Okay," he said, "I think we're ready."

Without a word, she cast the lines from the dock while he fired up the motors, and they eased away into the calm blue sea that sparkled in the light from the early morning sun. Being out on the water eased Jonesy's disposition and his focus returned to finding the artefacts. Their financial woes and marital issues would be a thing of the past when he surfaced with Sir Francis Drake's missing chest. Or what was left of it after 400 years on the sea floor. He piloted the Bertram to the general area they had dived yesterday and Ally directed him until she was sure they were close to where they had moored. Jonesy dropped the anchor and made sure it held fast as the boat slowly drifted south in the soft swells until the line went tight. Ally was already geared up when he stepped back to the deck so he hurriedly donned his own BCD. He wrapped the fabric weight belt around his waist and secured the metal clasp, then sat on the gunwale and pulled on his fins.

"Shall we start where we finished yesterday, and then do the deeper south portion?" Jonesy asked, glancing over at his wife seated on the opposite gunwale.

Ally looked back at him. "Do you know where you finished yesterday?"

He smiled; finally he had done something right. "I do. I left a marker."

She didn't respond, and back-rolled off the side of the boat. He followed her in, disappointed she didn't acknowledge his fore-thought, and quickly realised finding his coral stack wouldn't be as simple as he had hoped. Even with Ally's shoreline references, they would be lucky to be within a few hundred yards of yesterday's location, and all the inlets and fingers where the sand met the outer reef looked exactly the same. He checked the first ravine and saw nothing in the sand, so he kicked north, choosing one of the two options he had. It was all a guess. There, in the second inlet between two fingers was his stack of rocks. A surge of confidence raced through him, and just like that, he was sure it was going to be a good day. Fate, gods, karma; he didn't know or care what was aligning or guiding him, but the universe didn't want to waste his time today, and he was thankful.

He pointed the rocks out to Ally and signalled they would have three inlets to cover before moving over to the deeper side. That would put them where they had started yesterday. She finned over the reef to her position, and began searching amongst the fans and coral heads. She looked so graceful and elegant in the water, he thought. She moved as though she belonged there, not a creature from above the waves who could only visit through artificial means of breathing. Her slender body flowed and glided smoothly in fluid motion, her arms and legs extensions of her shapely torso, not flap-ping appendages like most divers. She was all he had known as a companion in his life, her days intertwined with his for as long as he could remember. He told her he loved her most days, but until now, faced with the possibility of losing her, he had never realised how deeply his happiness was bound to her presence. He couldn't imagine a world without her.

It took Jonesy ten minutes to search the three valleys between the fingers before they moved across the reef to the deeper side by the wall. Here, occasional ravines ran like giant cracks from the top of the reef cleaving a cut through the corner of the drop-off. Some were steep and angled, funnelling any debris like a chute that would deposit them over the edge. Others sloped more gently like a ditch running to the deeper ocean and captured stray objects and broken pieces of reef more easily. It was in these ravines that they both spent more time, figuring the gullies were more likely to have held something in their grasp for centuries. Heading south again, they took a while searching the first ravine, finding nothing but modern rubbish, before moving across the coral to the next indentation. They both looked around for a way into the cut, but the reef had grown over itself to fill in what had once been a small valley. At the outer wall it had grown over completely and he saw Ally shrug her shoulders and move on. Jonesy did the same.

They stayed out by the wall in deeper water for the rest of the dive, knowing covering the same distance by the sand with all the fingers and inlets would take longer. Jonesy found a few loose pieces of coral head to make another stack, this time on top of the reef at the farthest point they had reached to the south. They finned back at a shallower depth and returned to the boat for a break, and two fresh tanks.

"We need a magnetometer," Jonesy said, pulling a packet of crisps from the bag Ally had brought along.

"And where would we find one of them lying around?" she replied.

He ignored her cynical tone. "I'm just saying, we could be swimming right over the artefacts, and we don't know it. Four hundred years of coral growth and storms will have changed the reef an awful lot; a magnetometer would find anything metal down there. It's what the professional treasure hunters use."

"Know any?" she asked.

"Know any what?" he replied, crunching on the crisps.

"Professional treasure hunters with magnet-what-evers," she elaborated.

"Well, no," he mumbled.

"Anyone on the island even have one of these things?" she continued.

She seemed to be missing his point, but he guessed he couldn't win regardless. "Doubt it, they cost a bob or two."

"Don't suppose that will help us before tomorrow night then, you know, when we become homeless," she said, shaking her head.

"I'm just saying, maybe we could team up with a treasure group and split the money from whatever we find," he explained, while a nagging voice in his head told him to put the spade down again. "I understand that can't happen by tomorrow, but we could work on it after that." He thought a moment, then added, "If we don't find anything today, that is."

She scoffed and ate a few broken pieces of biscuit from the bag while Jonesy switched their gear to the fresh tanks and kept quiet. They had narrowed down this stretch of reef as the most likely spot to find anything, and they were about to explore the last section. Deep down he had a strong feeling that Drake's artefacts were close by somewhere, he just had to figure out where. Maybe, he admitted to himself, it was wishful thinking, but all the evidence he had pieced together pointed to the rowboat going down nearby. A thousand scenarios could have played out over the years in between; a likely one was them going over the drop-off to waters only accessible with a submersible, but if they were still on the reef, he was determined to find them.

By the time they descended to resume their search, Jonesy had renewed his zeal, and was sure this was the dive that would change their lives. He led them south at 40 feet below the surface until he spotted the rock pile he'd made on the reef below them. From there he turned east to the inner edge of the deep reef, and dropped to the sand. In and out of each inlet between the fingers, he rummaged through the debris and examined every unnatural shape he saw. Several fishing weights, an empty oil can and a length of coral-encrusted chain were the extent of his discoveries, none of them dating back more than a decade. By the time their boat was above them, Jonesy's enthusiasm and optimism were in his wake once more, and he and Ally ascended.

He took off his BCD in the water and hauled it aboard once he was on the boat, then did the same with Ally's rig. She popped out of the water onto the swim step, then over the transom to the deck where she grabbed two towels, handing one to her husband. She vigorously rubbed her hair and looked off towards the shoreline.

"I'm sorry," Jonesy said quietly. "I really thought we were in the right place."

She turned and looked at him with something other than contempt for the first time in days. Her face had softened and her eyes appeared sympathetic. "We might be," she replied. "It's a needle in a haystack. It's not like we're looking for a shipwreck, with cannons and ballast that are large enough to spot. We're searching for a handful of smaller items that might have survived the sea water."

He nodded. "A sixteenth-century rowboat was likely all wood. It rotted away years ago, same as the chest itself."

"What exactly was in the chest?" she asked.

"All we know from Drake's log was he lost his favourite compass and astrolabe," Jonesy replied. "Plus some number of gold coins he mentioned."

"What on earth is an astrolabe?" Ally asked, wrapping the towel around her waist.

"It's an old celestial navigational instrument, predating the sextant," he explained. "Would likely have been six or eight inches in diameter and looked like a disk with a ring that rotated. They used it to tell latitude."

Ally sighed. "Like I was saying, needle in a haystack."

Jonesy knew it was the truth, but a glint of light flickered at the end of his dark tunnel. She was speaking to him in a civil manner.

"Let's head back in and I'll refill the tanks," he said, moving to the helm. "We can make a plan over lunch."

He took her silence as progress over the sharp comebacks and started the motors. He slipped the boat in gear and idled forward, taking the strain off the anchor line, before putting it back in neutral. He started to walk around the edge of the covered helm when he noticed her staring towards the shore again. He looked in the same direction and spotted a large sport fishing boat halfway between them and the beach.

"Is that McGinnis's boat?" he asked.

"Yes, it is," she replied, not taking her eyes from the Viking Sport.

20

GRAND CAYMAN – MONDAY

Monday morning arrived chasing overnight showers away from the island, with blue skies accompanying the sunrise. AJ and Jackson took her van into George Town, where they filled the nitrox tanks with the various mixes they needed. Rasha was at the dock earlier than planned, so by 9am, Hazel's Odyssey was on its way to the dive site. They had been cleared by the Department of Environment to anchor in the sand instead of using the mooring buoy, saving them precious time to and from the cavern. AJ made her best estimate on where the site lay, relative to the buoy on Neptune's Wall, and Thomas released the anchor off the bow when they were sure they were safely over the sand and clear of the reef itself. She made a mark on her GPS to bring them back to the same spot, which she would erase and reset if they needed to get closer.

They took their time gearing up and Reg and AJ made a point of setting the alarms on their dive computers and adjusting them to read the 29% nitrox gas they would be breathing. Rasha was a certified diver and had brought her gear along, but AJ noticed she had left it under the bench.

"Are you sure you don't want to dive with us, Rasha?" she asked. "At least on the first one to make sure we set it up correctly."

Rasha smiled. "I trust you two, I'm sure you'll do it perfectly," she replied. "And to be honest I'm not a big fan of tight spaces, so I'm in no hurry to go down a tunnel into a cave."

"That's okay," AJ said, standing up, ready to go. "I don't fancy being around dead bodies, so you do that, and I'll dive the cave."

Thomas waddled past them in his fins to the swim step, with his heavy tank strapped to his BCD. "Might be doing both der Boss, who knows what's in da sand."

AJ pushed him off the swim step into the water.

They had positioned the boat perfectly. From where the stern swung around to the south, the ravine with the overhang was almost directly west. It still took them several minutes to manoeuvre the bag of weights and stakes, hung from the lift bag, adding air to the bag when they went deeper as the water pressure increased. Reg and AJ guided the bag while Jackson hauled the spare nitrox tank along. Once they arrived at the tight entrance under the overhang, they released the air from the lift bag and lowered the weights to the floor. AJ went through the snug opening first and between her and Reg they dragged, shoved and manhandled the weight bag towards the far end. Once they were both farther inside and the space opened up, they reinflated the lift bag and AJ led the way into the tunnel, pulling the lift bag behind her. The bag of weights dragged across the floor of the tunnel while the lift bag rubbed along the ceiling, but with care and gentle persuasion they reached the vertical drop where the rig slowly descended to the cave.

They both wore underwater headlamps, which eerily bounced beams of light around the cave with every movement they made. As AJ turned the corner at the base of the vertical tunnel, a mass of movement startled her as a school of yellowtail snapper swirled and funnelled out of the crack to the wall. She let her heart settle back down before pulling the lift bag in with her and making sure it didn't drag on the sand. She looked around the floor and a chill ran through her as she wondered if Mr. Jones was indeed hidden beneath the sand, waiting to be found. A shove on the lift bag from behind got her moving again and she finned forward to the end of the cave and released some air from the lift bag, lowering the mesh bag of weights to the floor.

Leaving a little air in the lift bag, they unclipped it from its payload and let it float out of the way, like a party balloon against the ceiling. They made quick work of opening the mesh bag and pulling all the weights and weighted stakes out, setting them gently on the sand. Reg took a tape measure from his BCD pocket and handed one end to AJ, who held it against the side wall as he did the same on his side. He wrote the distance down on a slate hanging from his BCD. They measured the width at the entry end, then the length of the cave, and finally the length actually covered in sand. Reg then began setting weights around the edge of the cave in two-foot intervals and AJ followed suit on her side. They then used the weighted stakes to complete the inner corners of their grid across the sand. Reg handed AJ the reel line then pointed to himself and the tank sitting at the end of the cave. She returned an okay sign, and watched him take the empty heavy duty mesh bag over to the tank and begin dusting off the old tank, readying it to be carried away.

She really wanted to watch Reg's careful process of extracting the tank, especially as she had been concerned it would crumble, but she had her job to do and time was limited. She wrapped the end of the line several times around one of the weights near the tunnel end of the cavern, then ran out the reel towards the outer wall, wrapping it around each stake on the way. At the wall, she stayed out of Reg's way as best she could, while doubling back to the first stake. From there she took the line to the side where it was wrapped multiple times around the weight before doubling back to the opposite side. By continuing to double back and make perpendicular runs, she was able to complete their grid forming twelve squares across the sand-covered floor without the need to cut the reel line, which she set down by the last weight.

AJ looked over at Reg, who appeared to have the tank already laid inside the mesh bag. He pointed to the lift bag over her head, and she pulled it over to him. He clipped it to the handles of the bag, then used his spare regulator purge to blast more air into the lift bag until it lifted the assembly lightly off the floor. He pointed to the exit and she returned an okay sign. She checked her dive computer which showed she had 1200psi left and plenty of bottom time available. She gladly turned and brought the lift bag along behind her. It had been a productive and efficient first dive of the day, on which they had completed the tasks they had planned. Leaving with plenty of margin in their tanks gave her a feeling of satisfaction, and confidence for the day ahead.

Back at the boat, they excitedly lifted the mesh bag from the water to the swim step. To AJ's relief the tank was perfectly intact and its trip out of the cavern had already shaken loose decades of sediment and superficial corrosion, revealing solid metal beneath. The tank itself had surface rust all over, but the valve and first stage looked remarkably clean. Once they were all back aboard and their gear in the racks, Reg carried the bag to the front and spread a towel on the deck under the shade of the fly-bridge. Rasha snapped some pictures of the tank in the bag, and then some more once Reg unzipped the bag, pulled the heavy tank out and laid it on the towel. Rasha placed a plastic toolbox on the deck and donned a pair of pale blue nitrile gloves. She opened a drawer and removed a small, clear evidence bag and a plastic scraper. Holding the bag under the first stage, she carefully brushed the scraper over the metal and caught the wet gunk and debris as it easily slid away from the shiny metal below. After several minutes of delicate cleaning by Rasha, AJ leaned closer and read the raised lettering on the wingnut-style tightening knob of the first stage.

"Blimey, that says ScubaPro. But I've never seen that kind of knob before."

Reg laughed. "That's 'cos you're just a baby. That's a Mark 10 first stage; it was the best available in the 80s and 90s until

ScubaPro superseded it with the Mark 25, which is still used today."

"Do you recall when it was first introduced, Reg?" Rasha asked.

He scratched his beard and thought a moment. "It was eighty-something, but I'd be…"

"1984," Jackson said, holding up his mobile. "Says here that the wingnut was replaced with a plastic knob from 1988 on."

Reg grinned. "That's bloody cheating."

Well, we know the earliest this gear could be in the cave is 1984," Rasha pointed out.

She carefully picked up the line from the first stage and placed another evidence bag under the end. Using the same method, she scraped away the build-up and debris to reveal the smooth glass face of a pressure gauge. The gauge read 300psi.

"Wow," Thomas exclaimed. "There's still air in dat tank?"

Rasha looked at Reg. "Maybe, I guess."

"Unless the needle stuck there," Reg replied.

AJ had an urge to reach over and tap the glass to see if the dial moved but resisted and kept her hands still. She figured with her luck the gauge would heave its final breath and blow the last 300psi all over the place, ruining their evidence.

"But let's think about this," Reg continued. "The regulator line has rotted away," he said, pointing to the metal fitting screwed into the first stage with nothing but a grubby nub left where the hose should have continued, "so air would have leaked out once the line began to corrode away and burst. That would take the tank down to 300psi, if the J-valve was set. So yes, I'd say it's possible there's still air in the tank."

They all stared at the tank in wonderment for a few moments before AJ spoke up.

"The regulator must be in the sand."

Reg nodded. "I reckon so. Be right next to where we found the tank, I imagine. Probably lay in the sand until the line rotted."

"So, if this is Jonesy's tank," Jackson said, "he didn't run out of air."

"Unless the J-valve didn't work," AJ said. "Right? If the lever stuck and the valve wouldn't open. That might explain him taking off the rig in the cave. He runs out of air and pulls the lever," she continued, pointing to the tank valve, "but it doesn't open, so he slips out of his BCD and tries to get it to budge. It won't, and he swims for it, leaving his gear behind."

Reg grinned. "Check out Miss Marple over here with her theories again."

Everyone looked at him blankly.

"Bugger me, none of you children know who Miss Marple is?" Reg exclaimed. "Agatha bloody Christie?"

"I know her," AJ said quickly. "And I think I've heard of Mrs. Marple, wasn't she on Netflix?"

Reg shook his head. "Doesn't matter. Anyway, your theory is bollocks because the J-valves didn't stick closed. If they had a problem, which they occasionally did, they leaked during the dive so when you pulled the lever, there was no reserve left. You'd already used it all."

AJ shrugged her shoulders. "So why did our man Jones take his kit off in the cave? We think he had air left…"

"I'll verify that back at the lab," Rasha said. "That's an assumption until we confirm whether the gauge is still working or not."

"Won't be too easy either," Reg added, gently tapping the metal knob on the tank valve stage. "Can't imagine the on-off valve will still turn; that thing has to be corroded and locked up. How else can you add a new gauge to the system without letting the air out?"

"Replace the first stage on the valve," AJ blurted out before the policewoman could reply.

"Exactly," Rasha agreed. "Even if I have to cut the yoke to remove the first stage. If the J-valve is still off, sealing the tank, I should be able to replace the first stage and connect a new one with a pressure gauge, then open the J-valve."

"Ha!" AJ said, giving Reg a shove. "See."

Reg chuckled. "And you both think after thirty-four years the J-valve will still open?"

"Oh. Right." AJ stopped smiling. "Maybe not."

"Surely it doesn't matter," Thomas said. "Like Jackson says, if dis is Mr. Jones's tank, he didn't run outta air. Don't much matter how much da man had left. Whatever it was, he didn't get to use none of it."

21

GRAND CAYMAN – MONDAY

Detective Roy Whittaker pulled up and parked in the driveway of a lavish house on South Sound Road, opposite the Cayman Island Rugby Club field. The home was a two-storey stucco overlooking the reef-protected sound, with beautifully stained double, wooden garage doors and wide tapering steps leading to a matching wood front door with etched glass sidelights. Walking up the steps, Whittaker was admiring the professional landscaping when he heard the door open. Before him stood an elegant woman in her late sixties with wavy, long grey hair, wearing a tan silk blouse and white trousers that discreetly complemented her slender frame.

"Mrs. Simmons?" Whittaker asked, extending a hand in greeting. "I'm Detective Whittaker."

The woman firmly shook his hand. "I am, but please call me Ally," she replied, and stepped aside. "It was quite a surprise to get your call this morning."

Whittaker walked into the foyer, which led into a large living room with floor-to-ceiling windows showcasing an unobstructed view of the ocean.

"Thank you for seeing me," he said, "and I'm sorry to bring up difficult memories from the past. I'll try and be as brief as possible."

Ally closed the door and led him down two broad steps into the living room which was open on either side to a well-appointed kitchen to the left, and a formal dining area to the right. She offered him a seat at a high-top wooden table by the window and he noticed a pitcher of water and two glasses already set out.

"Please have a seat and help yourself to a drink," she said politely. "And it's no bother. It was many years ago. Water under the bridge so to speak, but you mentioned on the phone you had some potential new evidence? Naturally I'm curious what that might be after all this time."

Whittaker sat and held up a hand. "I don't want to get too far ahead of ourselves. There's every chance what we've discovered has nothing to do with your first husband – I don't want to get your hopes up."

The woman smiled pleasantly. "When I left Grand Cayman in 1986, I left the hopes and thoughts from that part of my life behind me, Detective. I moved on and built a new life for myself. My interest in anything new that arises is nothing more than mild curiosity."

He was surprised how calm and detached she seemed from the events, and looking around, she certainly appeared to have built a far more affluent life than the one she had in 1986.

"You left the island shortly after Mr. Jones went missing?" he asked.

Ally poured herself a glass of water and offered Whittaker the same. He declined.

"I left as soon as the police cleared me to travel. There was nothing left for me here at that time," she replied. "I sold the boat and anything else I could get money for, and went back to England."

"What happened with your business, Mrs. Simmons, and the property?" he asked.

"Please, call me Ally, Detective," she insisted. "The business was nothing without the two of us. Without Charlie, I suppose. He was the fisherman and boat captain, he was also the diver. I mean, I could do all those things, but he was the one who really ran the charters and I handled the books. The business was in trouble anyway, we couldn't keep up with the rent and the day after he went missing was the day we were being evicted. The landlord had another tenant lined up."

"I'm sorry, Ally," he said. "That must have been very difficult."

She smiled, and he thought she might laugh, but she returned to her calm and dispassionate manner. "It had been difficult for a while, so nothing came as a surprise." She sipped her water and took her time. "Charlie was a dreamer, Detective, he wanted nothing more than to hunt for long-lost treasure and artefacts. But that didn't pay the bills, you see, which is why we were in the sad situation we found ourselves."

Her tone raised slightly as she spoke, the first indication Whittaker noticed of any emotional reaction to their conversation.

"That must have been quite a strain on your marriage?"

"It was a strain on us both, naturally," she replied. "When you live in paradise, you expect every day to be sunshine and toes in the sand. One big summer holiday. When the realities of trying to make a business work set in, paradise becomes a location, just like any other. You succeed or fail by the decisions you make. And we were failing."

"Were you planning on leaving before your husband went missing?" Whittaker asked.

Ally seemed to be caught off guard and hesitated a moment. "Every marriage has rough patches, Detective. As you pointed out, our financial woes were a strain, but I had made Grand Cayman my home, and I didn't want to leave. As you can see, I returned to stay once I was able to."

Whittaker took a moment to cast his eyes around the deck, with a pristine pool and manicured landscaping leading to a wooden pier extended out over the shallow, turquoise water.

"I imagine this is quite a contrast to your first time living here?"

"I've been fortunate over the years," she said carefully, "and my husband was willing to relocate here in the early nineties, so I was able to come back home."

"You met Mr. Simmons in the UK?" he asked pleasantly. "What does your husband do, if you don't mind me asking?"

"Yes, we met at a company I went to work for in Northampton, a small town in the West Midlands near where I grew up," she replied. "He worked as an architect for a builder. He's retired now, but that's what he did when we moved here too. He designed custom houses." She held a hand up and looked around the living room. "This house included, naturally. He's a talented man."

"This is a beautiful home," Whittaker added. "Talented indeed, and clearly successful."

Ally nodded and looked at the detective. "You haven't mentioned what this new evidence is you've found. I'm happy to help you in any way I can, but I'm sure reminiscing about the old days and talking about designing homes is a waste of your precious time, Detective."

Whittaker smiled. "Not at all, Ally, it helps me build a picture of what was going on back in 1986. It's all very helpful, and I appreciate your patience." He leaned forward slightly in his seat. "So, what do you think happened to your husband? You must have had an idea or theory at the time? Perhaps something that came to mind later about what may have happened."

Ally stared at him blankly, clearly recognising he had avoided telling her about his new evidence. "I've always said the same thing: I think he got himself in trouble diving on his own. He should never have gone back out. But quite honestly, it was all so long ago now, I can't remember all the details of that day, but I've never come up with any new theory that makes sense."

"Your husband was an experienced diver, was he not?" Whittaker asked.

"Sure, but he was hell-bent on finding these sixteenth-century artefacts he'd researched," she replied quickly, but her voice remained even. "In his mind they would save us."

"The artefacts from Sir Francis Drake's visit to the island?" Whittaker asked.

"Yes, and all this should be in the original police file, Detective, I went over it with them a hundred times back then," she explained. "I'd go by the statement I made in 1986 over anything I can or can't remember now."

"Did you believe him? About the artefacts I mean," Whittaker asked. "That would have been quite the find, surely? Very prestigious, not to mention incredibly valuable."

Ally sighed, and her expression tensed. "Charlie would come up with these theories all the time. We were broke and about to be kicked out of our home, so it wasn't a case of believing him or not. If he had spent half the time he wasted chasing ghost stories of lost treasure in drumming up paying customers, we could have made the business work. I'd heard so many of these tales, quite honestly, I'd stopped listening." She tilted her head to one side, her tone rising once more. "Do you know how much treasure he ever found, Detective?"

Whittaker smiled. "Naturally I do not know, but I'm assuming you're about to tell me it wasn't much."

"Four coins," she said bluntly. "Four coins was the extent of his treasure hunting resume." Ally waved a hand dismissively in the air. "They weren't even from the time period of the wreck he was searching for. Total blind luck he found them, and they certainly didn't have much value."

"So you think he went back out that evening and something went wrong on the dive?" Whittaker asked, pulling her back to the event itself.

Ally shrugged her shoulders. "Seemed to fit, and it hasn't crossed my mind much over the years since, Detective. I moved on and found a new life for myself."

"The landlord was questioned at the time too," Whittaker persisted politely. "You didn't think he could have had anything to do with it?"

"I certainly didn't care for Torsten McGinnis, believe me; he was a crude man, but there was no evidence of foul play to my knowledge. Unless you've now found something that says otherwise?" Ally replied, her voice back to her calm and even tone.

"In your original statement you had mentioned he appeared to be watching you and your husband – what can you tell me about that?" Whittaker asked.

"We owed him money," she replied firmly. "I couldn't stand him watching us, but I figured he was making sure we didn't skip town or something. Him and his daughter, they watched us like hawks. Torsten died years ago, but that daughter of his is still around, I believe. She's a piece of work."

"Brenda McGinnis?"

Ally nodded. "Yes, that's her, Brenda." She tapped her finger on the table and smiled pleasantly, but her tone was to the point. "So, Detective, are you going to tell me about this new evidence? I thought that's why you came to see me, or was that an excuse to ask me a bunch of questions I answered thirty-four years ago?"

"I apologise, I have taken up a lot of your time," Whittaker admitted. "Please forgive my curiosity, an occupational habit you might say. We've found some scuba gear that might be from the timeline matching your husband's disappearance, but as I said earlier, we're not sure as yet. Our forensic team will know more once we've completed our investigation of the site and thoroughly examined the evidence."

"Where was it found?" Ally asked keenly.

"Near the dive site known as Neptune's Wall," Whittaker replied. "Our divers are working out there as we speak."

Ally looked thoughtful and drummed her finger on the table a little faster. "That's where we were diving that day," she said quietly. "We hadn't found anything there, and we'd searched the whole area where Charlie believed the artefacts would be."

"Perhaps he went back out for one last look?" Whittaker suggested.

Ally slowly nodded. "Perhaps."

"You never had the urge to look some more?" Whittaker asked.

"I mean it truly would be a very valuable find. Actual artefacts belonging to Sir Francis Drake."

Ally stood up. "No. I never had the urge," she said.

Whittaker took the hint it was time for him to leave and stood. "Well, thank you very much for your time, Ally, I'll keep you updated as we know more."

She walked across the living room and he followed her to the foyer.

"Are you planning on talking to Brenda McGinnis, Detective?" she asked casually as she opened the front door.

"I thought I would stop by for a chat," he replied, exiting the house and turning back to face the woman. "Anything in particular I should ask her about, in your opinion?"

Ally frowned. "You could ask her if she knows what happened to my ex-husband, and see what she says, I suppose."

Whittaker laughed. "I could do that, but as you yourself said, there was no evidence to suspect her or her father at the time. If they were evicting you, it doesn't seem they would have much reason to do anything to delay that, especially as they had a paying tenant ready to move in."

"No motive, as you police people say," she replied.

"Exactly," he said. "No motive. Thank you again for your time."

She nodded and closed the door. As he walked down the steps towards his car, he mulled over the fact that there was actually one scenario that provided everyone involved with a motive.

22

—————

GRAND CAYMAN – SEPTEMBER, 1986

Jonesy piloted the Bertram up to their little dock, pulled in behind the dinghy, and Ally hopped over to the jetty and tied the boat into the cleats. He shut the motors down and began heaving the heavy steel tanks off the boat, onto the dock, and noticed Ally staring off into the distance again.

"What's up, love?" he asked, squinting in the direction she was looking.

He saw McGinnis's boat pulling up to their dock a few hundred yards north of them. "They follow us in?" he added.

Ally stepped back down to the boat to grab her bag and the towels. "Who knows? Seems like they're keeping an eye on us though, doesn't it?"

Jonesy peered over the top of their own jetty and noticed McGinnis was on the fly-bridge shutting the motor down. On the dock, next to the Viking Sport, was a younger woman who had tied them in and now stood, hands on hips, staring back at him.

"Who's that with him?" he asked.

Ally retrieved the empty petrol can from under the seat, and placed it on the jetty. She looked again towards their landlord's property.

"I think that's his daughter," she replied.

"I didn't know he had any family," Jonesy said. "I've never seen anyone else over there except the blokes he has working for him. Rough-looking lot they are too. Have you met her?"

Ally stepped to the dock. "Not really," she replied, hesitantly, "but I've seen her, and she sort of looks like him."

"Sturdy-looking woman," he said, and followed Ally up the dock, lugging a tank in each hand.

Jonesy refilled the tanks they had used over the past two days from their compressor in the gear room downstairs, while Ally fixed them both a sandwich. Once he was done with the tanks, he washed his hands and climbed the stairs to the flat. He grabbed a Hofmeister lager from the fridge, poured it into a glass then sat down at the small dining table opposite his wife. The cool drink and the breeze through the open windows felt good, and he let out a long sigh. His mind eased away from the disappointment of the morning and turned back to the envelope of copied papers from Drake's voyage. Maybe there was a clue they were missing, he wondered. He was about to suggest they take some time to revisit the logs when Ally spoke.

"Bit early for that, isn't it?" she said.

Jonesy was lost. "Early for what, love?"

She nodded at the drink in front of him.

"That?" he replied. "It's a bloody lager, love. It's gnat's piss."

She glanced at him, then looked away and took a bite of her sandwich. His first reaction was to defend himself further, but for once he bit his tongue and stayed quiet. Her silence was harder to swallow than her acidic comments. It felt like she had decided it wasn't worth it anymore. Why try and fix something that was completely broken? He wasn't sure what to say that could make a difference, other than screw things up worse than they already were, so he turned back to the only course of action he believed could save him.

"Let's take another look through those papers before we go back out," he said, trying his best to sound positive. "Maybe there's something I've missed that would help us narrow down the spot. You've got an eye for details, better than me, so you might pick up a hint I didn't see."

"Okay," she replied.

"After lunch, I'll run down to the petrol station and fill the little can again; that'll get us through the afternoon," he said and took a hurried bite of his sandwich, keen to get things moving now he had a plan in play.

Ally looked across the table at him and thought for a moment before she spoke. "I'll get the petrol."

"Huh?" he replied, as he finished chewing. "I thought you could start looking through the logs."

She took a deep breath. "Yesterday you went out to fill the can, and didn't come back."

Jonesy's heart sank. Again, he fought the urge to defend himself. He knew his actions were indefensible. He wanted to slam his remaining half a sandwich down on his plate in a show of frustration, but he held his anger in check. He was frustrated with his wife for pointing out his faults, but his true anger lay with himself, and he had run out of places to hide from it.

"Let me do it, love," he said, mustering up the calmest voice he could find. "I promise I'll come right back. I need you to give me the chance to prove that to you."

She wiped her face with a napkin and he could tell she was buying time while she considered his request.

Finally, she put the napkin down and nodded. "Okay."

He stood, eating the rest of his sandwich as he hurried to the kitchen sink, and poured the remainder of his lager away. He picked up the envelope, still sitting on the coffee table, and handed it to Ally.

"I'll be back in a bit."

He turned to leave, then paused. He fished his wallet from his pocket and confirmed it was void of any cash.

"I'm sorry, love, but do you have any cash?"

Ally opened her purse that sat on the table and took out three bills. She put two tens back in her purse and handed Jonesy a five. He sensed the unspoken statement behind her decision to leave him with the least amount of change, but he shook it off. He ran down the stairs, scooped up the petrol can and stepped out back to where his bicycle leaned against the building. He put the headphones on, hit play on the Walkman, and hopped on the bike as he wheeled it around the corner with Whitesnake's 'Fool For Your Loving' blasting in his ears. I am a fool for her loving, he thought with a smile, but she's worth it and then some. He pedalled enthusiastically along North Church Street, but coasted when he saw a woman ahead, standing by the side of the road outside McGinnis's place. It was the same woman he had seen by the Scotsman's boat. She watched him approach and he slowed, unsure of her intentions as she stood far enough out that he would need to swing into the road to go around her.

"What are you two up to then?" she asked in a broad Scottish accent.

He braked to a stop in front of the woman, and slipped his headphones off. She wasn't blessed with good looks, and had the build of a rugby player.

"I'm sorry?" he asked. "Who are you? If you don't mind me asking."

"I'm Brenda McGinnis," she replied. "And I dinnae mind you askin'."

"Pleased to meet you, Brenda," he replied politely. "I haven't seen you on the island before, are you visiting your father?"

She smiled the unfriendliest smile Jonesy had ever seen. "I live here now. Arrived last week. Helpin' ma da run things."

"Oh, well, welcome to the island then," he replied and started to move away.

"I'd like to know what you and your wee wife are up to out there," she said, stepping in front of him so he had to stop again.

"I don't see that's any concern of yours," he replied, trying to keep a courteous tone.

"Ye dinnae think so?" she asked, her voice becoming more challenging as she stepped even closer to him. Although she was much shorter than Jonesy, she had broad shoulders and a thick chest. He felt surprisingly intimidated. "Seeing as you're aboot to be kicked ootae oor buildin', I'd say we have a concern in whatever you're up tae, laddie."

"We'll get you paid," he snapped back. "Don't you worry about that. With the score we're hitting, we'll buy your damn building."

He wheeled around her and pedalled furiously away, cursing under his breath. He turned and saw her watching him go. Her grin was even wider.

Bloody hell, he thought to himself, I shouldn't have said anything. The pressure was killing him. He felt like every pebble that was added to the mountain was making the load unbearable, and he was living on the edge of falling apart at every moment. He filled the can with petrol at the station and paid the attendant. He put the change in his pocket and started the ride back, the petrol can handle hooked over the end of the handlebars, making the bike awkward to steer. He couldn't stop seeing Brenda's face, sneering that ugly smile at him. She was mocking him, as though she knew his failings and was happily watching his world implode around him. Worse than that, she and her rotten father were actively helping his life crumble. He was thankful she wasn't still standing out by the road as he raced by the McGinnises' and approached his building. He stopped pedalling and coasted, checking over his shoulder for traffic before crossing the road to the ocean side. His throat felt dry and his feet wanted to keep going. They began slowly turning the pedals again and Sandy called to him like refuge from a storm. All this madness and overwhelming stress would evaporate with her smile. A safe harbour, where the tentacles of life couldn't drag him beneath the churning seas. The voices thrashed and clawed at each other in a frenzied war within his conscience, until he felt himself floating above the chaos, a voyeur observing the voyage of his own demise.

He leaned his bike against the wall, set the petrol can down and stepped inside.

"Is that you?" he heard, calling to him.

He walked up the stairs and smiled across the room at his wife. "Yeah, I'm back," he said.

Jonesy wished his feeling of accomplishment at not continuing to the bar would win through and douse the guilt and sense of hopelessness attached to his desire to drink. But it didn't. If the change in his pocket had been enough for a drink, he may have made a different decision. Who was he kidding, he thought forlornly, there was no 'may' about it.

"I've gone through this stuff again, but I had looked at it for a while last night while you were…" she trailed off, and moved some of the papers around on the table. "Well, anyway, I'd had a pretty good look last night, and I think from the little we have, we're looking in the right area." She shrugged her shoulders. "Why do you think it would be on the reef, rather than in the sand flats east of the deep reef though?"

He sat down at the table. "Because I figured someone would have seen it in the sand, over the years, and they've dragged magnetometers across all of that, looking for wrecks. Several treasure hunting firms have spent years here looking all over the island."

"But aren't those magnet thingies looking for big parts, like cannons and anchors?" she asked.

"That's normally what they'll pick up first, if it's an old wooden wreck. Then they do finer sweeps and find the smaller stuff," he explained.

"Well, there isn't a wreck here, is there? It's only small stuff," Ally pointed out.

Jonesy thought for a moment. "I suppose, yes. So you think it could be in the sand and the treasure guys missed it?"

"Could be," she said. "But I don't know how we can do any better than they did. Like you say, no one's seen it on top of the sand; it's more likely to be buried underneath it."

"Several feet down too," Jonesy replied, scratching his head where the dried salt water was making his scalp itch. "The sands shift and move around all over the place in the storms. Small arte-facts could be taken hundreds of yards from where they were dropped."

"Needle in a haystack," she murmured thoughtfully.

They sat quietly for a few minutes until Jonesy remembered his recent encounter. "I met McGinnis' daughter," he said.

"Scary little wench, isn't she?" Ally responded.

"You're telling me," he replied. "She stopped me on the way to the petrol station, Her name's Brenda. She wanted to know what we were doing out on the water."

"She asked you what you were doing?" Ally repeated. "She's got some nerve."

Jonesy laughed. "She wasn't shy, that's for sure. I told her it was none of her business."

"What'd she say to that?" Ally asked.

"Nothing. I rode off," he said with a grin. "I was a bit worried she would come after me like a bloody bowling ball though."

Ally smiled, and it warmed Jonesy's heart to see a hint of happi-ness return to his wife's face.

"I've got an idea," Jonesy declared, and stood up.

"About our Scottish landlords?" she asked.

"No, well, I suppose it's all involving them at the end of the day, but an idea about diving this afternoon," Jonesy explained, and nodded towards the stairs. "Come on, I'll show you."

He led Ally downstairs into the gear room and moved several dive tanks aside to clear a path to his toolbox. It was a red rolling cabinet with a seven-drawer top box loaded with tools from his days as a mechanic. He opened the deep bottom drawer of the cabinet and pulled something from the side of the drawer and held it up.

"What's that?" Ally asked, with lukewarm enthusiasm.

"It's a magnet," Jonesy explained. "I have a pair of these big magnets I use for holding steel parts together while I weld them. We don't have a fancy magnetometer, but maybe we can find anything ferrous if it's not too deep in the sand."

Ally looked at him as though he had switched to speaking Mandarin. "You're thinking we're going to scour a square mile of sand with a pair of handheld magnets? Are you balmy?"

He wasn't expecting Christmas-level enthusiasm, but he had hoped for a touch more excitement for his idea. "Not the whole sandy area. I was thinking we'd try the inlets between the fingers where all the rubbish seems to gather."

Ally paused and appeared to consider the idea. "Do you think that will really work?"

Jonesy laughed. "Honestly, I doubt it, but I don't have a better idea, and maybe we'll pull up a nice watch."

23

────────

GRAND CAYMAN – MONDAY

AJ brought up a dry-erase board from below deck and set it on the bench under the fly-bridge, leaning it against the side. She took a black marker and drew her best version of the cave from her memory and dimensions she and Reg had taken. She then marked the lines they had run in red marker, forming the twelve squares. Across the top, she wrote A, B and C and down the side the numbers one through four, creating their references for each square. In the back of B1 she drew a blue circle representing where the tank had been found. She stood back, and the others gathered around to admire her artwork.

"That's perfect," Rasha commented. "Now we'll work by segments and I'll label everything you bring up accordingly."

"Where should we begin?" AJ asked.

"B1 I reckon," Reg said. "That's right in front of the tank and where we're likely to find the regulator and BCD parts, if there are any."

"I agree," Rasha added. "Start there as we've already removed items from that section."

"The buckle too, right Reg?" Jackson asked.

Reg nodded. "Yup, it would have been about here," he replied, taking the blue marker and drawing a 'D' shape next to the tank. "What about your piece of scrap metal?" he asked AJ with a grin.

She took a green marker and drew a small rectangle in B3. "There," she said with dramatic confidence, "and I used green to signify really old artefacts of great interest."

Reg rolled his eyes. "Blimey, she's Indiana Jones now."

AJ frowned. "More like Lara Croft I reckon," she replied, and gave Reg a karate chop on the arm.

"Who?" he said and walked over to his gear. "We diving, or what?"

AJ looked at her dive computer on her wrist. "Yup. We've been up 53 minutes; it'll be an hour by the time we're in."

"Video the grid before you start please," Rasha asked, as the group put their gear on.

She walked over and gave Reg and AJ a selection of clear plastic evidence bags which they both stuffed into their BCD pockets. She handed Thomas and Jackson one larger bag each, and gave AJ a stainless-steel beaker.

"Use the smaller bags to take a sand sample from the middle of each section, please," she explained. "Scoop up one beakerful, and make sure you seal the bag really well."

AJ nodded. "I'll shoot the video first thing, before we stir up a mess, and then we'll take the sample before we start sifting."

"Perfect, thank you," Rasha replied. "The larger bags are for whatever you sift from the sand. Bring up absolutely everything, organic or man made." She turned to Jackson and Thomas. "You have one each for back-up or in case you find something interesting under the overhang worth further examination."

Reg and AJ gave her an okay sign as they waddled towards the stern in their fins.

They splashed in and this time all they had to lug along with them was the sifting pan, which Reg carried. They descended swiftly to the overhang where the last of their bubbles were still finding their way out of the cavern from the first dive. A young hawksbill turtle saw the approaching divers and decided to hunt for a tasty sponge elsewhere, gliding over the reef towards the wall. One by one they funnelled through the tight entry, before AJ led Reg into the tunnel, leaving Jackson and Thomas to stand guard under the overhang. Once she arrived at the cave, she paused and shot a video of the cave showing their stakes and lines forming the grid. At the wall was a circular indention in the sand where the tank had rested. Perhaps for decades.

AJ put the camera away in her BCD pocket and finned gently into the cave. The bright morning sun found its way through the small fracture in the outer wall, illuminating a swathe of sand where life would begin to grow in years to come. They both slipped their fins off and set them aside at the edge of the cave, then released the air from their BCDs to settle into the sand either side of B1. AJ pulled out the beaker along with the wad of bags she had been given. She pushed the beaker vertically into the sand in the middle of the grid square, open side down, and wriggled it in until the top was about to disappear. She felt the beaker hit something solid and she hoped it was the floor of the cave, and not Mr. Jones. With that thought fresh in her mind, she tentatively pushed her hand into the sand until she could slide it beneath the beaker and trap the sand in the vessel. She carefully drew the beaker up while Reg held one of the bags open. She inverted the beaker once it was clear of the sand and removed her covering hand so Reg could slip the bag over. She slowly flipped the beaker upside down again and the wet sand poured into the bag, filling it with a cloudy mixture of brown-tinted sand and sediment. She pulled the beaker out and ran the slider across the closure, sealing the contents. She looked around and her headlamp beam lit up a hazy cloud of murky water, already reducing the visibility in the cave. That was from one scoop, and made her realise how they would be working solely by touch once they stirred more sand up.

AJ set the sample bag to the side as Reg pointed to the beaker in her hand and made a scooping motion. She quickly figured out what he meant, and used the beaker to scoop up the sand and pour it into the pan he held. She realised their first problem was what to do with the filtered sand that rained down from the perforated base of the pan. If they held it over the section they were searching, they were constantly recycling the same sand. If they held the pan over another grid section, they were contaminating it with sand that had already been sifted. Reg held the pan over B1 and AJ figured he had decided that was the best plan to start, so she continued scooping and pouring. She started near the wall where the tank had been and worked her way backwards into the cave. She could feel the beaker knocking and picking up large pieces of debris in the sand, but the visibility was already so bad she couldn't see what they were. There was something too big to fit in the beaker she kept nudging and moving and she dreaded to think what it might be. The sifted sand was piling up in the middle of the section, forming a hill which constantly scattered to the area she had cleared, until she noticed she wasn't feeling any more debris.

Reg's hand on her arm stopped her and for a minute they sat still, giving the water time to clear. Once they could see each other again, they both peered into the pan. Amongst the greyish-white pieces of dead coral were several black plastic parts and small tufts of faded material. AJ knew they had found what remained of the BCD that belonged to the tank. The fabric had rotted away, leaving only a few remnants and the plastic pieces of buckles and snaps that held the vest together. She looked down at the base of the outer wall where the tank had been, now the outer edge of their sand pile. There lay a much larger piece of plastic, rectangular with rounded corners and slightly curved in profile. She picked it up and they both examined the object in their headlamp beams. AJ was pretty sure it was the backplate from the BCD, the rigid part the tank strapped to. She placed it in the pan, opened one of the larger evidence bags Rasha had provided and they moved everything from the pan to the bag. Reg held a larger piece in his hand to show her and she recognised he had what remained of the regulator.

AJ checked her dive computer. They had been down for seventeen minutes already and she had used half the nitrox in her tank.

She knew Reg would have used more than she had, his larger size requiring more fuel than her. She wanted to finish the first section this dive, so she held up a hand to Reg, telling him to wait a moment. She took the beaker and began skimming off the top of the sand pile and moving it to the edge of the outer wall which she felt they had thoroughly searched. Once the hill was reduced to an even level with the surrounding sand, she began scooping a beakerful at a time into the pan again. Reg held the pan against the outer wall so the filtered sand fell closer to the edge, making the process a little easier.

Five more minutes and AJ figured they had searched the section as best they could. It was an imperfect process as nothing stopped sand from the adjoining sectors filling the gaps created as she scooped along the edges of B1. But they were collecting a lot of debris, and as long as they double-checked both sides of the reel line, she felt they had a good chance of capturing everything. They groped around in the white-out and added the last of the objects from the pan to the evidence bag, squished the bag down to evacuate most of the water and sealed the top. Leaving the pan in the cave, they slipped their fins back on and by the time they started up the tunnel, most of the visibility had returned. AJ heard an alarm beeping and pointed her headlamp at her dive computer on her wrist. It wasn't hers so she knew it was Reg who had reached one of the thresholds they had set.

She emerged into the dim light of the overhang, where she found Jackson and Thomas sitting with their backs against the side of the ravine, playing noughts and crosses in the sand. AJ laughed behind her regulator as she led the group out from under the overhang and began her ascent towards the boat. They had just completed a second successful dive on behalf of the RCIPS, and she was feeling relaxed and cheerful. She loved the diving, but beyond that, the teamwork amongst her friends and the feeling they were accomplishing something worthwhile filled her with satisfaction.

They spent three minutes on a safety stop at 15 feet to allow their bodies to dissipate more of the accumulated nitrogen in their systems and the gases to equalise, before returning to the boat. Rasha was keen to dig into the bag of goodies once they were back aboard Hazel's Odyssey. She diligently catalogued every item, including the natural debris, which she separated from everything non-organic and bagged on its own. When she pulled the larger piece of plastic out, they all gathered round and speculated over the new piece of evidence.

"It's a backplate from the BCD isn't it, Reg?" AJ asked.

"For sure," he replied. "And I reckon I can tell you the brand and model as well."

Jackson looked up from his mobile. "I was about to search for BCDs from the 1980s."

"Search away, see if you can find a picture," Reg said with a grin. "This is from the first jacket-style vest that was introduced. Seaquest came out with it in the mid-eighties. Changed the business for recreational divers. It was called the ADV, which stood for Advanced Design Vest."

Jackson typed the model into an Internet search and after clicking through a few pictures, found one to show the group.

"Here you go," he said, holding up his mobile for the others to see the screen. "This picture shows the backplate."

"Blimey," AJ muttered. "The old boy's right, that looks like the one."

Rasha laid out several more pieces of plastic and they compared them to the buckles they could see in the pictures on the mobile.

"I think we have a positive ID on the BCD," Rasha said. "I'll notify Detective Whittaker."

"What about the regulator?" AJ asked, picking up the second stage. "Can we tell what model this is?"

The regulator had a circular shape with an adjustment knob on one side and the mouthpiece and exhalation skirt missing. AJ handed it back to Rasha, who carefully brushed the gummy muck away, catching it in a bag. The metal below was dulled but not corroded.

"That's a 109," Reg said. "I used to have one of them."

AJ looked at the front of the circle where an 'S' emblem could be seen. "ScubaPro again, right?"

"Yup," Reg confirmed. "They stopped making the 109 mid-eighties, if memory serves, but it was popular throughout the seventies and eighties."

"Do you have da buckle Big Boss found?" Thomas asked.

Rasha paused her text message she was typing on her mobile and pulled a plastic evidence bag from a drawer in her toolbox. "Here," she said, and handed it to Thomas. "Keep it in the sealed bag, please."

Thomas took the buckle and showed it to Jackson. "Let's look at dose pictures for dis here buckle."

Jackson thumbed through the pictures he had found until he found one showing a rear view of the Seaquest BCD. "It looks like it should be the tank strap buckle, don't you think?"

Reg took the bag and examined the dulled metal piece. "I don't know," he said, scratching his beard. "What does the one in the pictures look like?"

Jackson showed him his mobile and Reg squinted at the small image. "That's not it, is it?" he said.

"Definitely not," Jackson confirmed. "The Seaquest buckle is half plastic and the metal part is a D-ring but it's thick wire. What you found is cut from plate."

Reg held the bag up. "This is from a weight belt," he exclaimed. "I remember these things. They were around in the sixties and seventies." He handed it back to Thomas and looked at Jackson. "See if you can find any history on weight belt designs, or classic weight belts."

"Hey," Rasha said, looking at her mobile. "Whittaker says the original report lists Charlie Jones's dive gear. He owned a Seaquest ADV dive vest, and it was missing when they recovered the boat."

"Bloody hell," AJ said thoughtfully. "I guess that confirms we've found Jonesy's dive gear."

"But still no Mr. Jones," Thomas added.

"Yeah, still no Mr. Jones," AJ agreed.

"And we still don't know why he took his gear off inside the cave," Reg said.

"Including his weight belt, it seems," Jackson pointed out.

They looked at each other, all trying to work out a situation where they would take all their gear off at 124 feet underwater.

"Doesn't make sense," AJ said, echoing everyone's thoughts.

24

GRAND CAYMAN – MONDAY

Detective Whittaker answered his ringing mobile phone as he parked on the ocean side of North Church Street, opposite the back entrance to Kirk supermarket.

"Hello Rasha, I've been reading your texts," he said. "Looks like we have a match on the dive gear, that's the BCD and the regulator listed in the original report from Jonesy's disappearance."

"When I'm back to my lab I'll write an official report after I make a more thorough examination and provide proof of identification, but I'm confident the ID is accurate," she replied.

"Excellent work, thank you, and please thank the divers for me," Whittaker said, looking over at the series of buildings, including a house that the McGinnises had owned for as long as he could remember. "I spoke with Alison Simmons, formerly Jones, this morning – seems like a pleasant lady. Done well for herself since 1986."

"I bet she was surprised to hear we've found her husband's dive gear after all this time," Rasha said with a chuckle.

"Actually, she was remarkably calm," he replied. "I might go as far as to say disinterested."

"Really?" Rasha said, sounding surprised. "Did she have anything new that might help the case?"

"Not really," he said thoughtfully. "She gave the impression she had moved on many years ago, and had little interest or memory of her first husband's disappearance, but she's sharp as a tack. I don't think she lied to me about anything, but I'm pretty sure she was guarded with what she was saying. She was strangely dismissive about the landlord and his potential involvement, which struck me as odd. Even pointed out their lack of motive."

"Are you going to see him, the landlord?" Rasha asked.

"He died a long time ago, but his daughter is still alive and kicking; she lives in George Town. I've had dealings with Brenda McGinnis before. I'm actually outside her property now," he replied, watching two men loading boxes into a van from one of the storage buildings.

"Does she have a criminal record?" Rasha asked.

"Not even a parking violation," Whittaker answered. "But I've had cause to interview her on more than one occasion. She's a clever woman. She owns legitimate rental properties, but we're confident she's also running book, high-dollar prostitutes, loan sharking, and dubious imports. We've never been able to make anything stick; even when we've arrested and prosecuted people who work for her, they never give her up."

"Wow, I'm guessing she inherited these lines of business from her father?"

"Yes, and back in the day he was arrested and prosecuted a couple of times," Whittaker recalled. "But his lawyers always wriggled it down to lesser charges, so he never served any time. On the island at least. Seems she learnt well from her father, and is even harder to catch. This ought to be an interesting conversation, she doesn't usually take too kindly to police visits."

"Well good luck, sir," Rasha said. "I'll make it quick as it sounds like you're busy, but I did have a reason for calling you."

"Of course," Whittaker said. "I apologise, I rambled on. What do you have for me?"

"I dropped the piece of metal from the cave off with my friend at the museum this morning, on my way to the dock," Rasha explained. "She texted me a few minutes ago and agrees it appears consistent with iron used around the 16th century. She thinks it might be a clasp from a chest. We'll need a metallurgy report to better understand the make-up of the iron, which will likely suggest a broad time period, as there's no way to truly date a metal. We'll have to send it to the US or UK for that report, and it will take four to eight weeks, I'm afraid. My friend is also trying to match it with styles of clasps from examples she has or has seen before. I'm hoping the divers bring up more pieces and maybe we'll find something with a more definitive style or shape we can match."

"Fascinating," Whittaker said quietly. "If we can prove Jonesy was in the cave and did in fact discover artefacts from Sir Francis Drake's visit, then I'd say motive just opened up for everyone concerned."

"I think we've proved he was in there," Rasha replied. "Or his dive gear certainly was."

"Okay, thank you again," Whittaker replied. "Keep me updated if they find anything else of note."

"They're in the water now for the third dive of the day," Rasha said. "I'll text you if there's anything new and interesting. Good luck with McGinnis."

Whittaker chuckled. "I might need it," he said, and hung up the phone as he opened the car door to a rush of hot, humid island air.

The detective walked down the tarmac driveway that opened into a wider parking area with two large storage buildings on the left and the McGinnis home on the right. The van he had seen being loaded pulled past him and continued up the driveway towards the road. The driver looked nervous and tried to avoid eye contact. The roll-up door where the van had just been rattled to the ground, and Whittaker heard the lock clunk. The second building had a door and window that appeared to be an office next to another large roll-up door. He decided to try his luck at the office. As he walked up, through the window he saw the large frame of Brenda

McGinnis behind a desk. She glanced up, ignored Whittaker, and continued reading the document in front of her. He knocked firmly on the door and waited.

After a few moments he heard a gravelly Scottish woman's voice. "Come in then."

The years had not been sympathetic to Brenda McGinnis, although Whittaker guessed her woes were self-induced. She was a large lady with thinning, grey wiry hair and bags under her dark eyes. The office reeked of cigarette smoke and piles of papers and assorted boxes littered every surface of the small room.

"Well isn't this my lucky day," she greeted the detective with a sneer. "Bring your bloodhounds with ye, or are you all on your tod?"

"Hello Miss McGinnis," Whittaker started politely. "My apologies for dropping by unannounced, but I was hoping I could ask you a few questions about your father?"

The woman laughed, and her whole face jiggled. "Still tryin' to pin crap on him after all this time, huh? Been deid and buried over twenty years and ye still cannae leave him alone."

Whittaker wondered at the stark contrast between the woman he had met with earlier in the day, and the one who sat before him.

"I'm meeting with everyone who was involved in a case back in 1986, Miss McGinnis; you and your father were mentioned in the investigation, so I'm making routine follow-ups."

"It's routine to follow up on cases from over three decades ago?" she growled. "Sounds like a waste of taxpayers' money if you ask me."

She took a noisy gulp from a can of Coca-Cola and Whittaker waited for her to finish before replying. "We follow up if new evidence comes to light."

"Ooooh, juicy, like *Cold Case* on the telly, huh?" she mocked. "So what's this ancient case you've drug up with your new evidence, then? Ye found Colonel Mustard's candlestick, did ye now?"

Whittaker smiled. "Do you recall a gentleman named Charlie

Jones? I believe he was a tenant of your father's in the building that used to be where the helipad is now."

"I dinnae remember a gentleman by that name," she replied, her eyes squinting below her saggy eyelids. "But I knew a deadbeat named Jonesy who couldnae pay his rent. That the fella you mean? Went oot diving on his own, and was ne'er seen again. Ye find his bones somewhere, Detective? If he had a wallet on him, I'll take dibs on anything in it. The piece o' crap owed us his rent."

"No body, as yet, Miss McGinnis," Whittaker replied patiently. "But we have recovered what we believe to be his diving equipment."

"I see," Brenda said, nodding. "And what does this have to do wi' me, then? 'Cos unless you're bringing me the money he owed, I couldnae give a toss what happened to the useless git."

"Like I said, I'm conducting basic follow-ups," Whittaker said, carefully gauging the woman's disposition. "What do you recall from the time surrounding Mr. Jones's disappearance?"

"I recall he bloody well owed us money," she snapped, leaning back in her chair, which Whittaker considered risky, unless the furniture had been suitably reinforced. "He was a drunk, slapped his missus around is what I heard," she said, looking past the detective and out of the window. "She was a hussy too. Came round trying to sleep her way ootae the rent," she laughed. "Ma Da sent her packin'."

Whittaker tried to imagine the elegant woman he had met with propositioning Torsten McGinnis, who he vaguely remembered meeting a few times. Chalk and cheese came to mind, but he had learnt over the years to never underestimate the ability of seemingly normal humans to commit unpredictable and often unthinkable deeds.

"She took off awful nifty after all this happened," McGinnis continued "You're not wonderin' aboot that now? Came back not but a few years later, she did, all drippin' in money, and with a fancy new husband on her arm."

"Miss McGinnis, are you suggesting Mrs. Jones made financial gain from her husband's disappearance?" Whittaker challenged politely. "My understanding was that she was left penniless, and homeless, as you and your father continued with the eviction."

"You're supposed to be the bloody detective," she retorted. "How aboot you do some detecting instead of wasting ma time." She waved a chubby paw in the air. "Or forget aboot the whole damn thing for Pete's sake; the dobber went oot on his own and topped himself most likely. That, or he's been livin' in Thailand for the past thirty years, ran off from his debts and that hussy of a wife."

Whittaker sighed. Speaking with Brenda was akin to having a root canal during a proctology exam, much as he had expected, and he was sure the stale, rank air in the office was reducing his lifespan. But the more she ranted, the more chance she would let something of use slip, so he kept prodding.

"Do you know why he was diving out on the reef?"

"How the hell should I know what he was doin'? Ask the hussy," Brenda grunted.

"You and your father were seen on the water near where he was diving," Whittaker pointed out, "on the day he went missing. Can you tell me why you were out there?"

Brenda leaned back again to the creaking complaints of her chair. She grinned at Whittaker. "Da had a very nice fishing boat back then, and this may surprise ye to know, but the fish live in the water, Detective. So to catch the fish, you take your fishing boat oot intae the water and catch the bloody fish. We tried inviting them ashore, but they didnae leap onto the dock for us, you see."

"You were seen over the reef, where even back in the eighties fishing was illegal, Miss McGinnis," Whittaker said.

"Well, best you dig up Da and give him a ticket for illegal fishing in 1986 then Detective," she shouted and wriggled forward in her seat, dipping her hand in a handbag on the floor beside her chair. "Here," she declared, waving a twenty Caymanian dollar note in her hand. "I'll pay the fine and save ye the diggin'."

"Were you following the Joneses, Miss McGinnis? Were you watching what they were doing?" Whittaker continued.

"I cannae remember what I ate for tea yesterday, so I certainly cannae recall what I was doin' thirty-four years ago. But likely I were doin' whatever it was Da told me to do." She shoved the money back in her handbag and pointed to the door. "It's been delightful to see you again, Detective, but I'm busy and you're wasting both our times, so toddle off now and help some old ladies cross the bloody road."

Whittaker took an official RCIPS business card from his wallet and placed it on McGinnis's desk. "Thank you for your time, Miss McGinnis, and please give me a call at the station if you recall any details you think might help the case."

Brenda snatched the card from the desk and used a corner to pick between her crooked teeth, staring up at the detective. He nodded and walked to the door, pausing as he opened it, savouring the fresh air that gusted in.

"Next time I come by, perhaps you could show me around your place here?" he said with a pleasant smile. "I've always been curious what you have in these buildings."

"Come back anytime," she snapped. "Anytime you have a legal warrant that is, I dinnae have time for your nonsense. Now git oot and close the door, you're letting all my air conditioning oot."

25

GRAND CAYMAN – SEPTEMBER, 1986

The wind had picked up and was bringing afternoon rain clouds across the island from the south-east, following Bottom Time out to the dive site. The hot, overhead sun played hide and seek behind the scattered clouds and the swells had picked up from flat calm to a light chop by the time Jonesy had secured the anchor and they had donned their gear. Ally had once again located them close to Jonesy's rock pile in the sand, which he found after a quick search below the boat. They split up and headed in opposite directions, magnets in hand, working the inlets between the coral fingers. Most of the sandy valleys extended 10 to 20 feet into the mass of the reef, and were no more than 6 to 10 feet wide. Taking his time, Jonesy brushed the large magnetic block across the sandy bottom, side to side of the inlets, working towards the point where the indentation into the reef ended. He had cleared most of the debris from the end of the valleys over the past two days, but was surprised how much had gathered back there again.

While working on the second inlet, he heard a light drumming sound all around him. He looked up and could see the surface, 55 feet above, dimpled with raindrops peppering the ocean. The cloud cover had dimmed the light at depth, but he found the steady rhythm of the shower calming and provided a soundtrack to work by. Jonesy's mood was buoyant. Deep down, he knew their chances of success with his magnets were slim, but Ally's demeanour towards him had softened, and if he could save his marriage then all was not lost. For a while, every object that leapt from the sand to his magnet gave him a burst of hope, but after a while of gathering rusty fishhooks and old bolts and screws, the novelty was wearing off. How many of the artefacts from 1586 were ferrous was another issue Jonesy contemplated as he foraged amongst the sand, natural debris and rubbish. Brass was a more popular material for most compasses and astrolabes of the time, but the compass needle had to have been magnetic and the hardware on the wooden chest would have been wrought iron. He hoped enough of the parts had survived to be found at all. There was also the question of whether they were scattered across the sea floor when the rowboat sank, or remained inside the chest all the way to the bottom. If the chest went down with its lid closed, then the likelihood of the artefacts being found in a small area was much higher.

Thirty minutes later they sat aboard the Bertram, where the rain had moved on, and compared their findings. Ally's biggest discovery had been several tin cans and a piece of angle iron. Jonesy had found a five-pound barbell gym weight, and they both puzzled over how such a thing could end up in the ocean almost a half mile from shore. Ballast for an illegal trap was their best guess.

"That took care of the east side of our reef section, what now?" Ally asked, between sips from a Thermos of water. "And please don't say we're gonna drag these bloody magnets over the sand flats."

Jonesy smiled. "No, I don't think that's worth it."

He sat quietly and thought for a few minutes. He felt defeated, but not in the desperate way he had before. Ally's warming had seen to that. Being homeless and penniless was certainly not appealing, but given time, he was sure they could find Drake's artefacts, so everything would work out in the end. A roof over their heads and money for food were details they would work out. They had friends who would take them in for a few nights or they could sleep on the boat. All they needed was a charter or two a week to keep them fed.

"Let's take one more dive along the wall," he replied. "I'll bring one of the magnets and we can investigate anything that looks interesting we may have missed before. If nothing else, we'll have a nice dive to finish the day."

Ally nodded, but didn't reply.

"I'm so sorry it's come down to this, my love," Jonesy said, trying to keep his voice steady. "I know I've made a pig's ear of things, and it's gonna be shitty for a bit, but I'm not giving up on finding this chest."

She looked over at him, and he tried to read her expression. Her eyes looked sympathetic but her face was stern.

"I know you won't," she replied, and looked away, across the water. "Bloody hell."

He turned to look. "That McGinnis again?" he asked.

"You think he'd have something better to do than watch us all day," she said angrily. "He'll have our home tomorrow – why doesn't he leave us alone?"

The Viking Sport was bobbing in the water halfway to shore; as they had been that morning, Torsten and Brenda were standing on the fly-bridge making no secret of the fact they were looking straight at the Bertram. Jonesy felt the tide turning with Ally's frustration pulling her away from him again.

"Let's get back in the water so we don't have to look at them," he pleaded. "Come on, we'll enjoy a nice dive, and then head back."

"What's the bloody point?" she scolded. "Take us home." She slammed the Thermos down and Jonesy heard the tinkling sound of shattering glass inside the container. "Home," she scoffed. "We need to start packing anything we care about keeping. This is a waste of time out here. Time we should be spending boxing up our belongings. We don't have a home anymore."

He had lost her again, and he knew it. He felt a lump rising in his throat as he stepped to the helm and started the motors. He took the tension off the anchor line, put the boat in neutral and carefully walked along the edge of the cabin to the bow. He wrenched and pulled until he freed the flukes from the sand, and hauled the anchor aboard. When he returned to the helm, Ally was in her seat, staring at the deck. He put Bottom Time in gear and swung her around, easing the throttles forward to head towards the dock. Off the port side, he looked over at his landlord atop his expensive fishing boat and wondered how the likes of McGinnis always seemed to come out ahead in this world.

Back at the dock, Ally marched up to the flat and left Jonesy to tie up the boat. He looked at their friend's dinghy and dreaded the idea of telling them they needed to come get it. Maybe he could drag it around behind the Bertram for a while, but he had to figure out where to put that too. There were guest moorings a few hundred yards offshore, he thought, looking out at the buoys. He could tie up there for a week or so. They could use the dinghy to run back and forth to the shore. At least he hoped it would be 'they', rather than just 'he'. He walked up the dock and into the gear room. Looking around, he was overwhelmed by the amount of stuff he needed to find a place to store. He could put a few more tanks on the boat, and some of the BCDs and regulators, but he would soon run out of room if they were going to sleep in the tiny cuddy cabin. It had a basic V-berth, but if he put the dive gear down there he would have to move it out to the deck every night to sleep. Well, he thought, it has to go somewhere, so that will have to work. He gathered up handfuls of gear and trudged back down to the boat. After six more trips back and forth he had the V-berth full, and all twelve fishing rods they owned strapped to the roof, alongside the two spearguns. At least they could dive from the boat each evening, he thought, and spear fish for dinner. Ally was a much better shot than he was, so that plan would work better – like every plan he had – if she was still with him.

He walked back to the gear room. He had four more tanks which he could squeeze aboard, but his tools and the compressor were a much bigger problem. Beads of sweat rolled down his face and his shirt was damp and smeared with dusty grime. He was thirsty, and wondered if Ally had calmed down yet. He took his shirt off, turned it inside out, and used it to wipe away some of the sweat. He stepped outside to where his bike was leaning against the wall and slipped the headphones on. Pressing fast forward on the Walkman, he hunted for the song he was looking for. Once he found it, he removed the headphones and ejected the tape from the deck, taking it with him upstairs to the flat. He cautiously looked around but didn't see his wife. Movement in their bedroom told him she was in the other room, so he walked quietly over to the stereo in the living room and popped the tape in, turned the volume up, and hit play.

Mötley Crüe's 'Home Sweet Home' filled their small flat as Jonesy walked over to the bedroom and opened the door. Ally stood next to their bed, looking back at him, with tears running down her face. He started to walk towards her, to sweep her up in his arms and let her know how much he loved her. Somehow, some way, he would make this all work out. All that mattered is that they were together. This was their song. It had become their fun way of saying their evening would turn romantic. He had carried her into the bedroom countless times with the tune playing, if they made it as far as the bedroom. But he froze after one step. A suitcase was open on the bed, filled with her clothes. Nothing else had been moved in the room, only her things. He had assumed she was crying because she heard the song and they would rush into each other's embrace. His feelings for her were so intense, he couldn't fathom how she wouldn't feel the same. Underneath her fear and anxiety brought on by their situation must lie the love she had always felt for him. Surely.

"What are you doing?" he asked, terrified of what she might answer.

"I'm going home, Charlie," she replied, crying and struggling to get the words out. "We've lost everything, I can't stay here anymore."

He took one more step towards her, but she turned away.

"What about us, Ally?" he managed to stutter.

She shook her head. "I can't do this anymore, Charlie, I can't."

"You make it sound like you've been living in hell, love," he pleaded. "I know I've made a mess of things, but the one thing we have is us." He forced a smile. "I even played our song."

She turned and looked at him, her eyes red and puffy, her lips quivering. "I'm not saying it's been hell, Charlie, but it's not turned out like we planned, or what we thought it would be. At least, not what I thought it would be."

"But I can fix this, love, I can get things turned around…" He started, but she cut him off.

"We're in this mess because of you, damn it," she snapped. "Don't you see that? How could I believe you'll make anything right anymore?

"Because I love you, Ally, and you're more important to me than anything," he said, his voice shaking and his eyes welling up with tears of his own.

"But I don't," she whispered and looked away.

"What?" he asked, hearing her words but unable to process what she had just said.

She turned back and looked him in the eye. "I don't love you anymore."

Jonesy backed away, somehow managing to keep his legs beneath him as his world crashed down upon him. He couldn't speak, he had no reply. All he wanted was to leave. Leave the building, and leave the reality of his life crumbling before him. He strode across the living room towards the stairs until he noticed Ally's purse on the table, next to the manila envelope of papers. He pulled out the two remaining tens, grabbed the envelope and continued down to the office. Anger welled up inside and he wanted to scream; he wanted to tear the place apart and leave a pile of rubbish for McGinnis to evict him from. He wanted to rip every shred of his broken marriage from his view, and from his mind. They'd had arguments before, disagreements and minor spats, but nothing like this. He didn't know this woman at all. If she didn't want him, then to hell with her, he didn't need her. Even as his rage shoved the thoughts through his mind, he knew they weren't true. He needed her more than he needed air to breathe, and he didn't know how he could go on. He put the cash in his pocket and threw the envelope down as his feet took him out the back door to where his bike leaned against the wall. He pedalled hard in the late afternoon sun, lying to himself that he was just getting away from the flat. Going for a ride to blow off steam. His ride ended outside Hogs Sty Bay Bar, where he propped his bike against the building. His guilt at his own weakness was lost amongst the pain and fury, blended together in an emotional cocktail that swirled in his head.

"Evening Mr. Jones," came a voice that sounded familiar.

Jonesy turned and faced a tall, lean man in a Royal Cayman Islands Police Service uniform. The policeman smiled.

"Whittaker," the man said, introducing himself, and touching his hand to his hat. "Perhaps you don't remember me from the other evening?"

"It's not altogether clear, I have to be honest," Jonesy replied. "But the uniform looks familiar." He extended a hand and Whittaker gave him a firm shake. "I'm guessing I owe you some thanks, and probably an apology."

Whittaker shook his head. "Think nothing of it. Happy to help, Mr. Jones."

The man appeared to want to say more, but Jonesy wasn't keen on sticking around and finding out. The policeman seemed like a nice chap, but pleasant conversation wouldn't bring Ally back, and wasn't helping him forget the image of her packing her suitcase. He didn't want to think about Ally, but the only other thing on his mind was his search for the artefacts, and that was a painful failure as well. What he needed was escape, and standing outside the bar was not accomplishing that. He nodded goodbye and quickly entered the building, walked down the hall and turned right into the bar. A couple sat at the stools in the middle of the row and a man he had often drunk with was at the far end. He couldn't remember the fella's name, but regardless, company was not on the agenda, so he gave him a nod and took the stool at the opposite end of the bar. No one was behind the bar, and the couple were giggling and chatting sweetly, as two people in love tend to do. Both observations aggravated Jonesy and he was about to get up and serve himself, when Sandy appeared from the back.

"Hey there, sugar," she greeted him and swiftly poured him a rum and Coke.

She placed the drink and two jars in front of him.

"This one's the balance from the other night, hon," she said, tapping the first jar. "This one will be tonight's."

He nodded. "Okay." And swooped up the drink.

"You alright, sugar?" Sandy asked, her voice sounding genuinely concerned.

He looked up. He would normally have assessed her outfit by now, primarily the twins' state of revelation, but he realised he hadn't even noticed. Perhaps that spurred her concern, he wondered.

"Rough day," he replied, unable to pull together a better or more elaborate answer.

Sandy looked at him and thought a moment. She leaned over the bar but folded her arms in front of her, covering her chest, rather than putting on her usual show.

"You sure this is where you need to be right now, sugar?" she whispered.

Jonesy swallowed, and fought back his tears. The ride over, Whittaker's friendly greeting and now Sandy's caring voice had stripped his veneer of anger, leaving his hurt filleted open and exposed.

"She's leaving," he murmured. "There's no saving it now."

Sandy reached over and touched his hand. "I'm sorry, sugar."

"Sixteen years," he said. "Only woman I've ever loved."

He stopped talking before his voice broke and she squeezed his hand before letting go.

"Sixteen years is a long time, sugar," she said softly. "Lots can change in that amount of time. People can change. The whole world changes in that kinda time."

He nodded. "That's the truth. Everything changes."

Sandy stepped back and Jonesy mulled over those words. Had he changed that much? Had she? He didn't think that either of them had, and a month ago he would have laughed if anyone had suggested his wife might leave him. But something had obviously changed. He couldn't face thinking about it anymore and his mind wandered back to his other failing. Four hundred years, that's a lot longer than sixteen, he thought, imagine all the changes that had taken place in four centuries. Imagine how much the reef had changed… He leapt to his feet, almost knocking the stool over. He grabbed one of the ten-dollar bills and hurriedly stuffed it in the jar.

"What's stoked your fire, sugar?" Sandy asked with a laugh, walking back over.

Jonesy leaned over and gave her a quick kiss on the cheek. "You did, sugar," he exclaimed. "You're a bloody genius."

He raced from the bar and grabbed his bicycle. He had hope once more. With two hours of daylight left he could get back out there, and just maybe, he would find Drake's artefacts. If he could walk in the house with the artefacts, he would prove he wasn't a failure. Surely Ally would see that? He could still fix this.

"Good night, Mr. Jones," Whittaker called from over the road. "Be safe now, sir."

Jonesy waved to the man with a broad grin, as he hastily pedalled towards the dock.

26

GRAND CAYMAN – MONDAY

After lunch on the boat and a longer break to let their bodies recover from the deep dives, the group made their third dive of the day. Reg suggested sifting all the edge sections as they were thinner where the cave floor curved up towards the walls, and narrower towards the entry tunnel where the cave tapered in. They suspected these sections were less likely to hide useful evidence, so knocking them out meant they could focus on the centre of the cave. AJ and Reg were able to work their way through all eight segments in a single dive, finding a rhythm to the process. Only one segment yielded non-organic matter. In the grid square A1, to the left of where the tank had been, they found two three-pound dive weights, and the other half of the weight belt buckle. Back on the boat, Rasha had nine sand samples lined up on the bench, an evidence bag for each of the matching grid squares, and AJ's dry-erase board now showed the weight belt parts.

By the time they had sorted everything they had brought up, switched their tanks over, and chatted excitedly about the next dive, their surface hour passed by and they stood on the swim step once again.

"Let's make this the last dive today," Reg said. "Four dives to this depth is plenty, we'll start going loopy if we do too many more. We can come back tomorrow and finish up."

"Or we could whistle through the last three squares, and be done with the whole thing," AJ suggested.

Reg nodded. "That would be fine in my book, but there's a lot more sand in the two middle sections than the edges."

"True," she replied. "Let's start from B4 and work into the cave then; that first one won't take long and then we'll see how far we get."

Reg gave her an okay sign and stepped into the ocean. She turned to Jackson and grinned. "And you'd better focus on your noughts and crosses, mister; Thomas is two wins up."

"I think he's being nice to me," Thomas beamed.

Jackson laughed. "I wish I was, but you're beating me fair and square."

"How many games have you played?" AJ asked.

"We ran out of pebbles to keep count at fifty," Jackson said, grinning. "And that was on the second dive this morning."

"Are you lot gonna bullshit up there all afternoon, or can we get on with it," Reg bellowed from the water, where he bobbed, impatiently waiting.

"Hush up, you grumpy old goat," AJ shouted back, laughing as she took a giant stride off the swim step.

Back inside the cave they quickly set about sifting through the sand in the centre section closest to the tunnel. It started as bare rock and sloped down until the sand was six inches deep next to the reel line for B3. AJ stretched her back and realised how much it ached from the constant balancing of the heavy tank while she worked. She had an idea, and unbuckled her waistband and slipped her arms from her BCD and let the tank drop to the sand. She moved it over to the side of the cave and made sure her regulator had enough reach for her to continue working. Every movement they made, they had to be careful not to drag the reel line and stakes around, ruining their grid. AJ felt clumsy and imagined it had to be much worse for Reg, who was twice her size. She looked over at him and he stared back at her with puzzled eyes. She pointed to her back and could see through the murky water he rolled his eyes, and she chuckled as she resumed scooping sand and dumping the contents into the pan.

They were soon moving on to the next section, and her back felt better, although it was harder to stay planted in the sand as her weights were integrated into her BCD and her buoyant wetsuit was trying to float her. AJ had completely forgotten about the chance of finding human remains, until her beaker hit something solid. The cave was a white-out of cloudy, silted water once again, and she hesitated, wondering what she would find if she reached into the sand. Somehow, it seemed creepier not being able to see whatever she was about to pull from its resting place. She took a few deep breaths and plunged her fingers into the grainy soup where the beaker lay unmoved. If it was bone, it was an odd part of the body, she decided. Whatever she was feeling had a uniform shape and as soon as she lifted it, the weight of the object told her it was non-organic. She fumbled for Reg with her free hand, and by touch they placed the item in the evidence bag they had started for B3. She went back to scooping beakerfuls of sand and pouring them into the pan that Reg held close by. She felt several more smaller objects knock against the stainless steel as she dragged the vessel through the sand. Once she was sure they had thoroughly searched through the section, she gave Reg three taps on the arm, their signal to stop and rest while the visibility cleared. It was strangely disorientating looking into a misty cloud illuminated by her headlamp. Its light was reflected, unable to penetrate the silted water. Shapes and patterns formed and dissipated like a crazed kaleidoscope that had lost its symmetry. Eventually, a ghostly apparition appeared from the haze and her sense of isolation faded as Reg's figure became clearer.

She signalled they could move on to B2, the final section, and he checked his dive computer. She did the same. Hers showed 12 minutes of no-deco time and a little under half her tank of nitrox remained. He gave her an okay sign and reached into his BCD pocket for another evidence bag. He pulled out one of the small bags they were using for the sand samples, but it was all he had left. AJ checked her stash and found she only had one small bag as well. She quickly dipped the beaker into the middle of B2 and, sliding her hand underneath, scooped the sample into Reg's bag which he held open. He tapped on his chest, pointed towards the tunnel, then drew a big square in the water column, indicating he would go up and get a large bag from the guys. AJ gave him an okay sign and shuffled aside to let the big man pass by once he had slipped his fins back on. He took the samples and the two larger bags they had already filled with him, and she watched him disappear from view in the hazy, particulate-strewn water as he entered the tunnel. She felt awkwardly alone.

Looking around, AJ decided to start on the last section. There was no point wasting time sitting there doing nothing when they were racing the clock to finish the project on this dive. She also hoped it would take her mind off her uneasy solitude. She set the pan on the adjacent section and began her scooping. She soon forgot she was alone and focused on the repetitive task that required concentration to move methodically through the segment. Once the sediment stirred up again she was blind and relied on muscle memory to return to the adjacent portion of sand from her prior scoop. Again, she could feel pieces of debris being scooped up and after she had half a dozen beakers' worth of sand in the pan, she shook the pan and sifted the grains away so only the objects remained. She picked out the pieces and dropped them into the last small evidence bag she had. When Reg returned she would drop the small bag inside the larger one and carry on.

She fumbled in the sand for the beaker and had just resumed her scooping process, when she felt a strange motion around her. The swirling pale brown hue of sediment illuminated in her head-lamp beam stopped its weaving dance, and began to vibrate back and forth. She felt the floor beneath her roll around as though it were trying to shake her from its back. A force in the water rocked her in time with the sediment shimmying before her eyes, as though a giant hand was rattling the cave. After a few moments everything settled back down and returned to normal, leaving AJ feeling slightly nauseous and confused. This was her fourth dive to over 120 feet in the past six-and-a-half hours, and although they had taken the necessary surface breaks, she knew the narcotic effect of nitrogen build-up in her body, or more specifically her brain, was probably compromising her perception and thought process. She closed her eyes and took several long, easy inhalations to clear her mind. If she could finish the last section of their grid, they could leave the cave, and not return. The thrill and gratification from the dives were wearing thin, and she was ready to be out of the confined space and lack of visibility.

AJ dug the beaker through the sand and continued her six scoops and shake the pan system for several more minutes until she felt she had finished the last section. The room was a cloudy mess but she sat and waited, letting the sediment settle. Her small evidence bag was crammed full, but she managed to seal the top, and for the first time she wondered where Reg had got to. Her sluggish mind jarred as she realised he had left and not returned. The water was beginning to clear and she shone her headlamp on her dive computer. Six minutes of no-deco time and 825psi left in her tank. It was time to leave. She looked around her as best she could to make sure she was taking everything with her. Well, she thought, I guess we're coming back down one more time to remove all the lines, stakes and weights, so I might as well leave the pan until then. She squeezed the small evidence bag of debris into her BCD pocket and dragged her gear closer to her so she could put her BCD back on. A beeping sound made her jump and she wondered where it was coming from. She brought her computer to her ear and realised it was the alarm sounding. Something blinded her for a moment and she squinted towards the outer wall. Through the murky water she could make out a bright patch in the wall where the crack was, but the light from the fracture was blinking at her. Her heart skipped as she thought something, or someone, was moving around at the end of the cave, back and forth across the sunlight peeking its way into the cave.

She wriggled into her BCD, keen to get the hell out of there, and reached for her fins. The light from the crack seemed to disappear altogether and then she was blinded again by a strong flash. When the beam of light dropped away she hurriedly pulled her fins on and when she looked up she saw the face of a diver at the crack. They had turned their torch around and were pointing it back outside at themselves so she could see them. It was Jackson. She scurried over to the crack, dragging grid lines in her haste, and he stretched his arm out to meet her. AJ was baffled. Why was Jackson outside the cave instead of standing by up above under the overhang? The idea that something must have happened to Reg surged through her mind and she felt a lump in her throat. Jackson firmly grabbed her BCD with his hand then let go and pointed his thumb urgently up towards the roof of the cave. She could see his eyes now. Those beautiful dark eyes so full of love and compassion. But they didn't look calm, and Jackson was always calm. They looked terrified. The realisation that something bad had happened consumed her. She had to get up and see what was going on. He pushed her away and kept signalling up.

AJ turned and finned across the cave, not caring if she stirred up the sand or kicked the lines. She reached forward and pulled herself around the corner of the vertical tunnel and ascended to the chimney fork. As soon as she turned the next corner she knew something was badly wrong. Ahead, there was barely any light reaching into the tunnel and her headlamp illuminated nothing but rock. For a second she thought she had made a wrong turn but as she lessened her depth, the narcotic effect of the nitrogen decreased, and her thoughts became crisper. There was no wrong turn she could make. The tunnel had become blocked.

Her hands met the rock that had filled the hole they had cleared from tunnel and she could see movement outside through two small gaps. She shoved a hand through the larger gap and waved. A hand clasped hers and pushed it back inside. Reg's big face filled the hole and in the dim light she saw the same terrified look as Jackson had had in his eyes. She was relieved he was safe, and he made an okay sign, but she knew nothing was okay. She held up her dive computer to the gap and Reg shone his torch through the hole so he could read it. He held up an okay sign again.

AJ lowered herself away from the rocks and looked at her computer herself. She had ascended to just above 100 feet so the no-deco time hadn't moved much; it was five minutes, and her nitrox remaining was 500psi. That wasn't very long to move a large boulder which they had undoubtedly been working on since what she now realised was an aftershock from the earthquake. This cave on Neptune's Wall, by her reckoning, had consumed artefacts from 1586, been the demise of Jonesy in 1986, and was now becoming her tomb. She switched off her headlamp and sat alone in the dark tunnel, trying to calm her breathing and conserve her air. Outside, through the two tiny gaps, she saw frantic movement.

27

GRAND CAYMAN – SEPTEMBER, 1986

Jonesy took a few minutes to secure all the dive tanks against the gunwales on the Bertram. The cuddy cabin was jammed full of gear but he only needed to go down there to get one thing. He reached across the BCDs and wetsuits and found a dive light. He hit the switch and to his surprise and pleasure, the batteries were good. He went back up top and checked his hurried lashing of the fishing rods and spearguns to the roof, which all seemed fine. He started the motors and hopped to the dock to free the lines. He paused and remembered the envelope of papers. He jogged up the jetty, past the dinghy to the back door and looked around the gear room. The envelope was still on the floor where he had thrown it. He scooped it up and returned to the boat. Stepping back onto the Bertram he glanced up at the flat. Ally was watching from the living room window, but moved away when she saw him looking. His heart skipped as her words from earlier echoed in his head. He eased the boat away from the dock and tried to focus on what lay ahead. Everything depended on what he was about to do.

He arrived in the general vicinity of the dive site and faced his first challenge. Ally had taken the lead on locating them each time, but he had paid attention after the first admonishment she gave him. His depth showed 50 feet and the paler blue water indicated he was over the sand flats. Lining up the straight section of land leading to the north-west point was tricky at such a distance, but he managed to get what appeared to be close, then looked to the south-east. A newer two-storey building on Seven Mile Beach stood out amongst the palm-lined shoreline. If he put himself directly in line between the flat of land and the Sundowner condos, he then had to judge if he was perpendicular to the sea wall at the north end of Boggy Sand Road. He ran back and forth a few times in line with his sightings and watching the depth. He glanced over at the sun lowering in the western sky and realised if he kept wasting time he would run out of daylight, not to mention petrol. Finally, by using his best guess more than an accurate gauge of his position relative to the sea wall, he dropped the anchor to the sand.

As he geared up, Jonesy's confidence had waned. He wasn't sure he had found the right spot, which made him think of Ally and how much he relied upon her. His epiphany in the bar seemed like a stretch; now he was about to dive down and find out. If he was wrong again, he didn't know what he would do. But she wasn't here, he reminded himself, and he needed to do this on his own. There was only one way to prove himself and that meant getting in the water. He pulled his mask in place and back-rolled over the side.

Swiftly descending, Jonesy kicked towards the deep reef and began searching the sand patches between the coral fingers for his stack of rocks. He checked three inlets to the north before changing directions and finning south, covering three more beyond his starting point. Nothing. He had already burned up valuable time and he still didn't know if he was in the right spot. He kicked west, over the reef itself, to see if he recognised any of the terrain they had spent so much time over in the past few days. Staying 20 feet above the coral gave him a wider view, and looking towards the drop-off, he spotted something on top of the reef. He kicked towards it and realised it was the second rock pile he had made, marking their southernmost point. He had anchored too far south, and what he was looking for now lay north of the boat.

Staying out near the drop-off, Jonesy kicked firmly back past his boat, which he could see silhouetted on the surface, and kept going. He crossed several ravines they had searched in detail until he came to the one he wanted. The gully almost completely closed over by an overhang protruding from one side. He had discounted it before as he didn't see a way below the overhang, so it was impossible for the rowboat or the chest to have ended up there. But what if the overhang wasn't there 400 years ago? Four centuries was plenty of time for the coral to have grown over, even at the slow rate in which the living polyps grew and reproduced. Now he had to find a way under the protrusion.

He poked his clunky dive light in the small gap along the side of the overhang, and saw below it opened into a wide cavern, littered with dead coral and debris. The end of the valley was completely blocked and it appeared there was no opening out to the wall. He followed the crack away from the drop-off and just as the overhang seemed to end and the gully merged with the reef, he noticed an entry point. It was low, but tall enough to slip through if he angled his body and narrowed his profile. He shone his torch ahead and the ravine opened up before him. How could he have missed this, he wondered, as he finned his way forward. Sand, silt and natural debris littered the ground where no light could reach and he cursed himself for not bringing his magnet. As he neared the end he forgot all about hunting through the sand. A few scattered rocks, some quite large, obscured a perfect view, but at the end of the gully he saw a large opening. He shone the beam across the overhang above him and noticed an unevenness to the underside. At some point the overhang had partially collapsed and dumped all the old broken boulders of limestone down to the floor, then built itself over the top once again. Some of the rocks partially blocked the cavern's entry but it was still easily large enough for him to swim inside.

Jonesy's excitement grew as he made his way down the gently

angled tunnel. Could this possibly be the place that had concealed a secret for 400 years? He paused as he considered the fact that two men also went down with the rowboat. He had focused on the artefacts and forgotten about the sailors. The idea of running into them now, in a dark tunnel, didn't hold much appeal. He kicked ahead and the tunnel soon turned steeply down where he noticed a smaller passage leading above towards the top of the reef. A slight opening in the top allowed a ray of light to sneak through, flickering like a candle. He guessed it must have fans and soft corals gently sweeping back and forth above the opening. He shone his light down the vertical cavern and saw a rock floor not far below. He could tell the wall on one side opened and guessed the tunnel took another turn. Head first, he finned down to the corner. His torch beam bounced off nothing but walls once he rounded the turn and levelled out. The cave was roomy enough to easily turn around inside, but offered no other outlet; this was the end of the road.

He knew he'd descended a good amount and ran the light over his wrist so he could check his depth gauge. It read 124 feet. He realised he wouldn't have long on his air supply at this depth. He swept the beam across the floor of the cave and allowed himself to drop to the sand. He dug a hand into the bed of fine, soft sand and silt, causing a small billowing cloud to rise up. His fingers touched rock when his palm was halfway in, telling him the covering was around five inches deep. He set the torch down beside him and began dragging his fingers through the sand like a rake, hunting for anything hidden below. After a few sweeps, edging forward each time, he felt something solid. He pulled the object from the sand and held it in front of the light. It was heavy in his hand and appeared metallic. Corrosion had taken its toll, but in the cave, buried in the sand and away from the sun, it had remained intact enough to resemble a hinge.

Jonesy's heart rate vaulted. He placed the piece aside and clawed through the sand again. He brought out a lump of broken coral, and another piece of metal. He fought to steady his breathing and continued the search, raking his fingers across the floor ahead of him in a pattern right to left. More pieces of metal. One appeared to be another hinge, and one he guessed was a clasp. His next sweep met a larger piece, as big as his hand. He pulled it from the sand that rained down in a cloud as he held the object in the beam of light. It was round, heavy, less than an inch thick, sporting a ring with which to hang it from, and an arm or needle across the face. He rubbed the surface, wiping away 400 years of grime and residue, revealing markings engraved in the face, and stared at Sir Francis Drake's lost astrolabe.

Jonesy wanted to sing. He wanted to cry. He wanted to race home and hold his find in front of Ally and see the amazement on her face. How he wished she was here to share this moment with him. They had been through so much together and just when they sat on the brink of disaster, he had now come through. He had pushed her to the point of saying those devastating words, but this changed everything. He wasn't the failure she had come to see. The same as he never meant his foolish outburst, calling her stupid, she hadn't stopped loving him, he was sure of it.

He looked at the pile of pieces on the sand and realised he had more than a handful to take up. He checked his pressure gauge and couldn't believe it. Less than 200psi. He gathered up what he could manage to keep hold of and still clutch the torch and turned to leave. He pushed off the bottom and finned back up the tunnel, going as fast as he could without risking the bends. He made each breath he drew on the regulator long and easy, making sure his lungs were full. He exhaled steadily, dreading the release of the precious air in case the next inhale was his last. When he reached the low entrance to the overhang he switched off the torch and left it in the sand. He would collect it when he came back down, freeing up a hand to safely hold his precious artefacts. He kicked from the deep reef at an angle towards the boat, which he could just make out at the surface to the south-east. Halfway up to the Bertram, the regulator became heavy to breathe and on the next inhale he ran out of air. He looked up at the evening sun glinting off the surface and smiled to himself. With a steady stream of bubbles leaking from the side of his mouth, he finned straight up the final 30 feet and surfaced. He took a few full breaths of warm, humid air, flipped onto his back, clutching his prizes against his chest like an otter, and kicked towards the boat less than 50 yards away.

Back aboard Jonesy wrenched himself away from studying the astrolabe. The sun would be setting in less than an hour and he didn't like the idea of finding his way to the cave in the dark. He placed all the items in the sink in the cuddy cabin and grabbed a fresh tank. This time he set the J-valve to closed, giving him a 300psi reserve if he was dumb enough not to pay attention to his pressure gauge again. He knew he was supposed to stay out of the water for a while after such a deep dive, but he didn't have the luxury of time. There was no stopping the sun setting and somewhere down there in the cave, he was sure was the missing compass. He couldn't leave the site knowing it was within his grasp. He stepped down to the cuddy cabin again and rummaged amongst the gear he had haphazardly tossed below in his haste earlier. Somewhere in the mess he knew he had a couple of mesh bags they used while spear fishing or collecting lobster. He finally found one and returned to the deck, dripping water all over the boat and out of breath from his excitement and rushing about.

He slipped into his BCD and sat on the gunwale as he pulled his fins on. He took a few long breaths to settle himself down and looked to the west at the clouds on the horizon beginning to glow in yellow and orange hues, preparing for another spectacular sunset. One more dive, Jonesy told himself. One more dive this evening, and tomorrow he would return with Ally to show her where he found the contents of Sir Francis Drake's long-lost chest. He laughed, as he considered the planets that must have aligned for the chest to land in the only ravine with a cave leading down into the heart of the reef. If they had hit the sea floor a little deeper they would have careened to the depths beyond the drop-off. Did the whole rowboat go down the cave, he wondered? There were so many scenarios that could have played out, it was too much to contemplate. He checked his pressure gauge, which read full at

2400psi; he had his depth gauge still on his wrist, the mesh bag stuffed through his weight belt and his torch waiting for him below. With a joy and confidence that everything had finally come together, Jonesy back-rolled over the side, and never noticed the approaching boat.

28

GRAND CAYMAN – MONDAY

Detective Whittaker checked his mobile phone in case he had missed any texts or calls while he had been driving. He hadn't. He tapped the phone anxiously on his leg as he gathered his thoughts. He hoped to have heard something more from Rasha, but he assumed they hadn't found anything new or interesting. He wasn't a diver, but he had been around scuba diving long enough to know what AJ and Reg were doing was dangerous work. He would like more clues, but mostly he wanted to hear that all had gone well. He looked over at the house facing the South Sound. Alison had reluctantly agreed to see him again. He got out of the car, walked across the driveway and up the steps to the front door. Once again it opened before he had a chance to knock.

"Hello again, Mrs. Simmons, I really appreciate you humouring me with a further intrusion on your day."

She didn't say anything but held the door for him to enter and closed it behind them. She led him across the living room to the same table where the water pitcher was refilled, and two clean glasses awaited.

"What is so urgent, Detective, that brings you back so soon," she said as she poured water into each glass, the ice clunking loudly. "Did you find my ex-husband?"

"No ma'am, we have not, but we do have further evidence that would lead us to believe it is Mr. Jones's dive gear we found," Whittaker explained, studying her face carefully as he did. "A steel scuba tank with a J-valve, the BCD appears to have been a Seaquest ADV model, and the regulator matches his ScubaPro. That all lines up with the equipment listed on the original report."

Ally's expression didn't change. She appeared relaxed, albeit tolerating rather than welcoming his second visit. "That's the gear he used. He bought us both those BCDs when they came out. We waited months for them to arrive and they cost a fortune to have them shipped to the island. But tell me," she continued, her face showing signs of curiosity for the first time, "if you found his gear somewhere on the reef, surely he would have been with it? Unless he, or someone else, tossed the stuff off the boat, I suppose."

"Where we found the tank, it is unlikely it made its way there from being discarded topside," he replied, and a line appeared between her brows as she considered what he had told her.

"Then how did his dive gear get wherever it is you found it, Detective?"

He smiled. "That is the question foremost on our minds, Mrs. Simmons."

Ally sat quietly, her expression returning to a neutral stare as she sipped her water.

"I noticed in the report there's no mention of you visiting Mr. McGinnis in the days leading up to your husband's disappearance?" Whittaker asked.

She took several moments to answer. "That was thirty-four years ago, Detective, I've long since forgotten the details of that time. If the report says I didn't visit the man, then I must assume it's correct."

"The report doesn't say you didn't visit him, but it has no mention of one," Whittaker corrected. "Did you visit Torsten McGinnis shortly before your husband went missing? I understand it was a long time ago, Mrs. Simmons, but perhaps you could think back and recall the events."

He noticed she didn't insist he used her first name anymore, as he gave her time to consider her response.

"I really don't remember, Detective, and I fail to see how this would have any bearing on discovering my ex-husband's dive equipment."

Whittaker smiled patiently. "As difficult as it is for you to remember the details from 1986, you can imagine it's tricky for me to piece the timeline back together as well, Mrs. Simmons. So I'm following up on all the loose ends from people's testimonies from the report."

"I'm sure you're doing a diligent job, but I'm afraid my memory is not that good anymore," she insisted.

Whittaker could tell she was trying to finish the conversation, but he pushed on. "It's just, I have a statement that you did speak with Mr. McGinnis, and in fact attempted to negotiate a deal to use other methods to square away the rent you owed."

The colour in Ally's cheeks grew slightly red and although subtle, he could tell she clenched her jaw. "He propositioned me," she replied curtly.

"So you do recall seeing him?" Whittaker quickly pounced.

Ally took a deep breath and composed herself. "Now that we're discussing it, I do recall going by his boat the day before Charlie went missing. I asked him to give us some more time to pay, and he offered me an extra week, if I would… You know…" She trailed off and stared out the window. "He was a crude and heartless man, Detective. Our situation was certainly desperate, but I was not ready to stoop to his level."

She turned back and looked at Whittaker with resolve returning to her face. "I'm sure it was that daughter of his that brought this up, she's cut from the same cloth. I wouldn't believe a word that wicked woman says."

"Did your first husband have a drinking problem, Mrs.

Simmons?" Whittaker asked, moving on with hopes she would keep opening up now he had her on the back foot.

"That awful woman say that as well?" she replied, with a hint of disappointment more than anger.

"The report contains a statement from the bartender at the Hog Sty Bay bar," he said, in way of explanation.

Ally's shoulders dropped and her perfect posture slightly withered. "Charlie liked a tipple every now and again, Detective. You know how things were back then. It wasn't a big deal to have a drink over lunch, or enjoy yourself of an evening. Things were tense, we were under a lot of stress, so he was drinking more than he usually did." She waved a hand in the air. "He may have been drunk when he went out on the boat that evening, who knows."

"I don't believe he was drunk, Mrs. Simmons; he may have had a drink, but he wasn't drunk," Whittaker corrected her.

"How could you possibly know that?" she retorted.

"Because I saw your husband shortly before he arrived at your residence and took the boat out. I spoke to him when he entered the bar, and when he left, which wasn't long after," Whittaker said and paid close attention to the woman's reaction.

Her lips parted but she took a while to speak. "Really? You saw Charlie?"

"I was the policeman who brought him home the day before, when I can attest to him being extremely drunk," Whittaker explained. "So I can tell you when I saw him on the day he went missing, he was sober. And excited."

"He was excited?" she asked thoughtfully.

"He was. I've no idea why, but he was in a hurry and he was quite upbeat. Certainly in better spirits than when he entered the bar," he clarified.

Ally stared at the detective. "You may have been the last person to see Charlie alive?"

"Possibly," he replied. "Or the second to last."

She started to question the statement, but stopped herself, clearly realising what he meant.

"You don't honestly think someone harmed my ex-husband, do you?" Ally asked.

"Can you think of a reason a diver would remove all their gear at 124 feet underwater, and swim away?" he asked.

She sat slowly sipping her water and thinking. Whittaker tried to read her emotions, but they were well guarded, and he couldn't tell if she was trying to come up with a genuine answer to his question, or just a believable one.

"Maybe he staged the whole thing," she said, to Whittaker's surprise.

"You found the boat, did you not?" he asked, taking a slightly different tack.

She nodded and her brow furrowed again. "I did. When he was gone a long time I took our friend's dinghy and went out looking."

"How would he have got to shore if the boat was adrift?" he asked. "The report said you found it drifting half a mile offshore."

Ally shrugged her shoulders. "I've no idea, maybe he had help? Or maybe the McGinnises were involved."

"Could he have found the artefacts he was looking for?" Whittaker probed.

"I strongly doubt it, Detective," Ally replied, looking back out of the window at the pale blue water of the shallow sound. "We had already searched all over the reef and found nothing, it was a lost cause."

A call lit up the screen of Whittaker's mobile, which was on silent, and he glanced at the caller ID. It was Rasha.

"Excuse me a moment, I need to take this call," he said and stood up, walked away from the table and answered his phone.

"Hello Rasha."

His face went ashen as he listened, and he turned to Ally with a hand over the mobile's mouthpiece.

"I have to go."

Ally lost no time showing him to the door.

29

GRAND CAYMAN – SEPTEMBER, 1986

Jonesy stayed at 30 feet as he finned above the deep reef towards the hidden cave. From that depth he could see the reef below but save his precious air. Once he neared the drop-off he descended to the overhang and chuckled to himself at the stream of tiny bubbles leaking around a large sea fan. Expelled air from his prior dive was making its way from the ceiling of the cave, up the tunnel, and taking the easiest route towards the surface through the crack at the top of the chimney. The only sign that a diver had been there. He wasted no time wriggling through the low opening, collecting his torch as he did so. He switched on the beam, scattering a school of blue-striped grunts, who funnelled through the edge of the over-hang and disappeared. He finned forward and entered the tunnel without pausing, sure of what lay below. Once he entered the cave, he could see the marks across the sand where he had previously dragged his fingers back and forth.

He was bursting with excitement, but tried to calm himself down and think about how he could work more efficiently. He pulled the mesh bag from his waistband and set it aside on the floor. Placing the torch in the corner of the room below the tunnel, he aimed it an angle across the cave, illuminating the sand where he would be working. He took two gentle kicks to the end of the room and deflated the air from his BCD until he was kneeling in the sand. Jonesy slipped his fins off and set them on the sand to his left at the back of the cave, out of the way. He removed his BCD and stood the tank against the back wall, where it settled firmly into the sand. From there, his long regulator hose would allow him to work from the back of the cave towards the centre where he had finished on the first dive. His weight belt kept him firmly anchored to the floor and without his rig he was unencumbered to move around. He just needed to remember once in a while to check his air gauge, which hung from his first stage on the tank.

He raked his hand through the sand and came up with broken coral and a few larger pebbles. He moved forward six inches and repeated the process, producing more of the natural debris. He raked, edged forward and continued, moving closer and closer to the centre of the cave. Jonesy began to see a pattern he hadn't noticed before. Silt and fine particles of sand billowed into the water as he dragged his fingers across the floor, and the outer edges had the whitish yellow tint he expected, but the middle three feet had a brown hue. He paused his sweeps and scooped up a handful of sand from directly in front of him and let it pour out slowly. It was laced with fine brown particles. He reached to the side of the cave and scooped another handful, which poured out in pale yellow and white granules. Was this what remained of the wooden chest? Or even the rowboat, he wondered. He turned and reached behind him, checking the sand near his tank at the end of the room. He brought the handful back around in front of him, into the light, and poured it out. A brown hue. Either the chest had scattered a long way as it decomposed, he decided, or the whole rowboat with chest still aboard made it all the way down into the cave. Amazed, he wished once again that Ally was here to experience these moments with him, first hand. The idea that he was kneeling on what once was a rowboat from Sir Francis Drake's flagship, Elizabeth Bonaventure, was mind blowing.

Jonesy reached back once again and grabbed his pressure

gauge, dangling from its line. He held it to the side so the light around him illuminated the dial and read the pressure. 1100psi. He needed to get to work. He turned back and resumed his raking pattern, now within two feet of where he had stopped working from the other end on the previous dive. His fingers finally came across something firm and metallic feeling. He pulled it from the clutches of the sand and waited a minute for the haze to clear so he could examine it in the light. It was a piece of corroded metal that resembled a handle. Convinced he was back to the area where the chest had rested, he hastily clawed and scraped through the sand, pulling several more pieces of metal out which he placed in the mesh bag. His final sweep, as he met the marks in the sand from earlier, produced a more evenly shaped, cylindrical object. Jonesy held his breath. He shook the sand away and studied the piece in the light from his torch, waving the particulate-strewn water away. Its bone-coloured exterior was smooth, with ridges and steps making slight variances to the 3-inch diameter. One end was solid but the other open, and he poured centuries of silt and fine debris from the inside. When he looked in the end, he saw a brass face etched with thirty-two points forming a compass rose. He turned the piece around in his hand and marvelled at the finely turned ivory housing and the intricate brass gimbal holding the compass face. The needle was missing, and he assumed as it would have been made of ferrous metal, it had corroded to dust.

Jonesy was frozen in awe. He breathed smoothly and calmly through the regulator and soaked up the moment, hoping he would never forget the feeling. He had no idea how much this discovery was worth, but it was certainly a lot more than a few months' rent to McGinnis. More importantly, it proved to Ally that her husband may be a dreamer, but she could depend on him when it counted. He closed his eyes and pictured the look she would have on her face when he walked into the flat. The thought wrenched him back to the moment and he realised he needed to hurry, his air was surely getting low. He hurriedly swept his hand through the sand and pulled out a round cone that matched the compass housing. It was the lid. He dug again and scooped up several small round objects. He pawed and groped, finding several more coins. Grinning behind his regulator, he added the compass, its top and his haul of coins to the mesh bag and turned back towards his gear. He reached out and lifted his pressure gauge into the light. Under 500psi. Plenty to get him safely to the surface if he left now. He dropped the pressure gauge and extended his hand to grab his tank, when he noticed his torch was bouncing its beam around the cave. That's odd, he thought, and wondered if he'd knocked it with one of his fins. Jonesy felt something thump him in the back, between his shoulder blades, and he gasped as the wind was knocked from his lungs. He reflexively reached to his chest, where his hand met a protruding shaft. Confused and light headed he looked down, but his body shaded the torch beam and he couldn't make out what appeared to be stuck to his chest. His fingers felt along the steel rod until it touched the barb and sharp point of the spear.

His life didn't flash before his eyes. No long tunnel with a bright light appeared before him, and the cave was absent of angels readying to carry him away. All Jonesy felt was a surge of pain in his chest, a desperate struggle to breathe, and an unstoppable approach of unconsciousness that fell upon him like a weighty dark cloak. Tunnel vision descended and he fought to hold on to his thoughts. No one would know what he had discovered. The idea tore its way through him with more pain than any spear. He had finally made things right, for them to be ripped from his grasp at the last moment. Ally would never know. As the lights faded and his thoughts ran from his mind like the sand granules had poured through his fingers, he choked on the idea that Ally would never know. His last, terrifying notion, the final lucid thought he took with him from this lifetime, was the incomprehensible idea that maybe she did.

30

GRAND CAYMAN – MONDAY

For several minutes, AJ could hear the dull thuds of tools levering, banging and digging from outside the tunnel. She kept her eyes closed and tried her best to think of pleasant things. Not long ago, Jackson had found himself in a bad situation, anchored to the sea floor with no air supply, and afterwards explained how he had stayed calm. He said he had made a decision to have a peaceful death and wouldn't let panic enter his mind. He consciously filled his thoughts with memories of her, focusing on how fortunate he was to have loved someone so deeply. It was the most powerfully beautiful statement she had ever heard. But as she sat motionless in the dark tunnel, facing the possibility of her own life coming to an end, she knew he had an inner strength and serenity that she didn't possess. As she thought about the man she adored, it overwhelmed her with sadness. He could look at their love and be grateful. She was consumed with grief for the future they would be deprived of. AJ had been in life-and-death situations before, but there had always been action to take, and her alley cat instincts took over. Trapped inside the cave, action simply meant air expended, and a hastened death. She was entirely at the mercy of her friends on the outside.

She peeked a look and saw the metal rod sticking into the small gap near her shoulder. They were trying to lever the boulder away, and she switched on her headlamp and shone it around the blockage. It appeared to be one large piece that had filled the hole they had made, too large and heavy for them to move with the tools they had. She watched the metal rod bending from the effort outside, but the boulder didn't budge. She wondered, with a surge of fear, if any of them were hurt when the rock fell or shifted. She switched her light back off and looked through the little gap. It was brighter outside the tunnel than she recalled, and it seemed consistent, not the sweeping beams of torches. The roof must have collapsed, she figured, that's where the boulder came from. All these thoughts and concerns were making her breathe more heavily, and she focused once more on calming herself. She had a desperate urge to look at her computer again, but she knew it held bad news and would only add to her anxiety.

Something nudged AJ in her shoulder and she looked over towards the gap. A hand was reaching in with a regulator, prodding her, with its hose dangling through the hole. She took the regulator and realised it was from the spare tank they had brought down. When she ran out of nitrox in her tank she could switch to the spare. By then she would be in deco for sure, but running out of air would certainly kill her; being in deco was a manageable situation. For a while. Eventually it would kill her too. None of it mattered if they couldn't find a way to open the tunnel back up. She let the regulator rest against the rock inside the tunnel, but the hand kept wiggling the hose and holding it up. She could tell by the skin tone it was Thomas, but why he was persisting she had no idea. Surely he had seen she had taken the regulator and knew it was there when she needed it? He shook the hose line, slapping the reg against her arm and she snatched it up, annoyed he wouldn't leave her alone. She switched regulators and breathed off the spare. Thomas held up an okay sign she could see silhouetted in the light from the small opening.

"Duh," she said into the mouthpiece, as she realised they

wanted her to leave the remaining air in her own tank for the swim out. Thomas pulled his hand back and moved away. She hoped there would be a swim out, but it was hard to see how. She relaxed again and took long gentle breaths from the spare tank. It was quite serene, if she ignored the impending death scenario she faced. Her slow, rhythmic inhalations and exhalations were the only sounds, and she sensed the nitrogen narcosis still dulling her thoughts slightly. Maybe she would die peacefully, she pondered, the narcosis slipping her into a blissful stupor, unaware of her own drowning. Some people became paranoid and panicked with nitrogen narcosis, but most reported euphoria, or tranquil confusion, which had been AJ's experience. But 100 feet was generally where narcosis, or the Martini effect as it was often called, started. It increased with depth and alleviated with ascent. It might be slowing her thinking, but it wasn't enough to anaesthetise her final moments.

It dawned on her that the overhang had become too peaceful and quiet. She looked through the gap and saw no one, and no movement. Her friends had all left. Had they given up? For a moment she was devastated; they had realised it was pointless and returned to the boat. She settled herself back down and fought to think clearly. Of course, they were low on air too. She switched on her headlamp and instinctively looked at her computer. It showed she had 280psi of nitrox, flashed a warning she was in deco with an arrow pointing up, and '30 feet' indicated over the arrow. She remembered the pressure on the screen was the remaining gas in her original tank that she wasn't currently breathing from. She had no way of knowing what was in the spare tank. The instruction on her computer was telling her to ascend to 30 feet, where she knew from experience it would then tell her how long to remain there before going shallower. The longer she spent at 100 feet, the longer her decompression commitment would be. The others would have needed to get more gas to stay down, and in turn they would end up going into deco trying to rescue her, if indeed they weren't already. Jackson and Thomas should be okay so far, she surmised, as they had been at 95 feet while she and Reg were deeper in the cave. Reg almost certainly would be pushing deco and out of air as he used more than she did. Then of course, she recalled, Jackson dropped to 125 feet to signal her from outside the cave.

What would she be doing if it was one of them in here, and she was outside? That question was a perfect distraction as she considered the options, fighting to keep her wits about her. They needed tools and they needed breathing gas, neither of which were available underwater. They would have to return to the boat, or at least send one of them up. Whoever had the least nitrogen loading she would send up to Hazel's Odyssey and have them lower fresh nitrox tanks down to the other two who would wait at 15 feet, off-gassing. Tools would be a problem. Someone had already been up to the boat as she had seen the metal bar and heard them working on the rocks. There was little on the boat to assist them more than what they already had, so they would need outside assistance. Whoever went up and retrieved the tools hopefully raised the alarm, but if they didn't, now would be a great time to call in the cavalry. Either way, help was not easily at hand, at least help that could move large rocks in a timely fashion. Plenty of people could be promptly on scene to witness her slow and unfortunate demise, but this situation wasn't one that required more people; they needed equipment.

Her thoughts arrived at a dead end. She had no idea what tool or piece of machinery would be useful in moving a large boulder, 95 feet below the surface of the Caribbean Sea, underneath a coral overhang. She fished the evidence bag from her BCD pocket and shone her headlamp over the contents. Most of it was natural debris, pieces of pale, broken coral, but she could also see a few more plastic items and some shreds of fabric. She pictured the tank standing at the back of the cave and the BCD parts they found scattered in front of it. All the pieces were in the two sections forward of where the tank was found, B1 and B2. Surely they fell to the sand as the fabric of the BCD rotted away over the years. Which meant the rig had been placed right where they found the tank, just as her own gear had sat behind her as she had worked, unencumbered by the heavy tank. She smiled to herself. Jonesy wasn't wearing his rig when whatever happened took place, he was working in the sand, just as she had been. If he was searching through the sand for the artefacts he was looking for, then surely he would have removed his fins as well? If he did, then where were the fins? And what about a light? He couldn't have been groping around in the cave in the dark. Whatever went wrong must have caused him to abandon his rig, which meant giving up his air supply, taking off his weight belt and putting his fins back on. Once again, it didn't add up. He would have kept his weight belt on while he worked, as it made it easier to stay planted in the sand. If he had lost his air supply, which would be the only reason to leave the tank behind, then he wouldn't have taken the time to remove the weight belt and put his fins on. Doing both would have taken too much time when he had a long, difficult swim on a single breath of air. Most people would panic and flee immediately when their air supply was lost. Which brought her thinking around full circle back to the tank. Their evidence suggested he still had air.

They had found several pieces of metal, which Rasha suspected were much older than the dive gear. Was it possible they were truly from Sir Francis Drake's visit to the islands in 1586? If they were, it suggested Jonesy had indeed discovered the artefacts he had been looking for. So, where were the artefacts? Bloody hell, she thought, he swam out of the cave with the treasure he found, fins on his feet, and the rest of his stuff abandoned where he figured no one would ever find them. He made himself disappear. The idea seemed to fit the evidence they had, but what would Whittaker think of her theory? He said there were two suspects in the original investigation, but without any evidence of foul play it didn't seem likely either were involved. One was the man's wife, and AJ had learnt recently that spouses, even wives, could be more ruthless than she had ever imagined. The other suspect was Brenda McGinnis, or at least her father, and AJ's dealings with that woman told her to not rule Brenda out.

She mulled the situation over some more and shuffled in the angled tunnel to try and get more comfortable. She felt tired and knew the nitrogen continuing to build in her system was taking its toll. Her body was working hard. At some point the large amount of oxygen she was taking on would also become a problem. Her computer no longer displayed her dive time as it was urgently flashing the necessity for her ascent, covering the other data displays. She looked at her Rolex watch. It was 4:47pm and they had started the fourth dive at 3:30pm. She had been at 100 feet or deeper for almost an hour and fifteen minutes, and probably had less than twenty minutes of nitrox left in the spare tank. She had felt a sense of hopelessness earlier, but she realised there had been a trace of underlying hope as she knew there was still time. Time that had ebbed away, leaving her feeling truly hopeless now. The almost imperceptible difference in reasoning made a cavernous change in emotion, and tears began rolling down her cheeks, trapped inside her mask. She felt exhausted and her chin dropped to her chest. Physically and mentally drained, she quietly sobbed, and allowed herself to start winding down and slipping away. Perhaps this was what Jackson was talking about, a calm acceptance of inevitability, no reason or energy to fight any longer. The sound of her breathing through the regulator became a distant, background sound effect to her dreamy, meandering thoughts, and she began to rock back and forth like a child in a crib, swaying to a soothing rhythm. The way her father would push her on a swing, his strong, adult hands gentle but powerful, moving her forward and catching her on the way back.

AJ jolted and realised someone's hand was actually on her shoulder, shoving her urgently. She shook the cobwebs from her mind and turned to the gap in the rocks. The hand released her and pointed frantically down the tunnel, then tugged on her regulator hose, the hose they had given her earlier. She struggled to bring her mind into focus, but the hand, Thomas's hand, yanked the reg from her mouth and kept pointing. She went to reach for the reg he had stolen from her, but her hand brushed her own regulator hose. She instinctively put her own reg in her mouth instead. Thomas signalled okay and pointed urgently down the tunnel. He wants me to go back in the cave? Going deeper again made no sense at all and she shook her head, taking precious breaths from her meagre supply left in her original tank. She saw Thomas reach in as far as he could, then he aggressively pushed her into the tunnel. She fell sideways and found herself aimed down towards the junction. Fine, she thought, I'm dead anyway, I might as well be dead down there. She kicked her fins and started back towards the cave.

Perhaps it was switching back to the 29% nitrox, or perhaps it was a final burst of lucidity, but for a few moments as she headed down the vertical tunnel, she sensed a confidence in Thomas's direction. She loved Thomas like a brother, and she knew he adored her in the same manner, so he would never send her towards harm. She turned the corner at the base of the tunnel and immediately noticed the cave was much brighter than she recalled. Oh bugger, she thought, I'm heading towards the light, wasn't that the final thing people saw when they died? The idea amused her, and she knew she was losing logical control again, succumbing to the exhaustion and narcosis as she returned to the deeper water. She spread her arms out in front of her and kicked her feet, gliding across the cave that she had become so familiar with. She felt herself pulled towards the light, and then she stopped. Rough hands were ripping her BCD from her body and the regulator was wrenched from her mouth. She opened her eyes but the light was too bright and she squeezed them closed again. Her head scraped along something rough and unforgiving, then her chest and hips did the same. She needed to take a breath, as the air had been knocked out of her, but she had enough reasoning to know she couldn't without drowning. Her legs slapped and banged and she felt herself lose a fin. 'Bloody hell, they're expensive' was the only thought that rattled around her head, until something was stuffed into her mouth. She instinctively breathed in and was rewarded with a gulp of cool air. She was moving through the water and managed to finally open her eyes. She looked straight into the barrel chest of a large person who gripped her tightly as they carried her away.

Like a hood being peeled from her head, the clarity and awareness returned with every foot they ascended, and as they neared the edge of the drop-off she looked up into the big grey beard of Reg. She was breathing from his back-up regulator. He paused and studied his own dive computer, so AJ checked hers. It still told her to ascend to 30 feet. Reg looked down at her and he signalled one finger and made a level sign. They needed to spend one minute here, which she guessed to be 100 feet. From her deep dive training she knew he was right. If she was using her tech diving computer it would give her one minute stops every 10 feet from here to 30 feet; her recreational computer wasn't designed to handle a complex decompression like the one she needed. From there she guessed they would have at least an hour of stops between 30 and 15 feet before it would be safe to surface. Thomas and Jackson joined them, appearing from the reef above. AJ stretched out a hand and Jackson took it in his. She felt a wave of relief flood through her body and she wished she could embrace him. And Reg, and Thomas.

31

GRAND CAYMAN – MONDAY

AJ looked up at the two additional hulls, bobbing in the water either side of Hazel's Odyssey. She and Reg had been below on their decompression stop for over an hour and one by one the boats had shown up. Thomas and Jackson had surfaced earlier, as they had shorter decompression obligations, and had brought down the tanks for Reg and AJ to use. She guessed they had reported everything was okay to whoever was topside as no one else had got in the water. Reg finally hauled himself up the ladder to the boat, and AJ followed. Tired and mentally exhausted, she was startled by the shouts and applause as she stood on the swim step. On either side were Police Marine Unit boats and all aboard were clapping and whistling. AJ was taken aback and blushed, but she managed a quick wave to them all. Jackson helped her drop her gear into one of the tank holders and once she was unbuckled and standing up, he embraced her and she buried her head under his chin.

"I thought I was losing you," he whispered and kissed the top of her head.

"That's a crappy feeling, huh," she replied and let him hold her tightly, the stress melting away in his arms. She wished they were home in her tiny cottage where she could curl up next to him and sleep for a day.

"I'm better being on the other side of things," he admitted.

"I'm not," she mumbled. "I'm a mess on either side."

He finally released her and gave her a towel to dry herself, as she sensed other people milling about the boat and talking. She looked over at Reg. He had kept a hand on her the whole time, from the moment he pulled her from the cave, up until they boarded the boat. Underwater they couldn't speak, but beyond their decompression plan, he had made no attempt to use hand signals or write on a slate. He saw her looking and got up from the bench and walked over, water dripping from his beard and scraggly hair. He took a seat on her side and she sat back down next to him. He looked her in the eyes, and she thought he was about to cry.

"I'm so sorry," he said, his deep voice cracking.

"Why?" she said, surprised. "You bloody well saved my bacon, you big ol' bear."

He shook his head and sea water rained down. "I left you alone in there. I broke the rule. The rule I made you swear to before we started. And sure enough, it almost cost us…" He broke off, unable to finish the sentence, and she was pretty sure tears were mixing with the salt water on his cheeks.

AJ put an arm around him, or as far as her arm could reach around the big man. "Even you can't stop earthquakes, Reg. You can start them, according to Pearl, but you can't stop them," she said, smiling and trying not to cry herself. "If you'd been stuck in there with me, then who would have got me out?" She tipped her head in and leaned her forehead against his shoulder.

Jackson was standing nearby drying his long hair with a towel, and obviously heard what they were saying. "I wouldn't be here if Reg hadn't come out of the cave," he said, and AJ looked up.

"When Reg came up, he signalled he needed evidence bags," Jackson continued. "We all moved to the other side of the overhang, under the crack, where the light was better. That was when the aftershock broke a big piece of the roof free. It landed right where I was sitting."

"Covered over dat last game we marked in der sand," Thomas added. "He'd a bin squished like a bug if he still been sitting there. Might a got me too."

AJ nudged Reg, but he shook his head.

"Maybe it worked out right, but still doesn't change the fact I did the wrong thing," he said. "I can never forgive myself." He looked over at her; his eyes welled up. "I was reckless."

"Don't you start," she said, punching his arm. "I have enough trouble with myself, I can't handle you getting all introspective and philosophical. It's all this time you're spending around my boyfriend. I reckon you're turning into a bloody hippie."

Reg laughed and wiped his eyes. "Nah, it's just the salt water doing this, I ain't no teary-eyed tree hugger. I'm a Navy man."

"Bull crap," AJ retorted, jumping to her feet. "You're a full-on environmentalist."

"Well, I suppose I am a bit," Reg admitted. "But I'm no long-haired hippie," he said, winking at Jackson.

All three of them stared at him in disbelief and Reg ran a hand through his mop of hair. "S'ppose I do need a haircut."

"Besides, I'm an environmental activist more than a hippie," Jackson added. "We do shit. Hippies talk about it."

"Ya did just bust out some coral though, Big Boss, so that's a strike against ya now," Thomas pointed out.

"Oh yeah, I'm pretty disappointed you couldn't find a better way than that to rescue me," AJ scolded him. "Big ox like you shoulda moved the boulder at the entry."

Reg shook his head. "You didn't see the size of that thing, it was half the bloody overhang fell down. Now we'll have to go back in through the opening we made in the wall to finish the job."

AJ scoffed. "Finish what job?" She reached into the pocket of her BCD and pulled out the small evidence bag stuffed to the limit. "I don't plan on ever going back in that hole."

"You finished sifting the last section?" Reg asked.

"Yeah, of course," she replied. "Figured I'd get on with it while you were gone. I was finished and about to come up when Jackson scared the crap out of me. I swam up and found the boulder in the way."

Whittaker stepped up to the group with Rasha, having come over from the police boat after they surfaced. "I'm so happy everyone is okay," he said. "I'm sorry helping us out put you in such a perilous situation."

AJ handed Rasha the last evidence bag. "Here you go, this was the final section."

Rasha looked at the contents. "Ooh, there's another piece of old metal in there."

"Scrap, you mean?" AJ said, elbowing Reg.

"My friend at the museum thinks they could be from the 16th century," Rasha replied. "It will be a while before we know, but early indications are promising."

"Does any of what we've found help with the police investigation from the 80s?" Reg asked, looking at Whittaker.

"Most definitely it does," the detective replied, "but I'm afraid without a body, it is unlikely we'll ever know what truly happened."

"Can't you get DNA or something from the dive gear?" AJ asked. "Or blood droplets from the sand?"

Rasha smiled. "Unfortunately DNA, fingerprints and blood don't hold up very long underwater, especially warm, salt water," she explained. "All of that would have been lost within weeks of the incident."

"Besides, so far," Whittaker added, "there's no evidence of wrongdoing. I have nothing to overturn the original assumption that Charlie Jones was the victim of a diving accident."

"Oh," AJ blurted. "I took my gear off inside the cave!"

"Why?" Jackson asked. "Were you trying to recreate the scene or something?"

AJ laughed. "Not deliberately. I took it off because it was easier to move around and search the sand without the tank on my back," she explained. "And I realised that was probably exactly what Jonesy was doing. We've been wondering why he took off gear we believe was in good working order – well that's why. It was easier to work that way."

"Which means he was searching the sand like we were," Reg added. "I guess he did find the artefacts then."

"The metal pieces we found tend to point that way, yes," Rasha said.

"Then why did he leave da cave without his tank den?" Thomas asked.

The group fell silent, all thinking.

"Only two reasons I can think of," Whittaker stated thoughtfully. "One, he deliberately swam out, hiding his gear. Or two, he was taken out by another party."

"You're sayin' he staged his disappearance?" Thomas asked. "Like he wanted to make it look like he gone missing?"

Whittaker shrugged his shoulders, "It's all hypothetical, but the man was broke. From what I can tell, his marriage was in serious trouble, and there's a possibility he found Sir Francis Drake's long-lost chest of artefacts. He wouldn't be the first person to fake their own death and slip off the radar with a fortune."

"That was the conclusion I came up with while I was hanging out waiting for you lot," AJ added. "Explains the missing fins and light as well. He must have had a light with him, right?"

"You'd think so," Reg answered. "And they were clunky big lamps back then." He turned to Whittaker. "Did you speak to his wife?"

"I did," Whittaker replied. "In fact I met with her twice today. She has remarried and done very well it appears. She had a slightly strange reaction and attitude towards her first husband, but again, there's no evidence to suggest any wrongdoing on her part."

"If he found the lost artefacts, surely he had the solution to his problems?" Jackson speculated. "Why would he go to all the trouble of disappearing? Seems like a lot of hassle instead of going home and living large from the treasure."

"Unless he really didn't like his wife," Reg pointed out.

"She didn't say it, but I got the impression she was leaving him regardless," Whittaker said. "When he went missing it saved her the trouble."

"Well there you go then," Reg replied. "He took the stuff and ran so she wouldn't get half."

Whittaker shook his head. "I don't think he knew she was leaving. He knew it was a possibility, but from what we know, and I recall from the time, his hope was that finding the artefacts would save everything. His marriage included."

"That's right, you said you were there when it happened," AJ recalled.

"I was," Whittaker said. "In fact I may have been the last person, or innocent person at least, to see Jonesy alive. I ran into him when he left the bar, sober I should add, and was heading for his boat to go out that evening. His wife claims she never spoke to him again. He was excited, and a man on a mission when I last saw him."

"A man on his way to collect his treasure?" Jackson asked with a grin.

"Possibly," Whittaker replied. "In the original report his wife told police they had quarrelled that afternoon, so she wasn't surprised he didn't ask her to go back out with him. She went out in a dinghy later and found their boat drifting, no one aboard."

"Woah," AJ exclaimed, throwing her hands in the air. "She found the boat? Sounds like she followed him out and once he found the artefacts, she knocked him off. You said she's living high on the hog now. I bet the wife did it."

Whittaker laughed. "I can't dispute that is a possibility," he said. "And to add to that line of thinking, the original report lists what was found on the boat. Missing was Jonesy's dive gear, and one of the two spearguns they owned."

"What did the wife have to say about the missing speargun?" Reg asked.

"She had no idea where it could have gone, according to her

statement at the time," Whittaker replied. "And I didn't get around to asking her about it today."

"Seems you'd have to be really ticked off with your husband to shoot him with a speargun," AJ said, wincing. "I wasn't thinking that when I said she knocked him off. I was meaning she bopped him over the noggin, or something less gory than harpooning the bloke."

"But the boat was out there drifting, you said?" Reg asked.

Whittaker nodded. "It was," he replied. "According to Mrs. Jones who found it, that is."

"So, if it was drifting," Reg continued, "anyone could have taken stuff from the boat."

"But what about da fins?" Thomas asked. "Why dere no fins in da cave? Best I see, 'cos da man swam himself outta dere is why."

"Maybe they rotted away," Jackson suggested.

"They would have been rubber fins, and quite dense," Rasha said. "I would expect them to have fallen apart a bit but still be there. It's not like the hoses that rot completely after a few decades."

"I wonder what fell out the back of the cave in the earthquake?" AJ pondered. "You know, when the fracture opened up a bunch of sand poured out. Who knows what else tumbled out to the depths below. If the crack had been closer to the middle of the cave the tank might have fallen out and we never would have known about it."

"I reckon he's living like a king in Belize, gave everyone the slip," Reg declared.

"If I'm runnin' off with my new-found treasure," Thomas responded, "I'm swimmin' outta da cave with all my dive gear. I can toss it into the deep as easy as I leave it behind in da cave. So why not use it to get out all safe, with no problems?"

"That is a really good point," AJ added. "I'm back to a foul play theory."

"As I said, folks, I suspect we'll never know for sure," Whittaker said, holding up his hands.

"The kid that spotted the tank on the video wants to write about the discovery for a school report," Rasha said. "Maybe the young sleuth will figure out something we missed."

"I hope he does," Whittaker replied with a smile.

"So that's it?" AJ asked. "A murderer might have got away with it?"

"I'll speak with McGinnis and Alison Jones again. But I doubt they'll shed any more light on the matter," Whittaker replied. "Sometimes we never get to know the whole truth. It's not like the TV shows where the bad guys break down and confess," he said, laughing. "In my experience they lie and deny until the very end."

32

GRAND CAYMAN – MONDAY

She sat alone in the dimly lit room, and stared at the only picture she had kept of him. Her thoughts often wandered towards the man, but never lingered there. No wishful thinking, regrets, unsaid words or remorse would change the past, and she wasn't one to waste her time on pointless reminiscing. She didn't need him to be successful. She had found a way to make things work for herself, over the years, a rugged independence she had forged through her own determination. Men had often played a role, but she dictated the terms and ran the show; they were reduced to bit parts as supporting characters. In her mind, men were inherently weak, too prone to emotions and desires, undependable. She glanced up at the view of the ocean through the window, silvery light from the moon sparkling off the softly ebbing water. Grand Cayman had become her home so long ago now, she couldn't imagine living anywhere else. The island, the people, and the opportunities, had woven themselves into the fabric of her existence. One day, not as far from today as it once was, she would pass on, and her ashes would be scattered on the water she now stared across, and she would join him again.

She thought about that day in 1986, the day the detective had stirred up after all this time. She had sure surprised him that day, she reminisced, looking at the picture again. He hadn't expected her to take control like that, to be so decisive. It had been over in an instant. A moment that changed her life forever. She never knew she had the strength until the moment it happened, but it opened up a new world. She remembered feeling invincible. Her aim had been perfect, and afterwards she lingered, looking into the far-off stare of a dead man, illuminated below his mask with his dive lamp she had picked up. She recalled feeling nothing but relief and power. No remorse, no regret, she wasn't shocked or devastated. She felt relieved to be free of the doubt and uncertainty. Power that she had proved her own strength in taking control. It hadn't been easy, dragging a grown man's body from the cave, but dropping the weight belt had made it possible. And now, after all this time, they had stumbled across Jonesy's dive gear. She grinned. They may have found his gear, but they won't find any trace of the man, and they certainly won't find Drake's long-lost artefacts or coins.

Brenda laid the picture of her father down on the table and closed her eyes. She could still see the surprise on Torsten's face when she dragged Jonesy's dead body to the surface behind their boat, and slapped the compass into her father's hand. He smiled and nodded, and at that moment she had known he believed in her. They were both even more stunned when they took the astrolabe and the papers from Bottom Time, realising the history behind their haul. From that day on, he treated her with the respect of an equal. He guided her through selling the coins on the black market in Florida, and they placed the compass and astrolabe in a safe deposit box. Family heirlooms he called them. She wished she could have them on display as a proud reminder of her father, and the day she became a fully fledged McGinnis, in his eyes. But there she sat, alone, without her trophies, without anyone to share the story with, or any story for that matter, contemplating the end of the McGinnis line. As the only child of Torsten, with no children of her own, she would be the last of the family tree. Where does an heirloom go after that, she wondered, as she lit another cigarette.

ACKNOWLEDGMENTS

Sincere thanks…

…as always to my amazing wife, dive buddy and partner in crime, Cheryl. Twenty years feels like a heartbeat.

…to my family for all their love and support.

…to my great friend James Guthrie.

…to my wonderful editor Andrew Chapman. I couldn't do this without you. He can be found at PrepareToPublish.

…to Drew McArthur for another great cover photo.

…to the Tropical Authors clan who provide wonderful advice, encouragement… and rum.

…to my advanced reader copy (ARC) group, whose input and feedback is invaluable. It is a pleasure working with all of you.

Above all, I thank you, the readers: none of this happens without the choice you make to spend your precious time with AJ and her stories. I am truly in your debt.

LET'S STAY IN TOUCH!

To buy merchandise, find more info or join my Newsletter, visit my
website at
www.HarveyBooks.com

If you enjoyed this novel I'd be incredibly grateful if you'd consider
leaving a review on Amazon.com
Find eBook deals and follow me on BookBub.com

Visit Amazon.com for more books in the
AJ Bailey Adventure Series,
Nora Sommer Caribbean Suspense Series,
and collaborative works;
The Greene Wolfe Thriller Series
Tropical Authors Adventure Series

ABOUT THE AUTHOR

A *USA Today* Bestselling author, Nicholas Harvey's life has been anything but ordinary. Race car driver, adventurer, divemaster, and since 2020, a full-time novelist. Raised in England, Nick has dual US and British citizenship and now lives wherever he and his amazing wife, Cheryl, park their motorhome, or an aeroplane takes them. Warm oceans and tall mountains are their favourite places.

For more information, visit his website at HarveyBooks.com.